KT-522-629

WHEN THE DEVIL DRIVES

The Liberty Lane Series from Caro Peacock

DEATH AT DAWN
(USA: A FOREIGN AFFAIR)

DEATH OF A DANCER
(USA: A DANGEROUS AFFAIR)

A CORPSE IN SHINING ARMOUR
(USA: A FAMILY AFFAIR)

WHEN THE DEVIL DRIVES

A Liberty Lane Mystery

Gillian Linscott

writing as

Caro Peacock

CRÈME de la CRIME

This first world edition published 2011
in Great Britain and the USA by
Crème de la Crime, an imprint of
SEVERN HOUSE PUBLISHERS LTD of
9–15 High Street, Sutton, Surrey, England, SM1 1DF.
Trade paperback edition first published
in Great Britain and the USA 2012.

Copyright © 2011 by Caro Peacock.

All rights reserved.
The moral right of the author has been asserted.

British Library Cataloguing in Publication Data

Peacock, Caro.
  When the devil drives. – (A Liberty Lane mystery)
  1. Lane, Liberty (Fictitious character)–Fiction. 2. Women
  private investigators–Fiction. 3. London (England)–
  Social conditions–19th century–Fiction. 4. Detective
  and mystery stories.
  I. Title II. Series III. Linscott, Gillian.
  823.9'2-dc22

ISBN-13: 978-1-78029-011-9 (cased)
ISBN-13: 978-1-78029-513-8 (trade paper)

Except where actual historical events and characters are being
described for the storyline of this novel, all situations in this
publication are fictitious and any resemblance to living persons
is purely coincidental.

All Severn House titles are printed on acid-free paper.

Severn House Publishers support The Forest Stewardship Council [FSC],
the leading international forest certification organisation. All our titles that
are printed on Greenpeace-approved FSC-certified paper carry the FSC logo.

MIX
Paper from
responsible sources
FSC
www.fsc.org FSC® C018575

Typeset by Palimpsest Book Pro
Falkirk, Stirlingshire, Scotland.
Printed and bound in Great Brita
MPG Books Ltd., Bodmin, Corr

Buckinghamshire
County Council

06 657 487 9

Askews & Holts | Nov-2011

AF | £19.99

COURT CIRCULAR

The Hereditary Prince (Ernest) and Prince Albert of Saxe Coburg Gotha landed at the Tower at 4 o'clock yesterday afternoon from the Continent. Their Serene Highnesses and suite were conveyed in two of the Queen's landaus to the Royal Mews at Pimlico, and shortly afterwards left town with their suite in two of the Royal carriages and four, for Windsor Castle, on a visit to the Queen.

Cutting from *The Times*, 11 October 1839, recording the arrival of Princes Ernest and Albert to visit Queen Victoria.

PROLOGUE

*J*ust after one o'clock on a damp October night, in Knightsbridge, on the south side of Hyde Park. Inside the grand new houses most people had gone to bed. In drawing rooms, servants put out the candles in chandeliers with long snuffers on poles, clumsy from tiredness, so that hot wax dropped and solidified on carpets. Trouble in the morning, probably, but that was five hours' sleep away. A police constable trod the pavement, slow and unworried. Knightsbridge was an easy beat. Most trouble happened east of the park in the livelier night time streets around Piccadilly. He was patrolling so that the sound of his feet, steady as a dray-horse, could reassure people inside the fine houses that they might fall asleep in safety.

The back door of one of the houses opened a crack. A girl came out of the door and stood in the candlelight from the scullery, listening. She was fifteen, with a pale round face, wearing the black dress and stained brown apron of a kitchen maid. When the sound of the policeman's boots died away, she let herself out of the yard gate and ran round the corner to the back of another house, much like the one she'd left.

'Stephen?'

The gate opened. A hand pulled her inside, as urgently as if rescuing her from a river.

'Jeanie. I've waited. Every night like I said.' He was a servant too and not much older than the girl.

'I couldn't get away till tonight. I can't stay, either.'

But she stayed for a while. They sat side by side on a rabbit hutch, his arm round her, the animals shifting on the straw inside. A vacancy for a maid had come up in the house where the young man worked. If she was lucky enough to get the position, they could be under the same roof, seeing each other every day. She was hardly able to believe in such luck, reluctant to give notice to her employers. He encouraged her: do it tomorrow. A shout came from inside the house.

'Stevie, where are you?'

'Got to go. You'll be all right back?'

They kissed. He disappeared inside. She unlatched the yard gate and stepped onto the deserted pavement.

Between the back of his house and hers were two corners and one short stretch of roadway. She worried she might meet the constable, who'd want to know what she was doing out so late and probably insist on escorting her home. Being absent from the house without permission would cost her a character reference and so any prospect of the position in the other house. The pavement was empty. She adjusted her shawl round her head and stepped out, walking quickly. She was halfway between the two corners when the carriage came along from the opposite direction.

It had the high rectangular shape of a gentleman's dress chariot and was drawn, at a walk, by two dark coloured horses, the coachman on the box in a black cloak. She couldn't make out any more because the lamps on the front were not lit. At first she was relieved, knowing that no gentleman would stop his chariot to take notice of a servant walking home late. It rumbled past, and she was only a few dozen steps away from her turning. Then it stopped. The rumble of wheels and slow hoofbeats gave way to brakes grinding, the jingle of harness, as the horses were reined in. She glanced up, saw the footmen at the back, opened her mouth and felt terror rushing into her whole body. Before she could even let it out in a scream the footmen had vaulted off the back of the chariot and were on her. She was plucked up into the air, blackness all round her. Blackness of the street or the sky, of their arms, their masked faces. She tried to scream, but one of them had his arm locked over her face. They carried her as easily as a stick of firewood and bundled her inside the chariot. One of them got in and slammed the door. The other jumped on the back of the chariot. It moved off, the horses going into a fast trot. The whole thing hadn't taken more than thirty seconds.

Later, while it was still dark, a different police constable almost tripped over the form of a girl, hunched in the gutter in another part of Knightsbridge. A damp shawl was wrapped round her head and she was so still that he thought at first she was dead.

He drew back the shawl and saw a pale face smeared with blood and tears. Her eyes opened, staring at him as if he were some horror from another world. She struggled to get away, weak as a butterfly in a boy's hand. He held her, spoke kindly, tried to soothe her. When she talked at last he could hardly make out what she was saying, but the word 'devils' kept coming up. Yes, he agreed, any man's a devil who does this to a poor girl. He tried patiently to get her to tell him where she lived. It took a long time.

When my part in the story began, I didn't know about the attack on Jeanie. The rape of a servant girl, with an hysterical-sounding description of her attackers, was not unusual enough to make a paragraph in the newspapers. I did not know Jeanie or anybody connected with her. It was only weeks later, after everything else had happened, that I found her and heard her account at first hand. By that time, her story wasn't hysterical at all and made perfect sense – not that that was much help to poor Jeanie. Looking back, I can tell myself that I should have known. It was no more than a mile away across the park from where I live. But then, most of us worry about what's nearest to ourselves and at the time I had enough to concern me. Such as the fact that rent day was fast approaching. Such as that Mrs Martley, my more-or-less housekeeper, kept dropping hints about the rising price of meat and coal. Such as what to do about Tabby. Then there was a certain gentleman who, I feared, was dangerously close to asking me to marry him. Altogether, I was looking the wrong way that October but so was almost everybody else.

Most people's eyes were on another event, which also passed me by. The Court Circular in *The Times* is not my normal reading.

The Hereditary Prince and Prince Albert of Saxe Coburg arrived in London yesterday by the Antwerp Company's steamship, *Antwerp*. They were accompanied by a small suite, and brought with them three carriages. Their Highnesses landed at the Tower, and immediately took their departure with their suite for Windsor by two of Her Majesty's carriages, which had been waiting from an early hour in the morning.

From the Court Circular, you'd have thought the arrival was all over in a matter of minutes. From the point of view of the two principals, it probably was. Two dark-haired young princes, one very dignified and upright with a Roman beak of a nose, the other with a softer and younger look, would have walked down the gangplank to be greeted by a line of top-hatted worthies, then been whisked away towards Windsor in the first of the carriages, the coachmen on the box in his blue Windsor uniform.

Even in the Court Circular, there's a hint of how far from immediate it was for everyone else involved. Those carriages waiting from an early hour in the morning; you can almost hear the horses shifting their hooves, smell the pipe-smoke of grooms and drivers who spend half their lives waiting. The second of the carriages would carry the more important members of the princes' small suite. There'd be no urgency about the servants' departure. They'd have had to wait on the quayside while the three German carriages were unloaded, along with trunks, crates, sword and gun cases, hat boxes and saddles. By the time this procession of servants and luggage set out to follow the princes to Windsor, it consisted of six vehicles. The three German carriages, plus a landau, a phaeton, and an indeterminate luggage cart bringing up the rear. At some point, I don't know when, a seventh vehicle fell in behind the luggage cart. It was a plain black gentleman's dress chariot, drawn by a pair of bay horses. Later, various people claimed they'd taken particular notice of it, but nobody commented at the time. All these details I found out later, at third or fourth hand. When they arrived, I had no interest in yet another party of European royals on the well-trodden trail to enjoy Little Vicky's hospitality at Windsor. I was a newly-fledged private investigator with a living to earn, and hadn't seen a serious client in a month or more.

ONE

'**D**ora will be totally lost in London,' the young man said. He was leaning forward in his seat from desire to convince me, long fingers clasping the edge of my table, fair hair flopping over his forehead. 'She's only nineteen. She'll be an abandoned fawn on a prairie of prowling lions.'

The sound that came from the girl on the other side of the table might have been a suppressed sneeze. Since the poetical young man didn't react to it, I hoped that was what he took it for, but I knew better. I glared at Tabby, to remind her of strict orders to keep quiet. From childhood, Tabby had survived by her own resources on the prairie of prowling lions, so had precious little sympathy for the fawns of the world. This interview was her first official appearance as my assistant and the start of what would probably prove to be an apprenticeship that tried the patience of both of us. At least she looked reasonably tidy in her grey dress, with hair clean and tied back. I picked up my pencil.

'You say you last saw Dora Tilbury at church on the Sunday before last. That's eleven days ago.'

He nodded.

'And that was at Boreham, in Essex?'

Another nod. It was, he'd told me, a village on the far side of Chelmsford, which made it about five hours from London by mail coach.

'And Miss Tilbury was living with her guardian?'

'Yes. Her parents died some time ago.'

'Shouldn't it be the guardian's role to start investigations rather than yours – since she's no relation to you?'

'She's everything in the world to me,' the young man said.

In his note, asking permission to call, he'd introduced himself as Jeremy James. He looked to be around twenty, some four years younger than I was, but there was still a schoolboy air about him. His lips quivered after speaking. Perhaps he was nervous of me and hadn't expected a businesslike air.

'Are you suggesting that her guardian cares for her less than you do?' I said.

'Not that, precisely. I'm sure he is concerned for her. He's her uncle, quite elderly, a clergyman who had to resign his living because of ill health. He's very conscious of people's opinion. And in a small village . . . you know.'

'You believe he might be too ashamed that his ward's run away to London to do anything about it?'

'She hasn't run away, I told you. She wouldn't do anything like that.'

'And yet she's disappeared from her home. Are you telling me that she's been kidnapped?'

'No.'

'So she went willingly?'

'She must have had a reason. She wouldn't just go. She's hardly been ten miles from the village since she was a child.'

I heard stubbornness as well as strain in his voice. He wouldn't be an easy client.

'Tell me what happened from Sunday onwards,' I said. 'You saw Miss Tilbury in church. Did you speak to her?'

'A few words. I asked her how she was and whether she was enjoying a book I'd sent her. Then Mrs Meek came up and hurried her away. Mrs Meek keeps house for Dora's guardian.'

'Why should she hurry her away? Does the guardian disapprove of you?'

'No, I think not. As I said, he is very conscious of propriety.'

'Are you engaged to Miss Tilbury?'

'In our hearts, yes. As the world sees it, no. My father says I should qualify for the bar first, then look for a wife.'

'Do you live in the same village as Miss Tilbury?'

'We have a small estate just outside it.'

'That Sunday, did she say anything to suggest she was thinking of going away?'

'Of course not.'

'So what did she say?'

He blinked. 'I've told you.'

'No, you've told me what you said to her. What did she say to you?'

He seemed at a loss. 'The usual things, I suppose. She was well. She thanked me for the book.'

I was tempted to say that was hardly the language of passion, but perhaps it had been one of those occasions when eyes did the talking.

'When did you find out she was missing?'

'The Thursday morning. Her guardian came round in his pony cart, demanding to know where she was. My father was furious.'

'With him or you?'

'With him. The old man was accusing me of eloping with Miss Tilbury. My father knew I wouldn't do anything so dishonourable, and in any case there I was, at home.'

'She'd said nothing to her guardian, left no note?'

'No. She went up to her room as usual, at about ten o'clock on Wednesday night. She didn't come down to breakfast. Mrs Meek went up to her room. Her bed hadn't been slept in.'

'Had anybody seen her leave?'

'Not leaving the house, no. But the landlord of the Cock saw a young lady getting into the coach for London at about six o'clock in the morning. I've spoken to the driver of the coach and there seems no doubt about it. His description matches Dora exactly, even down to her blue cloak and hood. He remembers her getting out in the yard of the Three Nuns at Aldersgate in the City when they arrived at about midday. After that, she seems to have vanished from the face of the earth.'

'Did he notice if she had any luggage with her?'

'A small bag, he thought.'

'Did she have money?'

'I believe about two hundred a year, from her parents.'

'Money in her pocket, I mean.'

'Her guardian allowed her pin money, for gloves and church collections and so on, but even if she'd saved it, she couldn't have had more than a sovereign or two.'

I put down my pencil. 'Miss Tilbury's been missing for six days now, so the trail's already cold. But I shall do my best. My terms are two guineas payable now, a further three guineas when the person is found, plus expenses whether we find her or not.'

'Expenses?'

'Omnibus or coach fares, payments to people who may have information. I try to keep them as low as possible. The initial two guineas covers two weeks of investigation.'

I'd been in business as a paid investigator for less than a year, but one thing I'd already learned was to establish the fee from the start. Clients who were prepared to promise the world when they wanted something would haggle over shillings once they'd been given it.

'And if you haven't found the person in two weeks?' he said.

'In my experience, if a person isn't found in two weeks, he or she is not likely to be found at all.'

So far my experience of looking for missing persons had amounted to three cases, two of them successful. Mr James looked doubtful, then slowly felt in his pocket and put two sovereigns and two shilling pieces on the table. I signed to Tabby to push pen and inkwell towards me and wrote him out a receipt.

'Now our work starts,' I said. 'I need a list from you of any friends or acquaintances Miss Tilbury has in London.'

'None.'

'None at all? Most people have an old schoolfellow or two.'

'Miss Tilbury was educated at home.'

'An aunt or cousin?'

'Apart from her guardian, the only relations I ever heard her mention were an aunt and some cousins in Scotland.'

'Had she any particular friends?'

'There are few young ladies in the area. Her guardian doesn't pay social calls because of his health.'

'Did you and she ever talk about London?'

'Not that I can recall. I may have mentioned a play or an opera I'd read about.'

'What were her interests?'

He thought for a while. 'She was very fond of her pet linnet and talented in embroidery.'

'Did she have any dreams involving London life?'

'Dreams?'

'Going on the stage, being the belle of the ball and so on.'

'Good heavens, no. Miss Tilbury is a modest and retiring young lady.'

I caught the expression on Tabby's face and had to look away quickly.

'Let's have a description, as detailed as you can make it.'

He seemed more at ease here, and rattled it off. 'Her hair is fair, complexion pale, eyes blue. Chin rounded, white and even teeth, a well proportioned nose, neither too long nor snub, height around average or a little below it, small and delicate hands and feet.'

I waited, pencil poised. He looked at me. 'Go on,' I said.

'I've just described her.'

'There are probably ten thousand young women in London who match that description. I need something that's particular to Miss Tilbury.'

'She's beautiful.'

'And I dare say for every one of those ten thousand women there's a young man who thinks she's beautiful.'

He tried to look fierce. 'I don't think I've done anything to merit your sarcasm, Miss Lane. When I heard about you, I hoped that a woman's heart would be touched to learn of one of her own sex in danger.'

'How did you hear about me, as a matter of interest?'

He mentioned a name of one of my clients and said he'd heard about his case from an old school friend, now a law student. Since I didn't advertise and could hardly put up a brass plate, all my clients came to me by word of mouth.

'I hope I'm not unsympathetic,' I said. 'But if I have any chance of finding her, it's my head and eyes I need more than my heart. You love Miss Tilbury?'

'Yes.'

'If you love a person, you notice everything about him or her. Not the things the whole world notices, like fair hair or blue eyes. A mole on the cheek, say, a particular way of walking or an expression.' (I thought of a man's face and his look when something amused him – a drawing together of the eyebrows, then the outbreak of laughter, revealing a tooth on the top right side slightly askew, from falling out of a tree when he was ten.) My client was telling me something and I had to drag my mind back to him.

'Dora has a pale brown birthmark on the inside of her left

wrist, about the size of a farthing piece. Her glove usually covers it.'

We could hardly go round London asking blonde young women to take off their left gloves.

'Anything else? Her voice for instance.'

'Soft and low.'

It would be. 'I shall report to you as soon as there's anything to tell you, and in any case at the end of a week, even if there's nothing,' I said. 'Are you going home to Boreham?'

'No. How could I stay there, knowing she's in London? I'm lodging with my law student friend, out at Islington. Any message from you will find me there.'

He borrowed the pen and wrote down an address. I stood up. He hesitated, as if hoping for something more, then stood too and picked up his hat and gloves. He'd kept his overcoat on through our interview. I only used my little box of an office when clients called, preferring to work in my own room next door, so the fire wasn't kept up and the temperature was scarcely warmer than the grey October day outside. I followed him downstairs, onto the cobbles of Abel Yard. Straw had blown into the spaces between the cobbles from the cowshed at the far end of the yard. Inside the carriage mender's workshop by the gateway onto Adam's Mews, the forge was roaring and the damp air carried the sound of hammering and the smell of hot metal. My client trod cautiously in his well-polished boots and gave me a puzzled glance as if wondering why I lived in such an artisan place. I could have told him: small fees and large problems.

After a reasonably successful summer, autumn had brought a falling-off in my business, along with the yellowing of the leaves and the first frost in Hyde Park. I told myself that was due to the rhythms of the rich. From May to August, the social season brought its crop of scandals, thefts, elopements and suspicious absences, with some of their consequences providing work for me. With the start of the shooting season, the wealthy and aris-tocratic carted themselves and their problems back to country estates. In the past fortnight, our only income had come from our reliable standby, Lady Tandy's marmoset. The lady was an elderly widow who lived in some luxury in Grosvenor Square. Instead of the more usual lapdog, she cherished a bright-eyed marmoset. Every now and then the animal would tire of a lifetime of sitting on velvet cushions, being fed peeled hothouse grapes, and make for the open spaces of the park. When that happened, a footman in gold and red livery would make his appearance at the bottom of our staircase.

'The monkey's gone missing again, ma'am.'

By now, Tabby and I had established a routine. She would inform the leader of the gang of urchins who hung about the mews, he would recruit his best climbers and off they'd go across the road to the park, where a group of bystanders looking upwards would instantly tell them what tree to target. The urchins would propel one of their climbers into a fork of the tree and he'd balance there holding out a palmful of raisins, which we'd discovered that the marmoset loved more than liberty. Once he was recaptured, Tabby would bring him to me and I'd present him at Lady Tandy's front door, where I'd be awarded a fee of half a guinea. That was broken down as follows: five shillings to the leading urchin, for distribution among the gang; two shillings to Tabby; three shillings to me for organizational costs and the embarrassment of walking through Mayfair with a marmoset in my arms; sixpence to replace the raisins borrowed from Mrs Martley's jar. So far, it was an arrangement that had worked to everybody's advantage. The marmoset had the exercise, our team earned the money and Lady Tandy appeared to enjoy the drama. The only drawback was my suspicion that Tabby and the leading urchin were conspiring to set free the animal in the first place, possibly with the assistance of some servant in the lady's household. If the escapes happened too frequently, I'd have to drop a hint to Tabby.

Back upstairs, I found her sitting at the table staring at the notes I'd made. No point, because she couldn't read. Over the past few weeks I'd made an attempt to teach her. She was so naturally intelligent and quick-minded that I'd expected it to come easily, but had reckoned without her core of stubbornness. Simply, she saw no place for reading and writing in her life and that was that. I put the notes in the table drawer and led the way onto the landing and through a doorway so low that even Tabby had to stoop. My two rooms had their own staircase down to the court-yard, but this was a quicker way to the living space next door that I shared with my more-or-less-housekeeper, Mrs Martley.

The landlord didn't know that I'd had the old door unblocked.
An alternative way of coming and going was sometimes useful.
Tabby hesitated at the doorway to our parlour.

'I'm not allowed in here, am I?'

'It's all right. Mrs Martley won't be back from Bloomsbury
for another hour.'

Mrs Martley wouldn't tolerate Tabby in the house. Since I
paid the rent, I could have insisted, but compromised for the sake
of domestic peace. I told Tabby to lay two places at the table,
carried a saucepan of Mrs Martley's good mutton broth to the
fire and roused the sullen and cindery coals. Tabby sat and
watched while I knelt on the hearthrug and stirred the broth. It
should have been the other way round, but she was about as easy
to domesticate as a March hare and it was less trouble to do it
myself.

'Well, what did you make of Mr James?' I said, carrying the
saucepan to the table. I thought she might have been impressed
by his sad story and his callow good looks. She made a face.

'Thinks the sun revolves round him, don't he?'

'Ah, so that struck you as well. Why?'

She chewed a nugget of mutton and thought about it. 'I reckon
it was him talking to her all the time, not noticing what she said.
You picked him up on that, not seeing or hearing her.'

More to the point, Tabby had picked up my picking him up.

'He says he loves her.'

'Oh, that.' She tore off a hunk of the loaf.

'Tabby, please use the bread knife. You don't think he means it?'

She shrugged, as if to say that was nothing to the point.

'I think he means it,' I said. 'I daresay he goes for long gloomy
walks and writes bad poetry to her.'

'What's poetry?'

I stared at her. She wasn't joking. 'It's words going together
and rhyming,' I said. 'Like "Where Alph, the sacred river ran
Through caverns measureless to man".'

'Oh, you mean what people sing when they're drunk. Kitty's
titties and things like that.'

'Well . . . but coming back to our client, how do you suggest
we set about looking for Miss Dora Tilbury?'

As far as the case offered any profit at all, it would make a prentice piece for educating Tabby in our business. Tracing missing persons is nine-tenths tedium, asking the same question time after time without result.

'She must have gone somewhere after she got off the coach,' Tabby said.

'Exactly. We start from the last thing we know about her. She gets off the coach at the Three Nuns in Aldersgate. Either she gets straight onto another coach, in which case the driver or the clerk who books the places will have noticed, or she walks out of the yard.'

I thought of a wise saying of my friend Amos Legge, the most fashionable groom in Hyde Park: Anyone who goes anywhere has to do it on two feet or four. When it came to inquiries in the world that went on four feet I could call on his help if necessary.

'If she walked out of the yard,' I went on, 'she has two choices. She turns left or she turns right. Young women travelling on their own aren't so very common. If we ask questions at and around the Three Nuns, we might find somebody who saw which way she went.'

This was where my new apprentice might prove her worth. Ragged boys who loitered for a chance to earn pennies holding horses or carrying bags might talk more easily to somebody who'd grown up like them, on the streets.

'She didn't know London,' I said. 'She'd have hesitated, wondering what to do and where to go.'

And yet I couldn't picture it. Something was wrong.

'Unless there was somebody meeting her,' Tabby said.

'According to Mr James, she didn't know a soul in London.'

'So he said.'

'You're suggesting there was somebody and he didn't know about it?'

She shrugged.

I looked at her, thinking that this made sense. Up to then, I couldn't understand how any creature who lived and breathed could have been as dull as he made Dora Tilbury out to be. By his account, this girl had lived nineteen years without acquiring friends, interests, dreams or any more experience of the world around her than a reasonably enterprising rabbit. It didn't match the young woman who'd got up on a dark autumn morning, walked on her own to the local inn and taken herself off to a city where she knew nobody.

'He said that in their hearts they were engaged,' I said. 'I wonder if he might be wrong about her heart.'

'You mean she liked somebody else better and he didn't know it?'

'It's possible, isn't it? If he thought he loved a girl, it might not even occur to him that she didn't return the sentiment.'

Looked at that way, Miss Tilbury's blankness became comprehensible. He knew nothing about her hopes or dreams because she hadn't chosen to confide in him.

I stood up and carried our empty bowls to the sink. 'Let's stay with the hypothesis that there's another man,' I said.

'Hypo . . .?'

'Let's assume for the moment it's true. It must be somebody her guardian didn't approve of, or she wouldn't have needed to run away.'

I wished I'd thought to ask if Miss Tilbury wrote or received many letters. There might have been some man she'd met only fleetingly and had fallen in love with by correspondence. I imagined her poring over a final decisive letter: *Come to me, my darling. I'll be there to meet you off the coach and whisk you away and marry you.* Had the fawn gone by arrangement to meet her own particular prowling lion?

'We'll be at the Three Nuns tomorrow to meet the coach,' I said. 'If we're there at the time she arrived, a week later, it might help to jog people's memories.'

'If it's another man, he might have wanted to get his hands on her money, then kill her,' Tabby said cheerfully.

I was about to ask what she was talking about, until I remembered that Miss Tilbury's two hundred a year would seem like a fortune to Tabby.

'I think a murderous fortune-hunter would expect more than two hundred,' I said.

I'd slipped Mr James' two sovereigns and two shillings into my pocket. I took out the shillings and gave them to her. 'Your wages.'

She looked at me doubtfully. 'I haven't done nothing yet.'

'You will. I'll meet you at the bottom of the stairs at nine o'clock tomorrow morning.'

Timekeeping was no problem with her. She could count up to twelve by the chimes of the workhouse clock on the other side of the churchyard. I watched from the window as she walked across the yard to the wooden cabin that was the nearest thing she'd ever had to a home. Tabby was fifteen years old, she thought. She could hardly remember a mother and she'd never met her father. I'd gathered from a few things she'd said that her mother's acquaintance with him had been fleeting and probably commercial. Until a few months ago, she'd survived on the streets of London, begging or running errands, flapping away pigeons to harvest crusts of bread from gutters, sleeping in doorways. Hopes of better pickings on the streets of Mayfair had brought her to Abel Yard, where she'd slept on old sacks in a lean-to next to milkman Colley's cowshed. Then she'd saved my life. She'd demanded nothing in return and if I'd offered nothing would simply have shrugged and turned back to the streets. I'd decided to try to help her by gradual stages. Mr Colley had a son-in-law who pretended to be a carpenter. Since the man was as idle as an aristocrat, his carpenter's shed was rarely used. Ten shillings from me persuaded him to partition it and make half into a space not unlike a ship's cabin, where a small person might sleep. Another ten shillings eventually produced a bed platform, three pegs on the wall and a small chest made from old planks for Tabby's few possessions. Bedding, blankets and a rag rug for the floor came from our living quarters, so cost me only an argument with Mrs Martley and remarks from her about taking riff-raff out of the gutter. When I'd first showed the cabin to Tabby she'd looked at me as if I'd offered her Blenheim Palace but she wasn't sure she liked the architecture.

'Do I have to stay here all the time?'

'Only when you want to. It's not a prison.'

For three days after that, we didn't see hide or hair of her. On the fourth night she slept in the cabin. Now that the evenings were growing colder and darker, I'd glance out to the yard most nights and see the glimmer of her candle through cracks in the wall.

I decided that I'd better clear away the evidence of our meal before Mrs Martley came back. The water bucket was empty, so I carried it down to the dark cubbyhole under the stairs that housed our pump and the drain for slop water. The pump valve needed replacing and every pull on the handle made a noise like a donkey braying. It took me a while to realize that somebody was shouting my name from the yard.

'Excuse me, where can I find Liberty Lane?'

I turned. The man standing there looked as if he hadn't rested or eaten for days. He was hatless, his dark jacket buttoned up to the chin, brown hair disordered, eyes feverishly bright. His voice and the whole of his long body were vibrating with urgency.

'Tom Huckerby,' I said. 'What's wrong?'

No mistering or missing with us. That had always been his way, from years back when I'd met him as one of my father's friends. I'd seen him twice since my return to London, once addressing a crowd at Hyde Park Corner on the evils of the new poor laws, once leading a march on Parliament. He was political to his fingertips, with a passion for justice and a contempt for possessions so total that if he ever happened to come by money or good clothes they instantly spun away from him like things in a cyclone. He'd twice served prison sentences for organizing demonstrations against the government.

'We need a hiding place.'

My heart sank. Politically, I was on his side but my way of life was precarious enough without having to harbour wanted men. Still, my father's daughter couldn't turn him away.

'How many of you are there?' I said.

'Not us. Not this time at any rate. It's our printing press. The devils sent the bailiffs in at first light this morning but we managed to get it away from them. We've been looking all day for somewhere to keep it where they won't find it.'

The authorities had several ways of dealing with protesters, apart from prison sentences. Heavy fines and legal costs meant that possession orders were constantly hanging over Tom Huckerby and people of his kind. Confiscating the presses that produced radical broadsheets or short-lived newspapers critical of the authorities was a tidy way of suppressing them.

'Where is it?' I said.

He led the way through the gateway into Adam's Mews. A

flat cart was standing there, with a small and weary-looking pony in the shafts. A plump young man standing beside the pony gave me a smile that was surprisingly cheerful in the circumstances.

'That's it.' Tom Huckerby pointed at an assembly of shapes covered in old sacks on the cart.

'Weighs a ton, it does,' said the young man in a strong Welsh accent. 'You should have seen us getting it over the wall.'

'We might just get it in behind the pump,' I said. 'Bring the cart up as close as you can.'

The young man led the pony and cart through the gateway. I cleared some old cans and buckets away from the cubbyhole, revealing a space behind the pump. Their muscles cracking from the strain, the two men slid the largest of the components to the edge of the cart and staggered with it over the cobbles. I tugged at a canvas sack, intending to follow, but could hardly move it.

'That's the type,' said the young man, coming back, his face shining with sweat. 'Solid lead it is.'

The two of them hauled it off the cart and I helped drag it behind the pump. The rest of the parts were lighter and we managed to get all of them wedged in and covered with sacks.

'We'll send for it when we can,' Tom Huckerby said.

I took one of the sovereigns out of my pocket. 'This won't go far, but it might save you sleeping in the park.'

Tom Huckerby received it without embarrassment and the young man thanked me. I watched them go, torn between shame that I hadn't given him both the sovereigns and regret that my small profit was melting away so quickly. Professionally speaking, I could not class it as one of my more successful days.

THE SUICIDE BY PRECIPITATION
FROM THE MONUMENT –
THE INQUEST ON THE BODY.

. . . he went out to see. He immediately saw a person lying near the entrance door of the Monument, and perceiving it to be a female went to the spot without delay. She was lying on her face in the frontage of the door. He thought at first that something had struck her from the upper part of the Monument, as she might have been sitting on the seats in the front, as occasionally ladies did. He saw blood flowing from the left arm, which proved to be completely severed from the body; and the attendant, then full of fright and fear, exclaimed, "She has fallen from the Monument."

Mr. Cowten, the ward beadle, was next called, and spoke to the depositing of the body in the watch-house of St. Magnus-the-Martyr. He searched the body: there was no pocket or any *memoranda* or papers discovered giving the least clue to the deceased's connexions. A ring was found on the wedding finger of the left hand. It was a gold chased ring.

> Short extracts from an account in *The Times*
> in 1839 of an inquest into a young woman
> who fell to her death from The Monument.

TWO

Next day Tabby and I took the omnibus from Piccadilly to the City and were at the Three Nuns well before the coach from Braintree arrived. Tabby stayed in the yard, striking up conversations with stable lads and loitering boys. I talked to the publican and established that nobody of Miss Tilbury's description had been seen inside his inn on the previous Thursday or at any other time. The booking clerk, in his booth at the end of the stable block, was sure that no such woman had taken a seat in any outward-bound coach that day. A crossing sweeper in the street outside thought he might have seen a young lady in a blue cloak, but it became clear that he'd happily claim sight of a waltzing rhinoceros if he thought there might be pennies in it.

Coaches came and went. In one of the lulls, Tabby caught my eye and walked over, looking dejected. 'None of them seen nothing like her.' She scuffed the cobbles with the toe of her shoe. When worried, she tended to revert to street urchin habits. 'Some of the boys think the devil's chariot took her off.'

'What?'

It was the first time I'd heard of it. She explained, still not meeting my eye.

'They say there's this chariot goes round the streets, drawn by two black horses with red eyes and footmen on the back with bulls' heads and horns. Girls get dragged inside and never seen no more.'

I sighed. For all the toughness of her life, or perhaps because of it, Tabby was as superstitious as a sailor. At this time of year, with the nights growing long and Halloween not far away, lads were always dreaming up ghost stories to make girls shudder.

'So you're suggesting Dora Tilbury got straight off the stage from Essex and was swept up by the devil?' I said.

She gave a reluctant shake of the head. I brought us back to business. 'What about men meeting people off the stage last Thursday?'

'Old man meeting two old women. Young man in a squashed sort of hat meeting another young man. Bad-tempered cove meeting a fat woman with a yapping little dog . . .' She ran through a list of seven or eight. It was a testimonial to her powers of extracting information and her memory.

'No good though, is it?' Tabby said.

I was inclined to agree, but didn't want to depress her spirits any further. 'It is in its way. Nobody noticed her. That almost certainly means that when she got off the coach she didn't ask anybody for directions or stand round wondering where to go. Since she doesn't know London, that probably means she was met.'

'But there isn't any of them being met that sounds like her.'

'No. So that might mean that whoever met her took care that they shouldn't be noticed.'

'So you and me was right. She was meeting some man she wasn't supposed to meet.'

'Exactly.'

But the conclusion was bad news for us. If Miss Tilbury had eloped with a secret lover, they were lost to us among London's two million citizens, or already gone from London to anywhere in the country or on the Continent. Any hope of tracing them would involve inquiries back at Miss Tilbury's home about her correspondence and all the men she'd ever met. That would not be welcomed by the poetic young gentleman, so there'd be no more money from him. The guardian, from what Mr James had said, was likely to turn his back on the whole unpleasant business. Only a determination that our client should get his full two guineas worth kept me waiting there to meet the Braintree stage, the *Sovereign*.

It arrived only five minutes late, turning into the yard at a hammering trot. The wheels had hardly stopped turning before the driver jumped down from the box and threw the reins to a waiting groom. He was a burly red-faced man, with a nose that looked like a squashed raspberry tartlet. I waited until he'd emptied a tankard that a waiter brought out to him before asking about the woman in a blue cloak a week ago.

'What is it about her? You're the second one asking me.'

He was bad-tempered, slurring his words. I guessed that he'd downed at least one tankard at the four or five stopping places between Braintree and London, probably with a warming measure of gin mixed in with the beer.

'Was the first one a fair-haired young man?'

He nodded.

'And you remember picking her up in Boreham early on Thursday morning?'

Another nod. He was watching the back door of the inn for the reappearance of the waiter.

'Did you see her getting off the coach?'

'No. Why should I? I've got enough to do with the horses and everything to see to.'

I was sure that then, as now, he'd have had his face in the tankard.

'Did she say anything to you at all?'

'No.'

'And you didn't notice anybody waiting to meet her?'

'No. No business of mine.'

He stumped into the inn, mumbling about the idleness of waiters.

That seemed to end our investigations at the Three Nuns and I was looking for Tabby to go home when I overheard a scrap of conversation. Two women were standing by the gateway to the street, listening to a clerk-like man.

'. . . didn't even know she was up there. First thing anybody knew, there she was on the pavement with her arm torn off and blood all over the place.'

Other people were coming up to hear him. I joined them and asked one of the women what was happening.

'Girl threw herself off the Monument last night.'

The man started his story over again, for the new arrivals. The Monument in question was the 200-foot high column on Fish Street Hill near London Bridge, built to commemorate the Great Fire in the time of the second King Charles. It was, sadly, a magnet for suicides. Beyond the fact that we were looking for a girl and a girl had died, there seemed nothing to connect it with our investigations. I felt a tug on my coat, and there was Tabby behind me.

'Are you going to ask him if she had fair hair?'

Somebody saved me the trouble by asking what the girl looked like. The man had to admit he didn't know. It turned out that he hadn't been there in person, but had talked to a man who had been. I walked out to the street, Tabby following me.

'One of the things you'll learn is not to jump to conclusions,' I said. 'There's no reason at all to think it's our Miss Tilbury.'

'But we're going to make sure all the same, aren't we?'

With her knowledge of London, she'd immediately registered the fact that we'd turned eastwards into a side street towards St Paul's instead of back to our omnibus stop.

'Another thing you learn is not to rely on everything you hear,' I said.

'If she'd decided to do away with herself, she wouldn't wait a whole week to do it, would she?'

'Probably not.'

And yet the patterns of suicide were strange. My missing person searches meant that I had to look for the small paragraphs in newspapers that recorded these lonely deaths. Some people did it simply and threw themselves in the muddy waters of the Thames. Others chose most elaborate ways, as if planning some scene on stage. I didn't talk about this to Tabby. We walked quickly past St Paul's and into Cannon Street. After a while the bright bronze flames at the top of the Monument came into view.

'I never been up there,' Tabby said. 'Sixpence they charge you. Is it true you can see the sea from the top?'

'No.'

Forty or so people were queuing at the railings round the bottom of the monument, waiting for admission under the disapproving eye of a City police constable. I told Tabby to wait and went up to him.

'Is it true a girl jumped off the Monument last night?'

He gave me an unfriendly look and nodded towards the queue. 'Can't you tell? Blinking ghouls.'

Normally, on a cloudy day in October, people would not be queuing to climb the three hundred or so stairs to the top.

'I don't want to go up there,' I said. 'Only, I'm trying to find out if anybody has identified her yet.'

He looked a little less unfriendly. 'You lost somebody, then?'

'An acquaintance of mine has been missing from home for a

week. A young lady of nineteen years old, with fair hair, average height or a little below.'

He thought about it for a while. 'Doesn't sound like her. From what I could see, she was a bit above the average tall. Right sort of age, though, give or take a year or two.'

'You saw her, then?'

He nodded. 'Didn't see her coming down, but I was there soon after they found her. I've been on this beat just under two years and this is the third one. They should have better railings or some nets at the top to stop people. The coroner keeps telling them, but do they do anything?'

'What colour was her hair?'

'Hard to tell. There was a lot of blood, but apart from that her hair was wet and that makes it look darker. Still, I'd reckon brown, not fair.'

'Her hair was wet?'

'Soaking wet.'

In spite of the clouds, it hadn't rained last night or this morning.

'How would her hair be wet?'

He shrugged. 'Funny things they do. Maybe she thought she'd wash her hair first.'

While we were talking, another half dozen people had joined the queue. The constable looked at them as if he wanted to spit, only police regulations wouldn't allow it.

'My woman had a birthmark on the inside of her left wrist, pale brown, about the size of a farthing,' I said.

'Left, was it?' He said it as if that made the thing more serious and came to a decision. 'Want to come and have a look at her?'

I nodded, heart sinking. He signalled to another constable standing on the corner to come and take his place and pointed to the church of St Magnus the Martyr at the bottom of the hill.

'That's where we took her.'

As we walked, I tried to steel myself. It wouldn't be the first time I'd had to look at a dead body, but it seemed to be harder rather than easier with repetition.

'The thing is . . .' the constable said, and hesitated. 'The thing is, her left arm got torn off. It must have caught on the railings as she came down.'

We stopped at a side door of the church.

'If you liked, I could go in and have a look first,' he said. 'Then if she hasn't got the mark on her wrist, you won't have to see her, will you.'

Cravenly, I thanked him and waited outside for what seemed like a long time. He came out, shaking his head.

'No mark there. Was your friend married?'

'No.' (Not unless she'd married in the past week.)

'This one's got a ring on her wedding finger.'

'Is it very new?'

'Might be. Funny looking thing for a wedding ring. Any road, we had a good look, me and the beadle, and there's no birthmark inside her left wrist or anywhere near it. So whoever she is, she's not your friend.'

We walked back to the Monument, where Tabby was chatting to a workman. He had a chisel in his hand and his jacket was grey with stone dust.

'He found her,' she said.

The workman nodded. 'I was on my way in to work. Nearly fell over her.'

'Does anybody know when she climbed up there?' I said.

The workman glanced towards the entrance to the Monument, where the attendant seemed to be refusing to let more people in.

'I reckon she spent the night up there. Mr Jenkins says he always checks the top gallery . . .'

'Mr Jenkins being the attendant?'

'That's right. Says he looked as usual before he locked up and she wasn't there, only he would say that, wouldn't he?'

'So you think she hid up there and waited?'

'Can't see otherwise.'

Waited for what, I wondered. For the streets to be quiet? For the first glint of light on the cold Thames?

'What time did you find her?'

'Half past six.'

'And nobody heard her fall?'

'Not that I know of. It must have been after midnight, because a man I work with was going home this way from the public house, and she wasn't there then.'

I wished him good afternoon and walked away, Tabby trailing after me.

'Aren't you going to ask anybody any more questions?'

'There's no point,' I said. 'She's not Miss Tilbury. She's too tall and her hair's the wrong colour and there's no birthmark on her wrist.'

'You saw her then?' She sounded envious.

'I didn't need to. The police constable told me.'

'Oh them.'

A vagrant's contempt for the police in her voice, I sensed that my apprentice had found me wanting, so I spoke severely. 'We do the work we're paid to do. Whatever happened with that poor woman is no business of ours.'

But as we walked away I couldn't help looking back at the Monument and its bright coronet of flames against a grey sky. There seemed something indecently triumphalist about it – as if it were exulting over another victim. I thought of the girl, alone and high up in the dark, hearing voices and seeing lamplight as people went on with their lives below, but her no longer being a part of their world any more.

'Still, it's a reminder to us,' I said, trying to sound brisk. 'When you're looking for a missing person, you must be sure to check reports of suicides or accidents.'

'How do we do that?' She sounded discouraged. Routine was a recently acquired word to her and she didn't like it.

'I read the newspapers,' I said.

Sullen silence.

'There's also a man I know who makes his living reporting on coroner's inquests for the papers. I may go and see him this evening.'

'Can I come with you?'

'Not this time.'

It might be interesting to see what Tabby and Jimmy Cuffs made of each other, but not yet.

As it happened I didn't make the journey to Fleet Street to see him because when I got home an invitation was waiting for me.

'A lad brought it while you were out,' Mrs Martley said, rolling pastry.

Embossed printing, my name written on the top left-hand corner in a hand I didn't recognize.

The Beethoven Appreciation Circle has pleasure in inviting
you to a recital to be given on Thursday 17 October at Lydian
House, Belgrave Square. 6pm for 6.30. Carriages at 8.

That was just over an hour away. Clearly, the decision to invite
Miss Liberty Lane had been taken at the very last minute. As it
happened, I knew about the recital. A French pianist whom I'd
been longing to hear was to perform two Beethoven sonatas. It
was a subscription concert, at a price that made clear it was a
society event, attended probably by people who had as much ear
for music as Mrs Martley's pastry.

What interested me – besides a wish to hear the music –
was that this kind of invitation was often the way my friend,
that ambitious young MP Mr Benjamin Disraeli, chose when
he wanted to talk to me. I could never decide whether it was
concern for my reputation or his that made him contrive our
business meetings in public places. His, probably, since he
had a dashing disregard for other people's needs. But that
couldn't be the case this time, because Mr Disraeli had married
his rich widow at the end of August and departed on a honeymoon tour of Europe. They were not expected back in London
until November. So if Mr Disraeli himself had not sent the
invitation, it must be from somebody close enough to him to
adopt the same etiquette. That meant another client, quite
possibly a wealthy one. I told Mrs Martley I'd be back soon
after eight.

'You be careful and take a cab back,' she said. 'It's not safe
in the streets on your own these days.'

My mind was already on my wardrobe, wondering whether
my blue velvet with the stand-up collar and silk facings would
be grand enough, but there was an edge to her voice that made
me turn and look at her.

'Why, *these days*?'

'Mrs Grindley's been talking to the cook at the Featherstone's
and she says one of the kitchen maids there was nearly carried
off on Monday night in a chariot with two devils on the back.
She's been in hysterics ever since.'

Odd, that this particular ghost story had already run all the
way from the City to Mayfair. I promised Mrs Martley I'd be

careful, ran upstairs and through the little door into my own room and changed into the blue velvet. It wasn't fear of devils in the dusk that made me spend money on a cab to Belgrave Square, only tenderness for my best shoes, which were black velvet and so didn't match the dress, but would have to do. The traffic was heavy and I arrived more than fashionably late, with just time to slide into a vacant seat in the back row before the music began.

THREE

The pianist was every bit as good as I'd been told. I only wished that some of my musical friends had been there to appreciate him, because it was clear that many of the present company did not. As soon as the first sonata finished, people left their seats and a babble of chatter broke out with a dammed-up rush that showed it was the main purpose of the event for some people. I was definitely underdressed. The recital was timed so that most people could go on to dinner afterwards. Women gleamed in silks and satins. Diamond pendants and earrings flashed light back to the chandeliers. Our hostess was a titled lady whose husband lived in the country, leaving her with the town house. Perhaps I should have gone over and thanked her for her hospitality, only I knew too much about her because she'd been on the fringes of an unhappy case of mine and she knew I knew. Assuredly, the invitation had not come from her. I accepted a cup of tea from a footman, perched myself on the end of a row of chairs and waited.

Almost at once a gentleman came and stood beside me. He was dressed in well-tailored but unshowy evening clothes, slim and tall. Not young, in his early forties perhaps. The dark hair over his forehead was touched with small flecks of grey like seafoam on waves. His eyes were brown and looked full of vitality. Something made me think he might be in the diplomatic service. He looked like a gentlemen who knew the world and was at home in it. Even before he spoke, I guessed that he wasn't English. Elegant Englishmen tend to be too pleased with themselves.

'Are you enjoying the music, Miss Lane?'

His English was perfect, but it wasn't his native language. I could tell that, without being able to guess his origins, which annoyed me because I pride myself on a quick ear.

'Very much.'

'You didn't think he took the second movement a little too slowly?'

'I think it might have been how Beethoven intended it, don't you?'

An inclination of his head, deferring to my opinion.

'You'll excuse my speaking to you without an introduction, Miss Lane. I believe we have a mutual acquaintance.'

He was cautious in naming names, even his own it seemed.

'Then you have the advantage of me,' I said.

He gave a fractional bow, nicely poised between politeness and irony. 'Sebastian Clyde, at your service.'

As he straightened up, he looked me in the eye and smiled, defying me to comment. Sebastian might be true, but I did not for an instant believe in the oh-so-British Clyde.

'Are you sure it isn't the river Avon?' I said. 'Or perhaps the Mersey or Ouse?'

The lifting of one eyebrow implied that well-bred people did not comment on little matters like false names.

'I met our mutual friend a few weeks ago in Stuttgart,' he said. 'He said that you had behaved with great discretion in the matter of . . .'

And he mentioned a case of mine, known to only a very few people. Disraeli was one of the few, and his itinerary had included Stuttgart. Mr Clyde glanced towards the piano.

'I see our maestro has not returned yet. There's somebody I should like to introduce to you, if you'd permit me.'

A group of men were standing near the piano, listening to somebody. There were seven or eight of them, ranging in age from twenty to eighty and every one of them was leaning his head with that unmistakeable indulgent air of a man listening to a pretty woman. As we came closer, the sound of their soft male chuckles filled the air, like a loft of pigeons on a summer afternoon. Mr Clyde managed to clear a path through them to the centre of attraction.

'Contessa, may I present Miss Lane. Miss Lane, the Contessa D'Abbravilla.'

The eyes that met mine were some of the most beautiful I had ever seen, large, slanting slightly upwards at the corners and deep violet in colour. Once, travelling the Mediterranean with my father and brother, we'd looked down from the yacht into the sea-filled crater of an old volcano, hundreds of feet below us. The sea at its deepest point was exactly the colour of her eyes. That memory came to my mind while it was still registering annoyance at Mr Clyde. Being introduced is one thing, being presented as to royalty quite another.

'I am so pleased to meet you, Miss Lane.'

My annoyance vanished at her open smile and the butterfly light touch of her white-gloved hand on my wrist. A polite nod would have met the case, particularly since we'd interrupted her, but she seemed as glad to see me as if I were an old friend. She spoke to me directly, apparently ignoring the men around her.

'I was telling them how much better it would have been if Beethoven had put some singing into it. Don't you think all music should have singing in it, Miss Lane?' Instantly, without pausing for breath, she trilled off a few bars of Rosina's aria from *The Barber*, in a small but tuneful voice. The male cooing broke out again.

'I'm sure Beethoven would have, if he'd heard you singing, Contessa,' the eighty-year-old said gallantly and was rewarded with a smile that rocked him on his feet.

She could afford to smile. Her little teeth were white and regular as a healthy child's. She was small in build, hardly coming up to Mr Clyde's shoulder, with tiny hands and feet. At first glance I'd taken her to be about my age, in her early twenties, but she was older by five years or so. Her dress was green silk, low in the bodice, embroidered with silver lilies of the valley. Another lily of the valley made of small diamonds set *tremblante* quivered in her dark curls when she moved her head. Before I was called on to take sides about putting arias in sonatas, a series of angry arpeggios sounded from the piano. Our hostess was standing at the keyboard, looking daggers at the contessa and our little group. Everybody else had resumed their seats.

'If everybody is *quite* ready . . .'

Mr Clyde escorted me back to my seat. 'I'd be grateful if I might have a word with you afterwards, Miss Lane.'

'Certainly.'

The second sonata was as beautifully played as the first, but this time I didn't give it the concentration it deserved. I could take a guess at the case I was about to be offered. Even a few minutes in the company of the contessa were enough to see that she was a breaker of hearts. There might be no intent or malice about it, no more than a cat leaping after a bird. A cat can't help it – but the bird's destroyed for all that. Some man was making a fool of himself over the little contessa so his friends were trying to rescue him. If I'd guessed rightly about the diplomatic background of Mr Clyde, that man was highly placed. So what would they ask me to do? Discredit her, quite possibly. Find something in her past or present that would disgust the besotted young man. Perhaps he'd written compromising letters which I was supposed to buy or even steal back. Well, I could always say no. I'd promised myself that I'd never take on a case my conscience didn't approve, not for any money. I was disappointed in Mr Clyde, though. When he'd first come to stand beside me I'd felt that lifting of the spirits and quickening of the heart that comes at the start of an adventure. It's as strange as love and as difficult to describe, and yet it's the thing above all that keeps me in my strange career. This time, it looked as if my instinct had been wrong. At least I'd had the pleasure of a couple of sonatas for my trouble, so I might as well enjoy this one.

Only my mind drifted away again. Why was I more than half decided on indignant refusal? Had I liked the contessa on sight so much? Not entirely. Her musical views were preposterous. She'd been charming to me, but that might be another way of appealing to her male audience. A clever flirt never does anything without being conscious of its effect, even when she seems impulsive. Especially when she seems impulsive. I wouldn't trust her an inch but – yes, I had liked her. The last chord was dying away. People were applauding and chairs scraping back as the audience realized it was already past the time for carriages. Our hostess was at the door to say goodbye to her guests, towering over the small maestro as if she'd taken possession of him and the late Mr Beethoven as well. Mr Clyde stood at my side.

'May I?

I nodded and he took the chair beside me, flipping back his coat tails.

'So, what did you think of her, Miss Lane?'

'A charming lady.'

'Indeed. Is she a lady you might think of making your friend?'

'I choose my friends according to my liking, not to order.'

'A friend for as long as is necessary, perhaps.'

'And I may have my own ideas on what is necessary.'

I was being annoying quite deliberately, to see how he reacted. His brown eyes registered interest, but no annoyance.

'Necessary for her safety,' he said.

'Is somebody threatening her, then?'

'Not precisely, no. But she is set on a course of action that may have the most serious consequences for her and for many other people.'

I waited.

'I must ask for an assurance that what I tell you will be treated in the utmost confidence,' he said.

'I regard my clients' affairs as in confidence.'

'I need more than that. Nothing that I'm to say to you from here on must be told to another person, under any circumstances.'

'Very well. But I still have the right to refuse the case.'

'Yes, though I sincerely hope you will not. Tell me, had you heard anything about the contessa before this evening?'

'Nothing.'

'Her father was a Prussian aristocrat, her mother from an ancient but impoverished Italian family. She married an Italian nobleman considerably older than she was. He died three years ago. There are no children.'

'Was she terribly young when she married?'

'Fifteen.'

'Poor girl.'

'She gained the title and a quite large amount of money.'

'A reasonable bargain, then.'

He pretended not to notice my sarcasm.

'After her husband's death, she took to travelling. Her parentage gave her access to many of the noble and even royal families of

Europe. She's an accomplished lady and speaks several languages fluently, so she was usually sure of a welcome.'

A widow, even a young one, enjoys more freedom than an unmarried girl. It sounded as if the contessa had been making the most of it. I waited for him to tell me at what point of her progress the contessa had captivated the man who was the point of all this.

'For some time, she lived in Dresden,' he said. 'While she was there, she met and formed a close relationship with a gentleman attached to the household of Prince Ernest of Saxe Coburg.'

He looked at me, as if asking whether he needed to explain. I knew at least that Prince Ernest was heir to the German dukedom of Saxe Coburg. The entire country is about the size of an English county. One of my disrespectful republican friends had described it as a place so aristocratic that even the palace pigeons flew backwards to show respect. The Saxe Coburgs have managed to marry into all the royal families of Europe.

'What was he doing in Dresden?' I said.

'At his father's wish, Prince Ernest has been gaining military experience as a cavalry captain in the Saxon army. He has his own house in Dresden. Several of his friends from Saxe Coburg joined him there and two or three of them have accompanied him on his visit to England.'

'One of them being the contessa's friend?'

'Yes. She considers herself engaged to the gentleman.'

'And he thinks otherwise?'

'I understand that his father will not allow it. He comes from one of the highest families in Saxe Coburg.'

'And a beautiful contessa isn't considered good enough?'

'For them, no.'

'And what about the gentleman himself? Has he just said "very well, papa" and abandoned her?'

He laughed. It rang round the room and made the footmen glance up at us. 'You look as if you're prepared to go into battle on her behalf.'

'No. But I'm certainly not prepared to go into battle against her.'

'You think that's what I want, Miss Lane?'

'I assume I'm being asked to befriend her and find out things this gentleman can use against her if she makes life embarrassing for him. The answer's no.'

'That isn't what I'm asking. Quite the reverse.'

I was on the point of standing up to leave, but the way he said it kept me in my chair. His voice was quiet and sad. 'Her friends are concerned that she may harm herself by doing something desperate. We want to prevent that at all costs.'

'So you're not representing the gentleman in the case?'

'No. It's her we care about.'

'When you say she might do something desperate, what do you mean?'

'She's determined to confront the man. When she heard that he'd be visiting England with the two princes, she immediately moved to London. I don't think she realized that the party would be staying at Windsor and how difficult it would be for her to see him. But she's a remarkably determined lady and has her own sources of information.'

'So her friends are concerned that she might jump out from behind a bush in Windsor Park and throw herself at his feet? Is that likely?'

'Something like that happened yesterday, Miss Lane. Only it was here in London, not at Windsor. That's why I decided to speak to you.'

I'd spoken lightly and his quiet reply seemed a reproach. 'What happened?'

'Prince Ernest and his brother had travelled up from Windsor to make a private visit to the Duke and Duchess of Gloucester at Gloucester House in Park Lane. The gentleman was accompanying them. The visit had not been announced in advance but somehow the contessa knew about it. When the party came out of Gloucester House, she was waiting by their carriage. Before anybody could do anything, she approached the gentleman and tried to thrust a note into his hand.'

'What happened?'

'People from the prince's retinue restrained her. The carriage drove away. To onlookers, it probably seemed no more than a case of a young woman overexcited by the presence of royalty.'

'And you want me to stop her trying anything like that again?

'Yes. At least, I want you to become her confidante, so that you can give me warning of anything she intends to do.'

'Are the princes and their friends staying in England long?'

'Six weeks. I'm quite certain she'll try again. She's becoming desperate and probably sees this as her last throw.'

'Desperate?'

'She's running out of money. She's sold all her serious jewels and is deeply in debt.'

I wondered fleetingly what it would feel like to live in circles where a spray of diamonds was not even counted as serious. Mr Clyde went on talking, dropping his voice so low that it was scarcely more than caressing the air. 'Then there's a commodity even more important and fleeting than money.'

'What?'

'Beauty, Miss Lane. You're too young to have known this, but the contessa is approaching the age where she might be described as "still" beautiful. You'll understand, for a lady like her, there's a deathly cold sound in that "still".'

The way he said it made me shiver too. I could see that he noticed.

'So why do you need my services in particular?' I said.

'Because I've heard about your resourcefulness and discretion. I believe you may win her confidence.'

'Why? I can't see many things we have in common.'

'She has few friends in London. She needs to find a foothold in society as soon as possible.'

'I should be a very poor foothold. Besides, it looks as if she's doing very well on her own account.'

'By being here this evening and letting men admire her? She needs more than that. She has five and a half weeks to find an entrée into the circles where the princes and their party move.'

'But he'll be at court, won't he?'

'Mostly, yes. She needs an introduction to court circles.'

'Then I'm quite the wrong person. Even if I had any ambition to move in court circles, which I most certainly have not, I'm sure I'd never figure in Victoria's guest list.'

'But the contessa doesn't know that.'

'I'm sure she'd very soon find out. I suspect there's a shrewd brain there, under the . . .' I hesitated. He supplied the word for me.

'Silliness? You're right. I'm not suggesting you should pose as somebody high in court circles, but unless I'm misinformed, you're clever enough to drop a hint or two that you know people who are.'

I still hesitated, knowing from experience how bad it felt to make somebody your friend for reasons other than friendship. Mr Clyde seemed to sense that.

'You'd be helping her. If she continues in this way, she may do serious damage to her reputation.'

'It sounds as if it's pretty badly damaged already.'

'Or even her freedom,' he said.

I stared at him. 'Are you hinting that they'd have her locked up?'

'Stranger things have happened.'

The flatness of his reply brought me up short. Yes, stranger things had happened. A touchy but well-connected little dukedom might have enough power to keep her locked in some comfortable asylum until the light in those sea-violet eyes had faded to sludge. He saw his advantage and pressed it.

'Miss Lane, if she can be stopped in time and made to realize the seriousness of her position, she might be saved from making a wreck of her life. I know there's a tolerant and well-born gentleman who would be more than willing to marry her at a moment's notice, in spite of everything.'

I looked at him, thinking, I understood now. I had very little doubt that the tolerant and well born gentleman who wanted to marry her was sitting beside me. A small spark of jealousy, of a woman who could be loved so much, flared and died in my sympathy for him.

'I'll try to befriend her, if that's possible.' I said. 'How am I supposed to set about it?'

He smiled, the brown eyes bright now that he'd got his way. Still, an attractive smile for all that, with just a hint of teasing in it.

'An appointment has been made for you at Madame Leman's, at eleven thirty the day after tomorrow.'

He took it for granted that he didn't need to explain. Madame Leman was currently the most fashionable dressmaker in London. Nobody ranking lower than a countess, a famous beauty or a royal duke's mistress could count on admission to her salon in

Piccadilly. Even if I'd wanted to be one of her clientele, which I didn't, her prices were far out of my reach.

'I have my own dressmaker,' I said.

In fact, an ingenious lady's maid with an enthusiasm for the latest modes, making some pin money in her spare time.

'I'm sure a lady can always use a new gown,' he said.

I felt his eyes on the silk facings on my bodice, then sliding down my sleek velvet skirt to my feet in their wrong-coloured shoes. I drew them under the hem of my skirt, feeling myself blush.

'Of course, the bill will be met,' he murmured.

I fought to keep the blush down, playing over a few cool bars of the Beethoven in my mind.

'The contessa has an appointment for the same time,' he said. 'These little slips will occur sometimes, won't they?'

He looked into my eyes. Although he hadn't stirred in his chair by as much as a feather's width, I felt as if he'd suddenly come much closer to me. We were conspirators.

'How am I to get word to you?' I said.

'Your maid will carry messages.'

'My maid?'

'Yes. Suzette, at your rooms at number four, Grosvenor Street.'

I stared, thinking he must have mistaken me for somebody else.

'The contessa has rented a house just round the corner in Grosvenor Square,' he said. 'You'll be nicely within calling distance.'

'As it happens, my real home is within calling distance too,' I said.

His smile said two things that didn't need words: he already knew where I lived, and the delicate contessa should not be expected to set foot among the cobbles and chicken droppings of Abel Yard.

'You might care to call at number four tomorrow,' he said. 'I hope you'll find everything to your liking. Now, if I may escort you home.'

He stood up, offering me his arm. I stayed sitting. 'Thank you. I shall see myself home.'

He didn't insist and simply bowed his head and wished me good evening. I gave him five minutes' start then followed him into the hall, where a yawning footman was waiting with my cloak folded over his arm.

'Has madam a carriage waiting or shall I call a cab?'

I said there was no need, thank you, and walked into the drizzling dark. Defiant both of Mr Clyde's courtesy and Mrs Martley's superstitions, I walked home, seeing nothing more alarming than the usual drunkards, several carriages of people bound for late dinners and a pair of police constables leaning against railings and smoking clay pipes, in defiance of the regulations. At home, Mrs Martley had already retired to her bedroom. I took off my cloak and gloves, stirred up the embers of the fire and found pen and inkwell.

> *Dear Mr Disraeli,*
>
> *I believe I may have met an acquaintance of yours at a concert tonight. He introduced himself to me as Sebastian Clyde but I suspect that may be a nom de guerre so I will add this description. He is slim and above average height, late thirties or early forties, dark hair just touched with grey, brown eyes, pleasant voice and confiding manner. His English is perfect, but I think he was born or has lived most of his life abroad. He says he met you in Stuttgart. We were discussing a matter of business. I should be very grateful if you could let me know as soon as possible if there is anything you think I should know about him. May I send my best wishes to you and Mrs Disraeli for pleasant travelling and a safe return.*

The Disraelis lived in his new wife's house, just round the corner and facing onto Park Lane. A man so avid of news and gossip would certainly have made arrangements for forwarding mail. If I were lucky, I might even receive a reply within two weeks or so. By then, I'd probably be too deeply in to draw back, but for the present it was the best I could do.

FOUR

Early in the morning, I went for my usual ride with Amos Legge. He had my mare Rancie waiting for me in the yard when I came down and as usual my heart rose at the sight of them and the sound of Amos's soft Herefordshire voice wishing me good morning. If Amos Legge and Rancie were not in my world, then it might stop turning. We crossed the road into the park and cantered along the carriageway, Amos riding a big skittish liver chestnut. When we slowed to a walk, we talked about the disappearing Miss Dora Tilbury. I always discussed my cases with him when I could, partly for his robust country common-sense, but more for his knowledge of fashionable London. In not much more than two years in the capital, he'd become one of London's best-known grooms. Sporting gentlemen respected him for his skill. He could sit on a horse that even crack riders from the cavalry regiments had rejected as uncontrollable and make it see reason by sheer persistence and a calm refusal to be thrown. He was never cruel, wouldn't wear spurs and carried a whip only for show. His wages at the livery stables in the Bayswater Road where he worked were supplemented by some high-class horse dealing. A gentleman might describe his new horse as 'one of Legge's', just as he'd drop the name of his Burlington Arcade boot or glove maker.

As for ladies – friendships had been broken by quarrels among female customers of the livery stables over whose turn it was to ride in the park with Legge as groom. Skill in horse-manship mattered to them too, only not so much as his height of six and a half feet, his broad shoulders and blue eyes. To have Amos Legge riding behind her in his faultless riding clothes and black top hat with a silver cockade complemented a lady's outfit very well. Often he'd be invited to come up alongside and chat. Amos loved gossip. He was careful about passing it on and listened more than he talked, but he had a way of listening that always made a story seem better. As long as the world moved around on hooves, Amos would be at the centre of things.

He agreed with my theory about Miss Tilbury.

'I'm not sure how far I trust that Braintree coach driver,' I said.

'You think he might have seen her go off with a man and been paid to keep quiet?'

'Yes. Or even that a man was with her in the coach all the way from Boreham and he'd been paid to keep quiet about that.'

'I'll ask a few people about him, if you like,' Amos said.

I was grateful for that. Aldersgate was a long way from Hyde Park, but the horse world spread a broad network.

'If they wanted to get away quickly, they'd probably have gone in a cab,' Amos added.

'Yes, I thought that. A pity.'

Cabmen were a different caste, lower than Hyde Park grooms or stage coach drivers. Although Amos, being no snob, would pass the time of day with one if he met him, he had no great knowledge of their ways.

We rode on in silence for a while. I'd have liked to tell him about my other case, but was bound by my promise to Mr Clyde. Still, there was one thing we could discuss without breaking a promise.

'I gather the Saxe Coburg brothers were paying a visit in Park Lane on Wednesday,' I said.

'That's right. Came up early in the morning in a calash from Windsor, stopped off at Kew, then changed to a landaulet at the royal mews. Couple of nice little dark bay hackneys, offside one a bit skittish. They called at Gloucester House here.'

He could probably have found out the names of the horses for me if I wanted.

'Did you see them yourself?'

'No, but one of the lads happened to be going past when they left Gloucester House. Bit of a business he said there was, with a lady trying to get into the landaulet.'

I was glad to have this part of Mr Clyde's story so easily confirmed.

'Why was she trying to do that?'

'The lad didn't see. I heard from somebody else that she was trying to give one of the princes a letter.'

Better still.

'You don't think it might have been for one of the gentlemen with the princes?' I said.

This was hardly breaking a confidence after all. Amos stared at me. 'What do you mean, gentlemen with them? It was a land-aulet, not a landau.'

'Meaning?'

'You can only get two people inside a landaulet. It was just the two princes. Private family visit without a lot of ceremony.'

This was a puzzle, although the rest of it seemed right. After a canter, Amos started talking about the devil's chariot. 'Me and the lads reckon it's some kind of gentlemen's secret society. You know the kind, swaggering to each other like cock pheasants only with less than half the brain, daring each other to all kinds of devildom.'

'Like the Hell Fire Club, you mean?'

'Something like, only a new bit of wickedness. Anyway, if it's going on round the park, we'll find where it comes from and put a stop to it. These secret societies are about as confidential as a dog fight in a fairground.'

'How will you find out?'

'If they're not out of the devil's own stables, the horses pulling that chariot eat hay and walk on iron like any others. We'll have 'em, don't you worry.'

The grooms of Hyde Park had their own code and even the London underworld knew better than to cross them. We turned and cantered back to the Grosvenor Gate. As we reached it, the clocks along Park Lane were striking eight.

'Get off here, if you want to,' Amos said.

I looked at him. Normally we'd ride back to Abel Yard together. Amos smiled.

'Don't worry, I saw him waiting there.'

Amos missed nothing. I too had seen the slim figure under a tree and greeted him with a slight lift of the hand that Amos might not have noticed.

'He's early,' I said.

'Well, he would be, wouldn't he?'

My heart was bounding and I knew the blood rising in my cheeks had nothing to do with our sedate canter. Amos slid off the liver chestnut, helped me down and remounted. I patted Rancie's neck and handed her reins up to him.

'Give my best respects to Mr Carmichael,' he said.

He wheeled the two horses round and went at a canter back towards the stables. Robert was at my side before they'd taken two strides.

'I was going to go home and change,' I said.

'I know. But I love seeing you so happy on Rancie. You're a different woman.'

'Meaning I'm not happy the rest of the time?'

'No, I don't mean that. You're happy when you're dancing or listening to music. Only sometimes you seem . . . well, preoccupied.'

I was tempted to add to his list of times when I was happy: 'and walking in the park with you'. But I didn't say it out loud. I was still feeling my way with Robert Carmichael, just as he was feeling his way with the world. We'd met only four months ago in strange circumstances and since then he'd lost somebody dear to him and come close to being killed. He was now convalescent from his injury and living in London, trying to decide what to do with his life. Not long ago, I'd been in the same circumstances myself and knew how raw it felt, how open to the winds of chance.

We walked on, past the round pond that was the water company's reservoir. I'd hitched up my riding skirt to make walking easier. At this time in the morning, there was nobody to stare. That was why we'd fallen into the habit of meeting there at this hour. I couldn't invite him back to my rooms in Abel Yard. My reputation was so precariously balanced because of the work I did that a breath of scandal would topple it irrevocably. Of course, any idea of visiting his lodgings was even more out of the question. We were too newly met to have mutual friends who might invite us to dinners or parties.

'Miles and Rosa have set the wedding date,' he said. 'I'm off to Ireland next week.'

My heart sank. 'You'll enjoy Ireland,' I said.

'To be honest, I'd prefer to stay here. But I think I should be there to support Stephen. He's braced to get through it, but it won't be easy for him.'

Miles and Stephen were his half brothers. Since the lovely Rosa had originally been engaged to the elder brother, Stephen, then transferred her affections to Miles, there would be tensions behind the wedding smiles.

'It looks as if I'll be away for three weeks, at least. Rosa's family are insisting I stay at the castle. There's talk of fancy dress balls and hunting and shooting, God help me.'

I talked to him about Dora Tilbury. I sensed that he was still uneasy about my way of earning a living, although it had led to our meeting. He might have preferred it if I were still a music teacher or had no need to earn a living at all.

We came close to Hyde Park corner and turned further into the park.

'Liberty . . .'

(It was still sweet to me to hear him saying my name. On the very rare occasions when we were in company, even the company of Amos, I was still Miss Lane.)

'Yes?'

'On this Ireland business . . .'

'You're wondering what fancy dress to pack? What about Hamlet?'

He stopped, taken aback. 'Why Hamlet? Am I being so very gloomy?'

'Not gloomy at all. A poor joke. Sorry.'

But it had come into my mind because I sensed that Robert had spent a long time trying to come to a decision. He started walking again, then suddenly made up his mind to speak.

'I was wondering if you'd care to come with me.'

This time I was the one who stopped suddenly. 'How could I? You can't simply produce a young woman the bride's family have never met and tell them to add her to the guest list.'

'Unless you came as my fiancée.'

I daresay my mouth dropped open. I stared at him.

'Is the prospect so very awful?' he said.

'You're suggesting that I should pose as your fiancée, simply to—'

He looked angry. 'I'm sorry if you think me capable of suggesting any such thing. There's no question of posing.'

'But . . . you're . . . proposing marriage.'

'You're surprised?'

Not entirely, but I hadn't expected it to come so suddenly. We started walking again. Part of my mind was glowing with happiness that he should have suggested it, but an older, calmer part held back. Robert wasn't ready for it. It was too early for him to know what he wanted. I'd be no true friend of his if I took him at his word and tied him to it forever.

'So the answer's no,' he said.

'Oh my dear, it's too early. You know that in your heart.'

He didn't argue. 'Only too early? Not no?'

'No. I mean yes, at least not no.'

Then, amazingly, we were both laughing. The glow of happiness grew, that he could understand me and take it without anger or bitterness.

'So I'm condemned to an Irish castle on my own?'

We walked back together and he took my hand and said goodbye to me as usual, at the gateway to Abel Yard.

Tabby was waiting at the foot of my staircase, eager as a terrier. 'Are we going to start looking for her then?'

At least her mind was still on Dora Tilbury, even if mine wasn't.

'Later. There's a letter I want you to deliver first.'

I went upstairs and gave her the note for Disraeli.

'It's for Number One, Grosvenor Gate, the house with the little round balcony. Tell them it's to be sent on to Mr Disraeli.'

When she'd gone, I walked along Adam's Mews, up Charles Street and round the corner into Grosvenor Street. Number Four was an elegant straight-fronted house with iron railings round the basement, sash windows and window boxes on the first floor with miniature box hedges, severely clipped. Mr Clyde had given me no key, nothing but the address. As I stood on the pavement looking up, something white bobbed up and down inside the window above the box plants. A maid's cap. I walked up three stone steps to the black painted front door and pulled at the bell beside it. The door was opened so promptly that the maid must have practically flung herself downstairs.

'Mrs Lane? Good morning, ma'am.'

She spoke before I could get a word out, and gave a bob that might have been a curtsey, although there was nothing servile about her. No ingénue of a maid, this one. She was older than I was, probably in her mid thirties, plump and short, with crinkly brown hair under her cap, shrewd dark eyes in a round face and a brown mole on her right cheek. I didn't like the fact that she'd been instructed to call me Mrs. It had a kind of spurious respectability that suggested I lacked the genuine kind.

'You're Suzette?' I said.

'Yes, ma'am.'

The frivolous French name didn't suit her. From her voice, she was as Cockney as drizzle on pavements, and about as cheerful. She stepped back for me to enter and closed the door.

'We're upstairs, ma'am.'

I followed her along a short corridor, past several closed doors, and up a flight of green carpeted stairs to the first landing. The house was clean and smelled of polish, but there was a lifeless air about it, like an empty hotel.

Suzette opened a door on the landing, stood back to let me go in first and waited to take my cloak and bonnet. I kept them on and looked round, hoping to find some more evidence of who Mr Clyde was. Nothing. I was standing in a drawing room, tastefully furnished but as lacking in character as the staircase. The colours were muted greens and greys, heavy curtains shutting out most of the October daylight. The piano was draped with a shawl, folded with right-angled precision as if defying anybody to lift the lid. I walked through to the next room. A small bedchamber done out in pink and grey chintz, with a four-poster bed that looked too wide for one but not comfortably large enough for two. A door next to the bed led to a tiny dressing room with a modern plumbed-in wash stand and water closet. Pink towels were folded on the wash stand, along with a fresh cake of soap. Geranium, and expensive.

'Is everything in order, ma'am?' Suzette, not letting me out of her sight.

'Yes, thank you. Where do you sleep?'

'Over there, ma'am.'

From the tilt of her head, I took her to mean across the landing.

Another door from the drawing room led to a dining room only just large enough for its mahogany table and four chairs. There was no sign of a kitchen. I assumed that people who lived here sent out for food.

When I went back to the drawing room, Suzette handed me a key on a silver chain.

'To that, ma'am.'

Another tilt of the head towards a rosewood writing desk against the wall. She was clearly not one to waste words, apart from the irritating habit of ma'aming me with every breath.

'No door key?'

'You don't need one, ma'am. I'll always be here to let you in.'

And to report back to Mr Clyde.

'Thank you, Suzette. You can go. I'll let you know when I'm ready to leave.'

She didn't like it, but withdrew. I unlocked the writing desk. It was as empty as a drum, apart from a note and a leather purse. The note said simply: 'Miss Lane, for incidental expenses'. The purse contained twenty bright new sovereigns. I put five of the sovereigns in my pocket, locked the rest back in the desk and went out to the landing.

'I'm going now,' I called.

Suzette appeared, prompt as a pantomime genie.

'You'll want me to go with you tomorrow, ma'am. To the dress fitting.'

Ladies able to afford Madame Leman's prices would certainly take their maids to help them undress. I said I'd call for her at eleven o'clock and escaped with relief into the street.

Tabby seemed to sense my mood and didn't ask many questions on our omnibus journey to Aldersgate. Outside the yard of the Three Nuns, I explained about cabmen.

'They're not easy to talk to because they're always looking out for a fare. The best time to catch them is when they're feeding or watering their horses. Like that.'

Two cabs were standing by the horse trough, their drivers beside them, smoking clay pipes.

'Don't talk this time,' I said. 'Just listen.' I wished them good morning and asked if they remembered picking up a fair-haired

young lady in a blue cloak and hood around midday the Thursday
before last, adding that she might have had a gentleman with
her. They were polite enough but had seen no such young lady.
When they'd gone, I waited and repeated the process with two
more cab drivers, with the same result.

'Do you think you could do that?' I asked Tabby, as we waited
by the horse trough.

'Should think so.'

At least it was serving a purpose in showing her the monotony
of our trade. When the next cab came to the trough I stayed
within earshot and let her do the questioning. She managed very
well. In her grey dress and bonnet she could have been any
ordinary servant. I was amused by some turns of phrase that
caught my way of speaking exactly. Tabby had a quick ear. When
the cab had gone I congratulated her.

'Wasn't any use though, was it?'

'It would be a miracle if it had been.'

'Why are we doing it, then?'

'Because we've got to do something, and at present I can't
think of much else. Can you manage on your own here for a
while? It's three o'clock now. Give it another two hours, then
come back to Abel Yard.'

I gave her money for something to eat and the omnibus fare.

'Where are you going, then?'

'Fleet Street. I'll see you later.'

I walked back past St Paul's to Ludgate Hill into Fleet Street.
I loved every grimy, crowded, purposeful yard of Fleet Street, from
the evil smelling Fleet Ditch at one end to Temple Bar at the other.
Far more than Whitehall or Westminster, it always seemed to me
the centre of what was happening in the country, or even the world.
Slow carts drawn by shire horses bringing supplies of paper to
feed the printing presses tangled in narrow side streets with discreet
carriages that brought cabinet ministers for confidential talks with
editors. Every fourth or fifth building seemed to be a public house,
with more laughter (always male) coming out of it than in any
other part of London. In between, print shops displayed caricatures
of those same cabinet ministers, and the journalists laughing in
the public houses probably knew more about the confidential talks
with editors than the prime minister did.

Jimmy Cuffs was usually to be found in the Cheshire Cheese, just off the street itself in Wine Office Court. The rule that respectable women do not enter public houses applied several times over at the Cheshire Cheese. Even unrespectable women weren't welcome. If I wanted to talk to Jimmy, I had to wait until a waiter or pot boy came out with an armful of empty bottles and ask him to take a message inside. Luckily, at the rate men drank in the Cheshire Cheese, empty bottles accumulated pretty quickly. The boy who took my message came back shaking his head.

'He's off at an inquest. There's three copy boys waiting already, so he should be back any time.'

I strolled up and down the street, wandering in and out of print shops. Several of them were selling pamphlets by the Chartists or other radical groups, urging people to unite against a government that kept the price of bread high in the interests of landowners, denied most labouring men a right to vote and locked them up in workhouses when there were no jobs for them. Most of the pamphlets kept just on the right side of the law on sedition, but a few went beyond it. I thought of the printing press hidden under my stairs and wondered which side of that dangerous line my father's friend Tom Huckerby walked. I thought I could guess.

When I went back to the Cheshire Cheese, the lamps were lit and Jimmy Cuffs had returned to his usual seat in the corner. I glimpsed him through the half open door, sitting very straight and writing as imperturbably as a country clergyman preparing his sermon, although his hand was moving at a speed nearer diabolic than reverend. As I watched, I was nearly bowled over by a copy boy rushing out of the door with a sheaf of papers in Jimmy's fine italic hand. Another boy was standing at Jimmy's shoulder, waiting to grab the pages away as he wrote them. After twenty minutes or so, that boy came rushing out with another sheaf of papers, followed at a more leisurely pace by Jimmy himself. He wished me good evening in his fine sonorous voice that might have brought him a career on the stage, except that he hardly came up to my shoulder and walked with a limp because of a club foot. He was one of the most learned people I knew and never seemed to resent the fact that he scraped a living reporting from the coroners' courts when lesser men held

comfortable fellowships at universities. I asked if his day had
gone well.

'Yes indeed. Three different papers and probably a half column
in all of them.'

'The Monument inquest?'

'Yes.'

We walked companionably into Fleet Street, then up another
side street to the back of a coffee house. Again, women weren't
welcome at the front of it, but Jimmy was friendly with the head
waiter, who kept a more welcoming salon at the back. We took
off our hats and coats and chose a settle by the fire. I waited
until our coffee was brought to put to him the case of Miss Tilbury.
He sipped and shook his head.

'Nobody of anything like that description in the past eight
days, neither accident nor suicide. I should certainly have known.
Young women invariably attract attention.'

That seemed to close another line of investigation. I came back
to the question of the Monument suicide.

'Did they identify the young woman at the inquest?'

'Yes. She was a Miss Janet Priest. Her father kept a stationery
and print shop in the City Road.'

'How did they find out who she was?'

'Yesterday evening a distraught young woman went to St
Magnus, saying that she thought the deceased girl might be her
younger sister, who had been missing from home for the past
week. They let her view the body and she fainted away. The poor
woman had to give evidence of identification to the inquest this
afternoon.'

Although it had nothing to do with my case now, I couldn't
help being interested.

'It's odd that she was missing for a week before she killed
herself. Or had she gone missing before?'

There were girls who slipped in and out of respectability as
financial need demanded.

'Nothing like that. According to the sister's evidence and an
older woman's who was a family friend, she was a model daughter
– helped her father in the shop and had few friends and interests
outside it.'

'No gentlemen followers?'

'No. And the surgeon who examined the body made it clear that she was not in a certain condition.'

Of course, with a young female suicide, pregnancy or otherwise would be one of the first things he checked.

'Had she been depressed in spirits?'

'The sister said not.'

'Did anybody have any idea where she went in the week she was missing?'

'No.'

I began to worry again about Miss Tilbury. There was a resemblance in that they both seemed to be two young women whose characters were a blank. Admittedly Miss Priest, doing useful work in East London, had lived a less sheltered life than Miss Tilbury, but both of them sounded too good and docile to be true. Miss Tilbury had been missing now for eight days. Miss Priest had been gone from home for a week before her body was discovered at the foot of the Monument.

'How did she get up the Monument without anybody knowing?' I said.

'The assumption was that she went up the afternoon before and the attendant, Mr Jenkins, failed to check before he locked up for the night. He insists that he did and that furthermore, if she had gone up in the afternoon, he'd have seen her and taken her entrance fee. He didn't.'

'Did they believe him?'

'On the whole, yes. Some of the jury were sceptical, but the coroner knows Mr Jenkins quite well.'

'And the entrance is locked at night?' I said.

'Yes.'

'So did they decide how she got up there?'

'No. Mr Jenkins' theory is that somebody must have borrowed the key and had it copied.'

'And then gave it to a young woman so that she could throw herself off? That's nonsense surely.'

'Nobody seemed impressed with the theory, but nobody produced any other.'

'What was the verdict?'

'That Janet Priest destroyed herself while labouring under temporary insanity.'

The usual kind verdict, meant to spare the feelings of relatives. I finished my coffee.

'Did anybody ask why Miss Priest's hair was wet?' I said.

'What?'

Jimmy had been staring into the fire. He turned to me, surprised.

'I was at the Monument yesterday afternoon,' I said. 'A policeman who'd seen her soon after the body was discovered said her hair was soaking wet. It hadn't rained that night or morning.'

'No, a workman gave evidence about finding the body and so did a policeman, but neither mentioned her hair.'

'I suppose he thought it wasn't relevant to anything. And by the time the sister saw the body, her hair would have dried. Strange though.'

'Very strange.' He was staring at me, reporter's instincts aroused. 'Another strange thing.'

'Another?'

'Yes, there was the question of a ring. Did your policeman say anything about that?'

'Yes. He said she had a ring on her wedding finger. I think he described it as funny looking.'

'Miss Priest wasn't married,' Jimmy said. 'The sister and the older woman were quite sure there was nobody even in prospect. The coroner and the jury gave some time to that and had to conclude that it was another of those inexplicable things.'

'So why should she wash her hair and put a ring on her wedding finger?'

'If she put it on her finger.' He was being provoking now, trying to lead me on.

'What do you mean?'

'The surgeon was a thorough man. He said there were abrasions on her knuckle. The ring was too small for her finger and it looked as if it had been forced on quite roughly.'

'By somebody else?'

'How could they tell? It's possible, after all, that she was so desperate to have it on her finger that she forced it on herself.'

'Why should she be desperate about that? I'm surprised that

they brought in a verdict of self-destruction. There are things not explained,' I said.

'Yes, but where was the evidence for anything else

We discussed it for a while, but it was no case of mine, after all. When we left, Jimmy insisted on paying for our coffee. He'd never accept money from me for his help. Once, as a thank-you, I'd been allowed to buy him an edition of *Martial* he'd coveted. That was all. He also insisted on walking me to the stop for the Piccadilly omnibus and seeing me on board.

'I'll let you know if I hear anything of your fair-haired lady,' he said.

Much though I liked to solve my cases, I hoped not. If Jimmy Cuffs had news of Miss Tilbury, it would be from a mortuary. Miss Priest had thrown such a gloom on my spirits that I did not want to contemplate another death.

FIVE

The contessa's white forehead was creased in doubt so deep that it looked painful. Her tongue tip, bright and plump as a strawberry, was clamped between pearly front teeth, hand to her cheek, her indecision reflected in half a dozen mirrors. The rest of us watched and waited. Six of us altogether, Madame Leman and her two seamstresses in plain black dresses, the contessa's German maid, my maid Suzette and myself, sitting on the end of a chaise longue, a swathe of velvet samples in my lap. The contessa was trying on a hooded cloak of mulberry coloured velvet, the hood edged with white fur. The effect was breathtaking, framing her deep violet eyes and dark curls to perfection. It was impossible to look at her without thinking of sleigh parties, harness bells and laughter on frosty air. But she wasn't satisfied.

'It's wrong, the feel of it. It's . . .' She swung round to me. 'It's the wrong animal.'

'The finest white coney,' Madame Leman protested.

The town's most fashionable dressmaker – or rather *couturière* as her bronze plate had it – was a plump woman, with rouged cheeks, several chins and the air of a put-upon duchess.

'Coney?' said the contessa.

I struggled to remember Italian for rabbit.

'*Coniglio.*'

The contessa flung the hood from her head as if the lining were live asps. 'Not possible.' She flew to a rail by the wall, where clothes for other customers were hanging, seized a white fur wrap and held it close to her cheek.

'This is what it must have. See.'

As far as the look of it went, she was right. The other fur improved on what had looked like perfection already, giving new lustre to her complexion, pointing up the whiteness of her teeth. Her great eyes took on a predatory gleam, as if from the nature of the animal that had owned the fur.

'Arctic fox,' Madame Leman protested. 'Very rare, very expensive.'

'No matter. It is what it must be. *Coniglio* – urrr!'

She let the fox fur slide to the carpet and began tearing at the trim of the cloak hood, managing to rip a seam with fingers that must be stronger than they looked. Madame Leman and one of the seamstresses hastily moved forward and unfastened the cloak. The other seamstress had picked up the fox fur and was stroking it like a person soothing a sentient animal.

'Very well,' Madame Leman said, with heavy politeness. 'But fox will cost ten pounds more.'

The contessa waved away a sum that amounted to three months' pay for a governess with a flicker of her fingers. 'No matter. And it must be done by Monday.'

The seamstresses exchanged looks. They'd be working all over the weekend. The expression on Madame Leman's face was one that would be recognised by anybody whose financial circumstances had ever been uncertain: she was wondering if her bill would be paid. She decided to give the contessa the benefit of the doubt, probably calculating that a woman with her beauty would always find some man who would pay.

'Very well, madam.'

Having carried her point, the contessa was all smiles again. 'All done, then. I shall send for everything else tomorrow.'

By my count, over the last hour and a half in the fitting room, that included two day dresses, a superb evening costume in jade silk with a bodice of Valenciennes lace and a matching mantle in silk taffeta, two cloaks and a muslin pelerine embroidered with seed pearls in flower shapes. Also a riding outfit in blue twilled silk with a close-fitting jacket, the garment of all of them that had most provoked my envy.

Suzette and I had arrived at Madame Leman's premises in Piccadilly at half past eleven precisely. There'd been no sign of the contessa, so for ten minutes or so we discussed my requirements. Since I'd presumably have to move in the same social circles as the contessa, a new evening gown seemed appropriate. We'd done no more than settle the colour (soft green with darker moss green trimmings, so much *le mode* she told me) and the materials (velvet, with silk pleating on the bodice) before a small commotion broke out downstairs. Madame Leman scurried out to the landing.

'Contessa, so pleased.'

The woman must surely have been complicit in the double booking. I wondered how much Mr Clyde had paid her and noted that he was being given a good performance for his money.

'So sorry, desolee, madame. One of my silly girls must have made a mistake.'

The contessa had swept into the fitting room, looking annoyed. When she saw me, annoyance gave way to a moment's puzzlement then, with hardly a pause, to recognition.

'We have met, yes?'

'The night before last,' I said. 'At the recital.'

'Yes.' The full force of her smile beamed out at me. 'You were taking my part against all those foolish men.'

Madame was still talking about the mistaken appointment.

'It's no matter,' I said. 'I'm sure the contessa made her engagement with you first. I can come back later.'

Of course, I had no intention of going. The contessa made it easy for me.

'No, you must stay and give me your advice. I know nothing, nothing, about English fashion. You shall guide me.'

'I'm sure you know more than I do,' I said.

Every pleat and tuck of the clothes she was wearing proved

it. She'd already untied her cloak and let it drop, to be caught by her maid, and her eyes were ranging round the room. I'd seen fencers at an academy look like that, choosing their weapons. The seamstresses produced the first garment for her to try and her maid undressed her to chemise, corset and petticoats. She stood there, in her white silk stockings and cream satin pumps, entirely unembarrassed at being in her underwear in front of a woman she'd only known for a few minutes. She was beautiful, a pocket Venus. For all her small size, her breasts were full and rounded, her hips curvaceous enough to give shape to a skirt. And yet there was one blemish to the perfection. When she bared her upper arm, four dark bruises such as a man's fingers might have made stood out against the white skin. She must have been handled roughly when she tried to get to the princes' carriage. She gave no explanation. Mrs Leman had probably seen worse and made no comment. Successions of muslin, silk gauze, velvet, were wafted over the contessa, patted into place and minute adjustments made. Now and again she'd ask me for my opinion, but only as a matter of form. After the business of the fox fur was settled and while her maid was dressing her in her outdoor clothes, she turned to me.

'We shall go together, yes? You'll come to have breakfast with me?'

Breakfast? It was one o'clock by then. I said I should like that.

I followed her downstairs, our maids behind us. A blue painted droshky was waiting outside. A palomino pony, hide gleaming like antique gold, stood between the shafts. The driver on the box was a lad as handsome as a young Pan, in sky blue livery with silver braid. He jumped down to help us in. As the droshky only carried two people, that left both maids on the pavement. The contessa's maid seemed quite used to this treatment. Suzette glanced at me.

'I'll see you later,' I said.

It would do her no harm to walk the short distance back to Grosvenor Street. The droshky went from a stand straight into a fast trot. Even in Mayfair, our equipage turned heads. We drew up outside a house halfway along the east side of Grosvenor Square. Before we'd come to a halt, young Pan had jumped off the box to help us out. He left the obedient pony standing and leapt up the steps to bang on the front door with the butt of his whip. Goodness knows why. There was a perfectly normal bell. The door opened immediately, as if of its own accord. When I followed the contessa inside, there was another young man in sky blue livery, standing to attention. She swept past him. I followed her upstairs.

'Such an exhausting morning.'

She collapsed onto a sofa. It was a spectacular collapse. She seemed to rise into the air then waft down onto the cushions, perfectly horizontal, like an acrobat. Her eyes closed, but her hand reached down to pick up a silver bell from the floor and tinkle it.

I settled into an armchair and looked around. At first glance, this room was as colourful and exotic as an aviary. Shawls in a rainbow of colours draped every horizontal surface, silk cushions plumped out chairs, a daybed, the window seat. And yet, once you were accustomed to the dazzle, there was nothing that couldn't have been packed up and carried away in a couple of hours. Behind the softness were the plain furniture and bland decoration of a rented apartment, much like the one that I was supposed to inhabit at number four Grosvenor Street. The place was not so much an aviary as a perch for a bird of passage. The door opened. The young man from downstairs came in followed by an angular maid, both carrying trays. If the contessa were deeply in debt, at least she was sinking in style. Still without opening her eyes, she fluttered her hand towards a table. They put the trays down and withdrew.

I was hungry and thirsty. There were a silver chocolate pot with two delicate cups, a decanter of what looked like Madeira and two glasses, a plate of thinly sliced seed cake, bowls of bonbons, hot house grapes with the bloom still on them.

'Would you like me to pour the chocolate?' I said.

She nodded. When I turned back towards her with a full cup, her eyes were open and she was watching me.

'I forget your name.'

I told her. We sipped our chocolate.

'You have no rings,' she said.

She was wearing four or five, mostly sapphires.

'No.'

'You are not married?' she said.

'No.'

'But you have a gentleman?'

'I have a gentleman.'

And yet I knew it was dishonest, because she would take it another way. I was unmarried but out in society and apparently not short of money. Therefore I must be a kept woman.

'You know many people?' she said.

'Yes, quite a number.'

'Have you been presented at court?' she said. Her pretence of exhaustion had gone. Her eyes were very bright.

'No.'

'But you know people who have?'

'Yes.'

In truth, very few. My friend Cecilia, now heavily pregnant so confined to her country estate. Two former clients, only one still on speaking terms.

'Tell me, how is it managed?'

'It's not easy,' I said. 'I believe the Queen keeps to quite a close circle of friends.'

Her chocolate cup rattled down on a table. 'It's a great mistake in a country, to have a queen.'

Although no defender of Little Vicky, I had to protest. 'Why not a queen? What about Queen Elizabeth and Catherine the Great?'

'Yes, and where were the chances for women in their time? With a king, if a woman is beautiful there's always a way in to court. What's the point of being beautiful if there's only a queen?'

She was as indignant as an orator attacking the poor laws. I thought I'd heard most political points of view but here at least was something original.

'I confess it's never occurred to me,' I said.

She stood up and began ranging round the room, picking up a sweetmeat from the bowl every time she passed the table.

'When I met you, I thought you knew people. I hoped you might help me.'

'Help you how?'

'To know how things are done. To be invited.'

'I'd have thought you knew much better than I do,' I said.

'Yes, but not in England. What do I know about England? I have no friends here, nobody.'

'Then why did you come here?' I said.

She didn't answer, apart from grabbing a stuffed date from a bowl and biting into it as if it had annoyed her as well. I noticed several newspapers on a table, which surprised me until I noticed that they were all turned to a page with the court circular. Her eyes followed mine.

'Look at them. They ride in the park, they listen to the band, they entertain the same boring people to dinner.'

'Are other courts more interesting?' I asked innocently, fishing for any reference to the Saxe Coburg household.

'It depends who's present.'

Since I'd been invited to breakfast, I took a date as well. Marzipan and rose water. Delicious.

'And you're interested in somebody who's at court at Windsor?'

She gave me a sideways glance and a sudden smile.

'You are?' I said. 'Who?'

'A gentleman who is attending on the princes.'

'Part of the Saxe Coburg suite?'

A little nod. I ate another date. She poured herself a glass of Madeira and looked inquiringly at me.

'Too early for me, thank you.'

'The doctor says I must drink it for my health,' she said. She finished the glass in a couple of gulps. If this was a sample of her eating and drinking habits it was a wonder she didn't have spots on her chin and breath like an old spaniel, but she was as fresh as a milkmaid.

'So you can't help me?' she said. 'You don't know anybody who can get me presented at court?'

'No, but I'm sure you'll meet somebody who will.'

Though whether young Victoria would welcome a woman with the contessa's beauty and reputation I very much doubted.

'It's not easy,' she said. 'I've been thinking about the horse riding. The paper says they ride in the park at Windsor every day. Is it like Hyde Park?'

'Larger.'

'And other people may ride there too?'

'I believe so, but I doubt if they're allowed to ride close to the queen's party.'

'I'm very good on horseback,' she said. 'I ride like a hussar.' She said it with such certainty that it hardly sounded like vanity, more of a statement of fact. I said that I enjoyed horse riding too.

'We shall ride in Hyde Park together then,' she said, good tempered again at the prospect of a diversion. 'You'll see to hiring horses?'

I nodded, not bothering to say that I possessed my own.

'When?'

'Tomorrow, if you like,' I said.

She shook her head. 'Tomorrow's Sunday. Nobody who matters rides on a Sunday. We shall ride on Monday.'

I told her the name of the livery stables where Amos worked and assured her that her driver would know it. I suggested meeting at eleven, knowing that she'd never dream of riding at my unfashionable early hour. Soon after that, she had to change to go and drink tea with somebody. She kissed me on the cheek and said how glad she was to have found a friend. She scared me. She had the ruthlessness of the self-absorbed, which is one of the most dangerous forces on earth.

Tabby was waiting when I got back to Abel Yard, with a self-satisfied look on her face that brought a brief flare of hope.

'Well, how did you get on yesterday?' I said. 'Did you find a cab driver who remembered Miss Tilbury?'

'Nah. They was useless. I found out something about the other one though.'

'Other one?'

'The one what went off the top of the Monument.'

I had to keep tight hold of my temper. 'Tabby, I told you, that case has nothing to do with us. Besides, it's all over. They had the inquest yesterday and decided she killed herself.'

'I know they had the inquest. I was there, outside the Old Swan.'

'You weren't supposed to be there. I told you to stay at Aldersgate and talk to the cabbies.'

'I did, for a long time. Then I could see I wasn't getting

nowhere, so I thought I'd walk over to the Monument and see what was happening there. When I got to Fish Hill Street, there was this crowd outside the Old Swan, with a policeman keeping them back. So I went over to find out what was going on and it turned out they were people who wanted to get in to the inquest but they couldn't because there wasn't enough room. And I thought if I could get inside, I could find out about it for you.'

She paused for breath.

'Tabby, I did not need to know about it because it's nothing to do with me.' Then I spoiled the effect by adding, 'Anyway, I've heard all about it already from somebody who was inside.'

'Did he tell you about the old man outside who saw the devil driving round?'

I turned away, intending to go upstairs. She stepped in front of me.

'He wanted to go in and tell the judge about him, but the policeman kept him back.'

'I'm not surprised. Now—'

'The policeman keeping the crowd back called him Gaffer. He seemed to know him. He's an old man, grey hair and beard all over the place, crawling with lice.'

(I supposed that was at least something on the credit side. A few months ago, Tabby would have taken that as a normal state of affairs.)

'And drunk, I suppose.'

'A bit. Somebody in the crowd says Gaffer's always seeing the devil at the bottom of a pint pot and they all laugh. So he walks off grumbling into a builder's yard next door. So I think I might as well follow him. He's got a bottle hidden in a woodpile there. I sit myself down beside him and ask what's all this about?'

I couldn't help sighing. Here was the best and worst of my apprentice. She was shameless and fearless and would talk to anyone anywhere, but when it came to everyday routine and following instructions, she was as unreliable as an untrained puppy. Yet she'd hooked me and I couldn't walk away from her story after all. I sat down on the bottom of the stairs and let her talk.

'He says he was asleep in the yard there, only a stone's throw away from the Monument, when he hears wheels on the cobbles outside. Not the usual wheels, he says. He knows the carts that come and go, and this wasn't one of them. So he thinks about it for a while, then he gets up to look.'

'What time was this?'

'Late. He says he'd heard midnight strike, and it was a long time after that. Still dark, any road. So he looks out, and there's this carriage standing at the back of the Monument. Gentleman's carriage, he says.'

'He can tell that in the dark?'

'There was enough light to see the shape of it. Then two people come out of it. One's holding a lamp with the shutter mostly round it so there's not much light coming out, and the other's the devil.'

'How did he know?'

'Because he had horns. Gaffer thought he had a hunched back too, but then it turned out that was because he was carrying something over his shoulder. Then when they got to the Monument, the devil took his head off and went inside with what he was carrying.'

'So devils can take off their heads?'

'Gaffer said this one did.'

Tabby was entirely serious. I couldn't tell whether she really believed it herself or whether she was faithfully recording the old drunkard's story.

'So what happened then?'

'He stands there looking, then he hears a sound from the other side of the Monument, the side he can't see.'

'What sort of sound?'

'Like a body hitting the ground. I thought he might just be saying that because he knew what happened, so I asked him what a body hitting the ground sounds like. He said like a sack of cabbages falling off a wagon.'

'No scream?'

'No.'

'Did he go round the Monument to see?'

'No. He says next thing, the devil and the man with the lamp come running from the other side of the Monument. Then they jump in the carriage and away they go.'

She stood, head on one side, waiting for my opinion.

'You don't really believe he saw a devil do you?' I said.

'He saw summat that scared him, I know that much.'

'Tabby, you know London's full of this devil nonsense. It's not surprising if it gets into an old drunkard's head.'

But was it possible that in his befogged state he really had heard something and embroidered the rest? Perhaps, if the policeman had been more patient, it might have helped to establish a time of death. Not that I intended to encourage Tabby's wild wanderings by admitting that. She looked down, disappointed.

'So what are we going to do now?'

'The work we're being paid for. Wait there while I go up and change.'

So we set off on a tour of police offices. By omnibus and on foot we trailed round offices from the territory of the City force in the east to Oxford Street in the west. At all of them I waited in a queue then asked the same question: was there any record of a young woman of my friend's description meeting with any kind of an accident in the past nine days? At all of them we drew a blank, sometimes given with a shrug but more usually after a careful examination of records. Knowing Tabby's attitude to the police, I'd forbidden her to utter a word, so she just stood beside me, glaring at the unfortunate officers as if they were maliciously concealing things from us.

'Tabby, why in the world should they lie to us,' I said after one such episode.

'Why does a dog bite?'

We took the omnibus home. I gave Tabby a shilling and told her she should take Sunday off.

'But we're no nearer finding Miss Tilbury,' she objected.

'It's like that sometimes.'

Too often for comfort.

Amos and I did not ride out on Sundays, so next morning I walked across the park to ask him to choose a horse for Monday, to suit a lightweight lady who fancied herself as a hussar. He promised to attend to it, but disappointed me by saying he wouldn't be there himself. He had to deliver a horse to Surrey, part of a complex piece of dealing, and expected to be away for two days. In the afternoon I walked over to Bloomsbury with Mrs Martley to visit my infant god-daughter, Miranda Liberty Suter. She kicked and gurgled in her wooden cradle while her parents glowed with content. When her mother Jenny took her away to feed her, attended by Mrs Martley, Daniel and I had the chance for a private talk. Daniel had been a family friend as long as I could remember and had stood by me in the sad and dangerous days after my father's death. At one time, I thought I might have married him, then he fell in love with Jenny, a dancer, when she was facing her own dark times. He was happy professionally as well as personally, composing again and in demand for directing and conducting at both Covent Garden and Drury Lane.

'And how are you, Liberty? Not working too hard, I hope.'

I admitted that as far as results went, I was hardly working at all.

He then said something that had clearly been on his mind. 'Liberty, you don't have to do this. I'm sure we could find some music teaching for you.'

'I'm well enough, for the while at least.'

'Now I'm on my feet again . . . if a few pounds would be of any help . . .?'

'Daniel, don't worry about me. You'll need to save all your money for Miranda, even if she does turn out to be the greatest musical prodigy since Mozart.'

'Jenny says she'll be a singer, from the way she gurgles in tune. I watch her kicking her little feet and say she'll be a dancer like Jenny.'

Besotted, the pair of them, as was right.

Robert came to meet us as we walked home along Grosvenor Street in the dusk. Mrs Martley approved of him, as far as she approved of any of my acquaintances, and walked a little ahead so that he and I could talk.

'Stephen and I are leaving by the mail coach for Holyhead tonight, then the Irish boat,' he said.

Our hands touched and clasped. I could feel the pulse in his wrist beating, through the thickness of our two gloves. At the gateway to Abel Yard we kissed for an instant, before Mrs Martley turned round to see if we were still with her. At least, I think we managed it before she turned.

'He looks thin. He needs looking after,' Mrs Martley said as he walked away.

I pretended not to hear.

That evening, I wrote two notes.

> Dear Mr James,
>
> I am sorry to inform you that so far I have not succeeded in finding any trace of Miss Tilbury. It may be of some comfort to know that exhaustive inquiries at police stations have produced no evidence that she has come to harm. If you recall anything Miss Tilbury may have said or done to give the slightest indication of her plans, it would greatly aid the inquiry. So far, my expenses amount to eight shillings and four pence, mainly on omnibus fares for myself and my assistant. I shall send a message to you at once if I have any news.

The other one was even shorter.

> Dear Mr Clyde,
>
> As planned, I met the lady in whom you are interested at the dressmaker's and shall be riding with her in the park on Monday morning. She is showing interest in the routine of the court at Windsor and makes no secret of her wish to introduce herself there. I shall report further after our ride.

I signed both of them 'your obedient servant' as was only businesslike. First thing in the morning, I'd give one to Tabby for the post, care of Mr James's friend at Islington. Suzette could deliver the other. Then I forgot about business and, in my mind, followed the Irish mail at the start of its long journey through the night.

SIX

'Your horse is better than mine,' the contessa said. She sounded like a child who'd been left with the smaller slice of cake.

'Yours is a very good horse as well,' I consoled her.

One of the finest in the stables, a 15 hand chestnut mare called Bella, bright as a new penny with a sweet temperament. Amos had done us proud there. In his absence, the groom riding discreetly two horses' length behind us was young Wiggins, newly promoted from stable lad to the glory of a cockaded hat. It was strange to be riding in the park without Amos, even stranger to be there at the fashionable time of mid morning, rather than the crack of dawn. At this hour, riding was like being at an assembly or rout that went on hooves rather than on feet. The broad rides through the park were thronged with open landaus and riders: ladies showing off their latest horse or riding costume, cavalry officers in uniform, invalids out for their health on slow steady cobs, lovers riding side by side, so close that their horses' flanks were almost touching. It might be sociable, but it meant very dull riding. Every time we broke into a trot or a canter, there'd be somebody waving good morning and having to be acknowledged, or a group of people stopping for a conversation in the middle of the ride.

We were in Rotten Row, on the south side of the park. So far, the contessa had reined in her horse at least half a dozen times. It was amazing how many people she knew after a short time in London, in spite of her claim to be friendless. Quite a few of them were foreigners. Some of her conversations were in German, some in Italian, most in English. Invariably, she introduced me as her dear friend. I wondered if all these other people were friends of as short duration. Sometimes too we had to stop for my friends and acquaintances, so I'd introduce her. After every such meeting, as we rode out of earshot, she'd quiz me about these people: were they wealthy, powerful, well-connected? Her interest was entirely shameless and always with the same aim: were they received at court? Sometimes I had to tell her I had no idea. She didn't believe me.

'You must know. Surely everybody knows.'

Something distracted her. She glanced towards a group of young men, lounging on their hunters on the far side of the Row then, without explanation or apology to me, started cantering towards them. I heard her call out a name.

'Courtney.'

One of the young men turned and went cantering towards her.

They met in mid ride and he raised his hat to her. He was a pleasant enough looking man, but had that callow look of some of the English nobility, as if he'd stayed in the nest too long. She asked him a question, urgently and without greeting or preamble. I couldn't hear what it was. His answer was short. When he'd given it, he looked down at his horse's withers, uneasy. She shot another question at him. He nodded, then watched her as she cantered back towards me.

I expected her to tell me who he was, but she said nothing. Whatever he'd told her had changed her mood. She was electric with excitement, so much so that the chestnut felt it and started dancing on her trim hooves.

'Let's race,' the contessa said, and loosed the rein.

The chestnut shot off, scattering a group of invalids, bringing ironic cheers from some of the sporting gentlemen. I smiled, taking my time. Bella had a good turn of speed but was no stayer, nowhere near a match for my Rancie. When I'd given them about a furlong's start, I let Rancie flow into a canter, then pressed my heel gently against her side. She went like a swallow into her gallop that was the nearest thing I'd ever know to flying, her hooves touching the ground only as a courtesy to gravity. We overtook them long before the end of the Row and I drew rein to wait for them. The chestnut's flanks were heaving, but Rancie had hardly broken sweat. Poor Wiggins, on a slow cob, was trailing along behind. The contessa looked wonderful, lips parted, cheeks glowing. She'd acquired a small following of gentlemen, riding a few lengths behind her. They did not include the young man she'd called Courtney. From their laughter, they'd been betting on the result of our race.

'I want to buy her,' the contessa said.

I just shook my head. Rancie wasn't for sale.

'May I ride her, then?'

I considered it, and nodded. The contessa was a good rider, with the light hands that were essential for managing Rancie.

'If you like. But no more than a canter. We're not racing again.'

Wiggins arrived and helped us change horses, making a step with his hands to lift us into our saddles. I had to admit, with a little envy, that the contessa looked very well on Rancie. We walked sedately back along the Row, pretending to ignore our following of gentlemen. Halfway along, a couple of rowdy young bloods were jumping their horses over a railing into a flower bed and out again.

'Could you do that?' the contessa said to me, eyes bright.

I was starting to say that I had more respect for my horse's legs, and for the flower bed come to that, but before I could get out more than a few words she'd turned Rancie and was cantering fast towards the railings. There was no time even to shout stop, though it wouldn't have helped. The young rowdies looked on, amazed, as Rancie soared over the first railing, into the soft earth of the flower bed and out again on the other side. By that time, she was without her rider. In landing, Rancie had at once understood the danger of her situation and faced it with her usual courage and intelligence, taking off again immediately in a long leap that landed her safely on the turf on the far side. If I'd been on her back, I'd have known by instinct what she was going to do and kept my seat, but the contessa had expected her to take a short stride in between, as the men's horses had done, so was taken by surprise. She was lying there on her back, senseless, on the earth.

Pandemonium. A woman was screaming, men shouting. Several threw themselves from their horses and leapt over the railings to help her. I slid off the chestnut, threw the reins to Wiggins and walked round on the grass to Rancie, not caring much if the contessa were alive or dead. I was so furious with her that I'd have felt like knocking her unconscious myself if the ground had not done it for me. Rancie was standing there, nostrils flaring, knowing that something was wrong. I took the rein and stroked her muzzle.

'It's not your fault, Rancie. It's mine. Forgive me. I should never have let her touch you.'

I walked Rancie a little way and found her mercifully undamaged. By then, Wiggins had come to join us, pale faced and looking as if it were his fault. 'The poor lady's alive at any rate,' he muttered.

I just stopped myself saying that she didn't deserve to be. I left the three horses in his care and went over to the flower bed. Some of the men were lifting the contessa over the railing. She gasped and briefly opened her eyes. I didn't think they should have moved her but it was too late now. Two of them spread their coats on the grass and laid her down. Another vaulted onto his horse saying he'd fetch a doctor from the barracks. I noticed that the skirt of her riding habit was rucked up showing a shapely knee in a silk stocking and a calf booted in black leather. Perhaps the gentlemen were too polite to touch the skirt, or more likely they enjoyed looking at her leg.

I kneeled down beside her, and at first sight thought that a bone must have broken so badly that it was making a bulge along her boot. Then the light caught something metallic in the top of the boot close to the calf, only visible to me kneeling down. I might have made some sound of surprise, because her eyes sprang open, full of pain, and fixed on me.

'Don't touch it.' She hissed it at me, winced and closed her eyes again.

I pulled her skirt down and stayed kneeling beside her until a doctor came galloping up. Under his care, and a gulp of brandy from a gentleman's flask, she recovered enough to sit up. After some time, the doctor pronounced her fit to be moved and a charitable lady offered to see her home to Grosvenor Square in her carriage. As she limped to the carriage, supported by several gentlemen, her eyes met mine again. Challenging eyes, as if daring me to say anything. Wiggins and I watched the carriage roll away.

'Don't worry,' I said. 'You were certainly not to blame and I shall make sure Mr Legge knows that.'

We rode slowly back to the livery stables, Wiggins leading Bella. As soon as I'd seen Rancie untacked, I went straight across the park and knocked on the door of 4 Grosvenor Street. As Suzette let me in, I heard piano music coming from upstairs. Mozart, and very well played as it happened, although I was too angry to notice at the time. I stamped up the stairs and opened the door of the drawing room that was supposed to be mine. Mr Clyde turned on the piano stool, smiling as if the music had put him into a pleasant dream. He stood up and the smile faded when he saw my face.

'What happened? Wouldn't the contessa ride with you after all?'

'Oh, she rode with me,' I said. 'She nearly killed my horse and has probably broken her ankle.'

'Where is she?'

'Somebody took her home.'

'I must go to her.'

'Not yet,' I said. 'There's something that won't wait.'

'What's that?'

'I'm not accepting your case after all.'

'Why not?'

'Because I can't do my work if my clients lie to me,'

If he'd denied lying, I'd have walked out. (Even though curiosity might nag me for the rest of my life.)

He stood looking at me, his eyes sad. When he spoke, his voice was low and tired. 'Would you sit down, at least?'

I sat on the edge of one of the armchairs. My riding boots were muddy from the flower bed and had left smears on the carpet. He sat back down on the piano stool and waited for me to speak.

'You told me that the gentleman she's obsessed with is part of the prince's household. He isn't. She's in love with one of the princes himself.'

'She told you that?'

'No. But there were only the two princes in the carriage when she tried to deliver her letter.'

I could see that he wanted to ask how I knew that. 'So which is it?' I said. 'Ernest or Albert?'

'Oh, Ernest. Albert's far too shy for anything like that.' His reply was prompt, with a wry twist of a smile.

'So the contessa was Prince Ernest's mistress?' I said.

He nodded.

'I should have told you from the start, I admit. But I'm sure you'll understand the wish to avoid scandal, particularly since the princes are on an official visit here.' He waited. I said nothing.

'Please, Miss Lane, accept my apology and don't give us up. I can't tell you how relieved I was when you agreed to help me. If you walk away now, I don't know where to turn.'

I guessed that he wasn't accustomed to plead for what he wanted.

'There's something else you didn't tell me,' I said.

'What?'

'That she carries a pistol. It was hidden in her riding boot, but I saw it when she fell off.'

He looked startled. I didn't know whether it was because of the pistol, or because I knew about it.

'Did anybody else see it?'

'I'm almost sure not. But did you know?'

He hung his head, looking away from me for the first time. 'I didn't know. Perhaps I feared it.'

'Why?'

He raised his eyes. 'A person may carry a weapon in self-defence.'

'This is Mayfair, not some blasted heath full of highwaymen,' I said. 'Why should she expect to have to defend herself? Have any of Prince Ernest's people threatened violence against her?'

'I don't believe the prince would countenance anything like that.'

'If not the prince, maybe one of his overenthusiastic followers?' I persisted. 'After all, if she's such an embarrassment, it might have occurred to somebody to try to scare her away.'

'The contessa is not easily scared.'

'Exactly. She wasn't scared this morning, out in the park, and yet she was carrying a pistol. There are two reasons for carrying a weapon: defence – or attack.'

He looked at me and said nothing.

'So who is she planning to attack?' I said.

'Like you, I can only guess.'

'Who, then?'

'The man she thinks has wronged her.'

'If every woman who was wronged by a man decided to shoot him, half the human race wouldn't reach the age of thirty,' I said.

'She is not every woman. She's passionate, perhaps reckless.'

'Desperate too, you said. So, Prince Ernest?'

'Yes.'

I thought about it, aware of his eyes on me. He'd won one round at any rate. I hadn't walked out.

'Assuming you're right,' I said, 'how could she? He must be surrounded by people nearly all the time. Even when she was trying to deliver her letter, she didn't get to him.'

'But suppose she'd had a pistol in her hand at the time, not just a letter. Would she have been close enough for that?'

I thought the answer was probably yes.

'There's another point about that. She knew somehow that he'd be making a private visit to the Gloucesters in Park Lane,' I said.

'Exactly. I've thought all along that she's getting information, either from somebody in the princes' suite or even at Windsor.'

'She met a young man in the park named Courtney,' I said. 'He told her some piece of news that excited her.'

'Did you know him?'

'No.'

'And she didn't say what the news was?'

'No.'

'You might ask her when you go to visit her.'

'I'm not sure I shall be visiting her.'

'Wouldn't it be the normal thing to do, call and ask after her injury?'

'Except that the injury was her own fault and she could have broken my mare's leg.'

He waved that aside, but then he couldn't have known all that Rancie meant to me.

'Miss Lane, I should have taken you fully into my confidence from the start. Now you know the worst of it, you must see in all humanity that you can't walk away and leave her.'

'If you're even half right, that's exactly what I should do. You're asking me to protect a woman who might try to assassinate a visiting royal.'

'No. I'm asking you to help prevent it.'

'Then tell the police or even the Foreign Office what you suspect. I'm sure you have friends in high places.'

'And have her arrested? You can't ask me to do that.'

'Even if she tries to kill him the next time he makes a visit somewhere?'

'Then we must stop it. That, and something else she might be planning.'

'What else?'

He hesitated, turned to the piano and held down a low key. When he spoke, his voice was not much louder than the dying vibrations of the piano wire. 'She might be planning to shoot herself in his presence.'

I could imagine that, more easily than seeing her as a murderess. I even pictured the scene: a public occasion with His Highness and courtiers on horseback and in uniform. A lovely, desperate young woman rushes forward, perhaps grips the prince's stirrup with her small hand. *See, see to what you have condemned me.* Her other hand produces something from her heaving bosom. Before the courtiers can recover from their horror, a shot rings out. The young woman slumps to the ground, heart blood pumping over the white lace at her breast, pistol falling from her hand. The other hand clings for a few seconds to her betrayer's stirrup then, as the fingers reluctantly surrender their grip, falls beside her lifeless body. A scandal of European dimensions has occurred.

'I think, in cases like that, people don't really imagine they're going to die,' I said, almost to myself. 'They picture themselves floating over it all, seeing people being sorry for what they've done.'

'Exactly that. You see, you do understand her. That's why you can't desert us.'

'You mentioned a gentleman who wanted to marry her in spite of everything,' I said. 'Does he know about all this?'

'Yes.'

'Then if I were that gentleman, I think I should try to kidnap her.'

He opened his eyes wide. 'Kidnap?'

'Yes. According to what you tell me, she sees this visit to London as her last chance. The prince is only here for a few weeks. If the contessa could be got out of the way until the visit were over, she might see sense at last.'

'So you're advising him not only to kidnap her but keep her locked up as well?'

'If you're right, she's at risk of being locked up in any case, and for a lot longer than a few weeks.'

'You take my breath away. I wasn't aware I was dealing with a lady of such ruthlessness. But she would surely hate the poor gentleman very much for dealing with her so roughly.'

'Yes.'

'And he doesn't wish to be hated by her.'

'If he loved her, he might have to suffer that hatred as the price for preserving her freedom and possibly her life,' I said.

I was testing him. He sighed.

'Well, I shall put to him your interesting suggestion, if I have the opportunity. Meanwhile, will you go and visit and let me know how she is?'

My riding habit and muddy boots were hardly suitable for visiting the sick, but I wanted to get it over. I stood up.

'Above all, don't say anything to her about this conversation,' he said. 'Don't even mention my name.'

'Really? Would *Mr Clyde* mean anything to her if I did?'

He dropped his eyes. I still wasn't completely in his confidence, whatever he said.

At the contessa's lodging, I had to wait in the hall while the blue and silver footman took my name upstairs. When he ushered me into the salon, the contessa was lying on the chaise longue in a rainbow chrysalis of silk and merino shawls, with her dark curls and those amazing eyes giving promise of an especially exotic butterfly. And an impatient one.

'Where have you been? I have been waiting for you.'

'How's your ankle?'

The leg sticking out from the chrysalis was swaddled in bandages and the smell of comfrey ointment hung in the air.

'The doctor says it's only sprained, but what does he know? I think the bone's broken. And he tells me I must not put weight on it for a week.'

'Is that so bad?'

I thought it might at least keep her out of action while we decided what to do.

'Impossible. I must be in Kensington tomorrow.'

Less than two miles away, but she made it sound like the end of the earth.

'Why?'

'Because he'll be coming there from Windsor.'

I played ignorance. 'Who?'

'The gentleman I told you about.'

'The one who is in the service of Prince Ernest?' I said. I let her understand from my tone of voice that I'd guessed where her true interest was centred. She was too desperate to care.

'Yes. Tomorrow afternoon he'll be paying a private call. I must see him, give a letter to him.'

'You've tried that once already,' I said.

Again, she either didn't hear me or didn't care.

'You must come with me. We'll go in my carriage, then you must give the note into his hand.'

'On certain conditions,' I said.

She listened. She didn't like what I said to her, but had little choice.

Half an hour later, I was back at 4 Grosvenor Street reporting to Mr Clyde. 'That's obviously what she heard from the man Courtney,' I said. 'Somehow she's found a spy at court who lets her know the prince's movements in advance.'

'She has the address in Kensington?'

'Yes. We're to wait outside it in her carriage. Since she can't put her foot to the ground, I'm to get out and deliver the note to him.'

'While she sits in her carriage and takes aim with the pistol, or turns it on herself? Suppose it's a suicide note you're delivering.'

'I don't think so.' I took out the pistol that was weighing down my pocket and gave it to him.

'I made conditions. One, she should hand this over to me. Two, I must be allowed to read the letter I'm to deliver. Three, I'm to be present when her maid dresses her, just in case she possesses the twin to this one.'

He laughed, a good genuine laugh. 'Miss Lane, you are a wonder. She's lucky to have you, even if she doesn't think so.'

'She doesn't. And we're only buying time. This won't solve the problem.'

'If we can buy enough time, the problem solves itself.'

'There's still a month or more of his visit to go. I can't be with her all the time. I suggest you have some urgent words with her other friends about getting her out of the country.'

I wondered whether there really were other friends or if his were a one-man crusade. I thought he might resent my tone, but he took it calmly.

'Yes. I've been thinking over what you said to me. Kidnap may be the answer. But it's important that she must have no suspicions and go on trusting you.'

I did not much like the idea of being the one to lure her into a cage, but it had been my suggestion after all, and the other possibilities were even worse.

'I shall let you know what happens tomorrow,' I said.

'It's getting dark already. May I not escort you home?'

I said no thank you, wanting time to myself. On the landing, he waved Suzette away and came downstairs to open the door for me himself. On the step, he took my hand and held it for a moment.

'I am more grateful to you than I can say, Miss Lane. Go safely.'

As I walked through the gateway into Abel Yard, there was Tabby in her street waif clothes, idly throwing stones at the pump under our stairs. Then, as a well-aimed cobblestone made the metal clang like a bell, it struck me that the onslaught looked anything but idle.

'Tabby, have you gone mad? You'll break the pump if you go on like that.'

She turned, scowling. 'There's a man hid himself behind there. I'm trying to get him to come out.'

'Who is he?'

'Dunno. I saw him looking out, then he saw me and ducked back in again.'

She stooped to pick up another stone. I took it from her.

'Whoever he is, that isn't going to encourage him to come out.' I walked towards the dark place under the stairs. 'Who is it?' I called. 'Come out of there.'

'I can't come out. There's somebody chucking rocks at me.' The voice sounded only mildly annoyed about it.

'Tom Huckerby?'

'The very same.'

'You can come out. No more rocks.'

'Nor bailiffs?'

'No bailiffs either.' I turned to Tabby. 'It's all right, it's a friend.'

'What's he doing at the back of our pump, then?'

'It's just how he lives.'

She accepted that and watched as Tom Huckerby emerged from the dark. He looked more dishevelled and strained than when I'd last seen him, but Tabby's target practice might be enough to account for that. I asked him what the trouble was.

'Apart from Boadicea here, you mean?' He gave Tabby a

friendly grin, not returned. 'I'd just come to see the press was safe, only there was a man out in the mews and I thought I caught a whiff of bailiff off him, so I ducked in here.'

He jumped at the offer of a cup of tea and a sandwich, so I left him with Tabby while I went upstairs to prepare them. Mrs Martley was at the table working on her scrap book and looked over her spectacles at me when I brought out the loaf and ham.

'Are you giving our good food to that ragamuffin again?'

Now I thought of it, feeding Tabby seemed a good idea too. I carried three cups of tea and two doorsteps of sandwiches downstairs on a tray. Tom Huckerby and Tabby were sitting on the mounting block, chatting like old friends.

'He's been in Newgate,' Tabby said, in tones that put it several notches above Eton.

'Just for five weeks on remand,' Huckerby said modestly. 'They were trying to put me away for years on a charge of seditious libel, but the jury wouldn't have it. Here's to the incorruptible British jury.'

He and Tabby toasted it in tea. I guessed she had no idea what he was talking about. He told me, through mouthfuls of sandwich, that they were thinking of moving the press to Wales as soon as they could get transport organized. He thought the workers of Cardiff and Newport might be more likely to stand up for their rights than spoiled Londoners.

'Thought you might like to see this. Latest edition of *The Unbound Briton*. We got five hundred copies printed off before they came for the press.'

He pulled a much folded newspaper from his pocket and gave it to me. I perched on the step of the mounting block and scanned the front page, laughing.

'Oh, that really is very wicked.'

It was mostly taken up with a caricature of Queen Victoria. She was sitting on the lap of our old roue of a prime minister, Lord Melbourne, like a wide-eyed china doll. He was pulling a string that guided her hand while she put her initials to a stack of new laws. In the background, a line of haggard men queued outside a building marked 'Workhouse'.

'Good, yes?' Huckerby asked.

Undoubtedly. But a little unfair too, since the little Vicky had shown signs of having a mind of her own, even if she did lean heavily on Lord Melbourne. It was a fairly mild sample of Tom Huckerby's productions. I turned the page and there was another Victoria cartoon, this time simpering like a girl on a Valentine, hand in hand with life-size tin soldier with 'Prince Albert' written helpfully on the sash across his chest. Moneybags with pound signs on them were heaped at his feet. A couplet underneath, in Gothic type, read:

> He comes to take, for better or for worse,
> England's fat queen and England's fatter purse.

'You couldn't quite describe her as fat,' I said. 'Plump maybe. Is this Albert going to marry her then?'

'So it's said.'

I couldn't help laughing, though my heart sank at the thought of what Mrs Martley would say if she knew that the press producing these disloyalties was hidden practically under her bedroom. Tom and I talked politics for a while, then he said he should go. He departed with a courtly bow to Tabby.

'Farewell, Boadicea. We shall meet again.'

Thinking about it later, it struck me that if Prince Ernest's younger brother really were going to marry Little Vicky, that made the contessa's position even more precarious. A scandal over a minor visiting royal would be bad enough, but ten times worse if it involved the monarch's future brother-in-law. Did the contessa, with her mysterious sources of information, know that? It made me worry even more about what I'd committed myself to do.

COURT CIRCULAR

WINDSOR, Oct. 22.–The Queen rode out in the Park soon after 3 o'clock this afternoon, accompanied by Prince Albert of Saxe Coburg, and attended by Lady C. Barrington, Baroness Lehzen, Miss Quentin, Viscount Melbourne, Viscount Falkland, the Hon. Colonel Grey, The Hon. C. A. Murray, Count Kolowrath, Baron Alvensleben, Sir Frederick Storin, and Sir George Quentin.

Prince Ernest of Saxe Coburg, attended by Lord Alfred Paget, left the Castle this morning for town. His Serene Highness is expected to return to the Castle this evening.

Extract from The Times, 23 Oct 1839.
Albert rides in Windsor Park with Victoria.
Ernest makes a visit to London.

SEVEN

I needed Amos. That was the thought in my mind when I woke on Tuesday morning. True, it would mean compromising my promise of confidentiality to Mr Clyde, but I didn't need to tell Amos everything, just enough to have him keep a close watch on the contessa while I carried out her errand. At our usual time for a ride, I waited for him by the gate. He didn't appear, so I guessed that his trip to Surrey had taken longer than expected. Later in the morning, I walked across to the livery stables in Bayswater Road and asked one of the lads in the yard if Mr Legge had come back.

'Yes, ma'am. But he's not seeing people.'

Puzzled, I found a groom who was a particular friend of Amos. 'Is Mr Legge out on a ride?'

'No, ma'am. He said if you asked for him, I was to tell you he's sorry not to have been with you this morning, only he's indisposed.'

'Indisposed?' Amos was an oak tree. Illnesses glanced off him and rebounded to softer targets. 'Do you mean he's been hurt?'

The groom muttered an apology and disappeared into a loose box. I strode towards the owner's office. On the way, I was aware of a movement behind the closed door of the fodder room.

'Amos Legge, is that you?'

A shuffling inside, then Amos's voice, through the wooden wall. 'Miss Lane? I'm sorry. One of the lads'll look after you.'

The voice was husky. I pushed the door open. He was turned away with the lid of a feed bin up.

'Amos, what is this? Are you really ill?'

He turned reluctantly, letting the lid bang down. I gasped. 'What's happened? Were you thrown, trampled?'

Until then, I'd have sworn that no horse ever foaled could throw Amos.

'Something like that.'

His left cheek was discoloured by a great purple bruise, his right eye shut and the skin round it shiny and stretched like an overripe plum. He pulled his hat down, but not quickly enough to hide the bandage round his forehead, clumsy because his fingers were swollen and bruised, his knuckles raw.

'You weren't thrown, were you? Someone attacked you.'

'More than one, it was.'

At least a flash of pride there. No one man could have done that to him.

'Was it horse dealers?'

Then I saw the expression on his face and knew that I'd made the wrong assumption and he was relieved about that.

'It wasn't, was it? It was something else. Something more serious.'

He looked at me almost as if I had turned into an enemy. 'Don't ask questions. It's my business and I don't want you having anything to do with it.'

It was the first time he'd tried to keep me out of anything and we'd been in some dangerous circumstances together.

'Do you want them to get away with what they did to you?' I said.

He looked at me, face hard. My heart sank even lower. Amos was slow to anger, but any man who did him a deliberate wrong would pay for it.

'When will you be well enough to ride out with me?' I said, letting him know from the coldness of my voice that he'd hurt me.

I was too worried to care much, but I had to find some way of making him talk to me. He touched his bruised cheek.

'Tomorrow, if you don't mind being seen out with this.'

'Amos, as if I'd care about that.'

It went to my heart how much his pride had been hurt. We agreed to meet in the morning as usual. The owner of the livery stables was lingering outside. He was a decent man and a worried one.

'He won't tell me what happened,' I said.

'He won't say much to any of us. He told you he was going to Surrey on Sunday? He was delivering a horse somebody had bought from us and going to look at another two on his own account. He expected to be back late last night. He arrived this morning, looking like you see him now, only worse, and all we could get out of him was that half a dozen men had set on him and attacked him.'

'Here or in Surrey?'

'Here, just across the park in Knightsbridge. Later, I got him to talk a bit, mostly about the horses. He'd delivered the one of ours, then he stayed down there overnight Sunday and had a look at the other two. One suited and one didn't, so he rode the one back. It was late yesterday evening when he got back, but he delivered it straight to the stables of the man who's thinking of buying it. He'd started walking back across the park, in the dark of course by then, and they jumped out of the bushes and attacked him.'

'Did they steal anything?'

'Not a brass farthing. He still had the money he got for our horse in his pocket, first thing he said to me, as if that was all that mattered.'

I walked slowly home, knowing that in spite of his injuries and the new coldness between us, Amos would be there to help me if I'd said the word. Only I couldn't say it, so would have to manage without him.

Four o'clock on an overcast afternoon saw the contessa and me bowling westwards along Rotten Row towards Kensington. Even in that blasé thoroughfare, the contessa's bright blue droshky with a golden pony drawing it and young Pan on the box turned heads. She was comparatively soberly dressed by her standards in a blue velvet mantle edged with chinchilla and a matching hat with a plume of silver-dyed feathers. Her small hands were coddled in a chinchilla muff that had caused me anxiety back at her lodgings. I'd picked it up from a chair while she'd turned away to consult with her maid about stockings, trying to look casual about it. She'd pirouetted round on her unhurt leg, grabbed it from my hands and turned it inside out to show the grey silk lining.

'Nothing, you see.'

Although she'd had to agree to my conditions, she didn't like them.

'You think I'm an assassin?'

Although I'd insisted on being present when she dressed, I couldn't help feeling more embarrassed by the situation than she seemed to be. As she sat back in an armchair to let the maid re-bandage her injured leg, I'd walked across to the dressing table where the contents of her jewel box were spread in a glittering sweep. None of the pieces would have been classed by Mr Clyde as serious jewels, but there were pretty things all the same: silver and jade bracelets, pendants and earrings of garnet, turquoise, topaz, tourmaline. One of her rings, a heavy gold signet, looked more like a man's. It had a fine carving of a bull's head, the lines clear and deep as if newly made. A white hand came over my shoulder and snatched it. The contessa had limped across the room, one stocking off, one stocking on. She scooped up the jewels, put them back in their velvet lined box and slammed the lid shut. At the time it struck me as petty revenge – she thought I was regarding her as an assassin, so she was treating me like a thief.

Now, side by side in her droshky, we seemed to be in a state of truce, though she was as tense as a cat about to pounce.

'So you know exactly where he'll be visiting?' I said.

She nodded.

'And when?'

'Not exactly. But before evening.'

'Royalty usually keeps to a strict timetable,' I said.

'It's a private visit. He has been to London before. He has an aunt in Kensington.'

'Is Brother Albert visiting too?'

A firm shake of the head. Either she was bluffing or well-informed.

'And are you quite certain your gentleman friend will be with Prince Ernest?' I said.

She turned to me, surprised. I think up to that point she'd forgotten her own fiction: that it was a gentleman of the royal household rather than the prince himself who was the object of her obsession. She recovered herself quickly.

'He is always at the prince's side.'

We turned out of Rotten Row, into the tree-lined suburb of Kensington Gore. Houses here were set back from the road, refuges for the rich who preferred to keep their distance from

London society. From there, we made a right-handed turn into a street of elegant straight-fronted houses, a stone's throw from Kensington Palace. Pan on the box seemed to know where he was going. He turned the droshky into a side street before glancing over his shoulder for instructions.

'There.'

The contessa signed to him to turn into the driveway of a tall and narrow house. The windows were shuttered, the gravel of the drive furred with grass under the almost bare branches of an old plane tree.

'Turn here.'

Pan turned the pony on the sweep in front of the deserted house and came to a stop under the tree. We were facing outwards to an equally tall but broader house across the street. That one was inhabited, curtains drawn back, a lamp already glowing in one of the downstairs windows. From the intent way the contessa was looking at it, this was the house where the prince was expected. How had she known that there was an empty house opposite, so suitable for keeping watch? My admiration of her staff work increased.

We waited in the droshky. Young Pan slid off the box to stand beside the pony, feeding it tidbits from his pocket. A drizzle set in, painting a gloss on the fallen leaves of the plane tree, hazing the light from the lamp in the opposite window. The contessa sank back in her seat and put up her fur-lined hood.

'You have the letter?'

'Yes.' It was in my reticule. I'd read it before we left her apartment. It was written in very correct German, in her school-girlish hand.

> My Dear,
>   I have not deserved this neglect. Only send me a line to assure me that I am not forgotten and, if you can, call on me and permit me to tell you in person what I say to you daily and hourly in your absence, that you are forever in the heart of your devoted and unhappy friend.

Then her signature, looped and curling back on itself like a slow river. The light under our tree took on the grainy look that comes just before dusk. Several more windows of the house opposite yellowed into lamplight. The contessa sighed.

'Is he worth this?' I said.

The hoplessness of her situation was coming home to me.

'Have you never loved a man?' she said.

I hesitated. When she spoke again she sounded triumphant.

'You haven't, have you?'

I'd been thinking of Robert, and if I'd torment myself like this for him. He'd be in Ireland by now. In the hiss of drizzle on leaves, I spoke the truth.

'I don't know.'

'Then you haven't,' she said.

'Isn't it possible to love a man without pain?' I said.

From the movement of the fur hood, she was shaking her head.

'What if a man loved you and wanted to spend his life with you? Wouldn't that be better than risking hurt like this?'

When I said it, I was speaking for Mr Clyde. I guessed what her answer would be, but never knew for sure because the sound of hooves, wheels and creaking leather came from the corner and a carriage turned into our road. Her fingers clamped my wrist.

'Him.'

A plain black landau, drawn by a pair of greys. On the box, a driver with a groom beside him. The hood at the back was up, but as the carriage slowed and turned to enter the drive of the house opposite, I could make out two men sitting inside, their top hats on their knees. One was dark, the other yellow-haired.

'Now.'

The contessa let go of my hand and gave me a shove on the shoulder.

'Which one?' I said, knowing full well.

'The dark one.'

Prince Ernest and his brother had dark hair. Even I knew that. I took my time getting down from the droshky because the landau was still manouevring its way close to the steps of the house opposite.

'Hurry,' she hissed at me.

No need to whisper. The men wouldn't have heard a shout

above the grinding of wheels on gravel. I crossed the road, her
note in my hand. The landau came to a halt and the groom jumped
down to open the door, by the steps on the far side from me. I
walked quickly round the back of the landau, judging my moment.
The door was open, the groom holding it. The fair-haired man
came out first, put his hat on and stood back. As soon as the
other man's shoe gleamed on the step, I moved.

'Sir, I've been asked to give you this.' And I held out the
note.

Close to, in the lamplight over the door, he was good looking
enough although not a man for whom I'd break my heart. Quite
tall, standing like a soldier, curling side-whiskers and a beak of
a nose that was almost Roman, coming nearly straight down
from a high forehead. He had an arrogant air, as if modelling
for his own statue and was giving me a stony stare down that
long nose. From what had happened to the contessa, I was
expecting a rough handling, ready to run once I'd done my
errand. Instead, the two gentlemen and the groom seemed frozen.
Then the yellow-haired man reached out and took the note from
my hand.

'Allow me, Your Highness.'

The door was open now, a flood of yellow light coming down
the steps. The dark-haired man gave one nod of the head, turned
and walked up the steps. The yellow-haired man followed, holding
the note between gloved fingers, and turned for one glance back
at me. I walked back across the road with a sense of anticlimax.
Young Pan was already on the box and our droshky was moving
before I'd even had a chance to sit down. I fell onto the seat
beside the contessa.

'What did he say?'

'Nothing.'

'You gave it to him, into his hand? I couldn't see.'

'The other man took it. His *aide de camp*, I suppose. At least
he didn't throw it down.'

'And you saw him up close?'

'Inevitably.'

'What did you think of him?'

'A man like other men.'

She gave a great sigh and flopped back on the cushioned

seat. I thought it was a sad sigh, until I looked at her face in the dusk and saw an expression of deep satisfaction, as if she'd achieved something difficult and dangerous. Was she imagining the prince reading her note, relenting? I couldn't help feeling pity for the undoubted disappointment she'd suffer. We parted at her door, after I'd helped her get down from the droshky and limp across the pavement. She didn't thank me, but then I hadn't expected it.

At nine o'clock, by arrangement, I met Mr Clyde at the apartment in Grosvenor Street to report what had happened. Suzette was on the premises, as a token chaperone I supposed, but we talked alone in the drawing room, one lamp lit. He listened, expressionless, while I told him about our excursion.

'So it all went as she wanted?' he said.

'Yes, but what good will it do? When he doesn't reply, we'll be back where we were before, only she'll be more desperate.'

He nodded. I wondered if he were thinking seriously about the kidnap proposition but decided not to mention it again. I stood up and picked up my cloak from the piano stool. Instantly, he was on his feet, helping me settle the cloak round my shoulders. His hands lingered for a moment more than was necessary and the tip of his little finger brushed my neck, light as a moth's wing. I turned and found myself looking into his eyes.

'Miss Lane, I'm more grateful to you than I can say. You're a true friend to her – and to me.'

A paid friend, I should have reminded him. Not a true friend at all. And yet I couldn't say it. I let him lead the way downstairs and open the door. He raised his hand for a cab and one arrived almost instantly.

'I don't need a cab,' I said. 'It's only a step or two.'

He said nothing, only opened the front of the cab for me and handed up money to the driver. I was jolted the few hundred yards home in the old leather and tobacco smelling dark of the cab. Take her away and take yourself away, I said in my thoughts to Mr Clyde. I was still feeling that moth-touch of his finger on my neck and the trouble was, I'd liked it.

EIGHT

I was awake through most of the night, counting the chimes from the workhouse clock. At last I fell asleep, but it felt as if I'd been unconscious for only a minute or two when running footsteps came up the stairs. A fist thumped against the door, followed by Tabby's voice, hoarse and breathless.

'There's a lady dead in the park.'

I jumped out of bed and opened the door. She was wearing her old boots with a shawl over her head, much as she'd been in her pre-apprentice days. I think she wandered in the dark for old time's sake.

'Where?'

'By the naked statue.'

I guessed she meant the enormous Achilles at Hyde Park Corner, set up in honour of the Duke of Wellington's victories and so anatomically detailed that delicate ladies averted their eyes.

'Did you see her yourself?'

'No. One of the boys that works in the mews just told me.'

'When did they find her?'

'He said she wasn't there last night. Some man found her just now.'

'Have the police been sent for?

'S'pose so.'

I told her to wait on the landing, while I dressed and scrawled a note to leave on the mounting block for Amos, saying I was sorry I'd been called away. We walked together across Park Lane and through the park. The dark was lifting, but it was still too early even for the earliest riders and the paths were deserted until we came near Achilles. By then it was light enough to see that a small crowd had gathered round the pale granite base of the statue.

Two police constables were standing in front of something lying by the base, trying to keep the crowd back. They had the edgy look of men waiting for somebody to tell them what to do. I told Tabby to wait and went up to the nearest one. He spread his arms, blocking my way.

'You wouldn't want to see, ma'am.'

Under his arm, I glimpsed the dark fabric of a woman's skirt, horizontal.

'I don't especially want to see, only a young woman acquaintance of mine is missing.'

'Missing how long, ma'am?'

'Just over two weeks.'

'Well, it won't be her then, ma'am. This one wasn't here last night.'

Before I could discuss the logic of that, the constable caught sight of somebody over my shoulder and snapped to attention.

'We're just waiting for the coffin shell to be brought from the church, sir, then we'll get her away.'

A sergeant had arrived, with the washed-out air of a man who'd been dealt one incident too many at the end of a night duty. I stepped back, but kept within hearing distance. The sergeant asked the constable if the deceased had been identified.

'No sir. Young and respectable by the look of her.'

'Who reported her?'

'Park keeper, out early walking his dog.'

'Was she dead when you got here?'

'Dead and cold, and the blood had congealed. We took note of that.'

The constable sounded pleased with himself but the sergeant was unimpressed. 'Not so very much blood, with her throat slit,' he said. He was looking at something over the constable's shoulder.

'But then, she wasn't very large, was she?' the constable said.

I took a step forward, unnoticed by either of them. I could see a pair of feet now. They were small, but the black shoes were more clumsy and scuffed than seemed likely in a woman of Miss Tilbury's class. The sergeant asked the constable if they'd found anything on her that might identify her.

'No sir, no reticule or anything, unless it's lying underneath her. No jewellery, apart from her wedding ring.'

'She was married then?'

'Looks like it, sir. Quite bright and new looking, the ring is.'

I must have made some sound, because the sergeant turned towards me and frowned. 'This lady knows another young lady who's gone missing,' the constable explained. 'Only she's been gone two weeks.'

'My acquaintance is nineteen years old, fair-haired and a little below average height,' I said. 'Her name's Dora Tilbury.'

The two men looked at each other then at me.

'Do you feel able to look at this lady?' the sergeant asked. 'If it's not her, at least you can feel easy in your mind.'

I nodded. It was not the time to admit that I'd never actually set eyes on Dora Tilbury. The constable stepped aside and the two men formed a screen behind me as I stepped up to the body.

My first thought was simple and terrified: *He's destroyed her.* I'd never been so close to the Achilles statue before. The monstrous size of the black metal god towering on his plinth twenty feet above us, the upraised sword and the shield blotting out the rising sun, made it seem as if the statue had slaughtered the creature lying far beneath its feet and was celebrating a triumph over his victim, out of all proportion to its size or the small force needed to take its life. For a heartbeat, I hardly thought of the woman and stood frozen by a terror out of myth. If the two policemen noticed, they probably thought I was reluctant to look at the woman. That too. The smell of blood was in my nostrils. I looked down. Her neck was wrapped in a cotton scarf or tucker so deeply encrusted in dark blood that only a few patches showed it had once been blue. Her eyes were closed, head flopped at an angle. More blood had soaked into her grey jacket and the plain white bodice beneath it. Some had pooled on the stone beside her upper body. Her arms lay neatly at her side, gloveless with palms facing upwards. The left wrist had a diagonal slit across it, encrusted with more blood. It looked as if she might have raised her arm to try to fight off her attacker. Her hair . . .

'Her hair's wet,' I said.

It was scraped neatly back from her face, so presumably coiled in a chignon at the back, a dark straw colour that would probably have been fair when dry. It wasn't wringing wet, but thoroughly damp as if she'd washed it an hour or so before. Whatever the two police officers had expected from me, it wasn't that.

'Is she your friend?' the sergeant asked, doing his best to sound gentle.

'I . . . I'm not sure. Dora Tilbury had a pale brown birthmark on the inside of her left wrist.'

The sergeant nodded to the constable, who walked round her head and kneeled down by the left hand.

'Can't tell, sir. Too much blood on it.'

'Then go and get some water.'

The sergeant nodded towards the pool in the Dell. The constable took a handkerchief out of his pocket and pushed his way round the growing crowd.

'So you're not sure?' the sergeant said.

'I didn't know her well. She was a friend of a friend.'

It was too complicated to explain then about being a private investigator. We stood in silence with our backs to the body until the constable came back with his wet handkerchief. In his hurry, he skidded on the stone pavement surrounding the statue and almost pitched over onto the body. The sergeant told him to be careful, took the handkerchief from him, kneeled down and sponged.

'Slippery here,' mumbled the constable, shamefaced.

I thought he might have skidded on the blood, but there was none where he'd stepped. I supposed even a police officer's nerves weren't cast iron.

'If you could come and look, ma'am,' the sergeant said.

It was only a small mark, no more than an inch long. The horizontal gash in the slim white wrist had just missed it.

'Yes,' I said. 'She must be Dora Tilbury.'

With her hand palm-up, we could only see the back of the gold ring on her wedding finger. It looked new and rather loose.

'I'd be grateful if you'd wait over there, ma'am,' the sergeant said.

The sergeant and the other constable kept the crowd back while the beadle and constable lifted the body into the shell and then onto the coffin cart. It was trundled away, with some of the crowd following.

'Nothing to see now. Go about your business,' the sergeant said to the rest of them.

Slowly, they drifted away. At some point, Tabby had arrived at my side.

'Is it her, then?'

'Yes, I'm afraid so.'

She stayed with me until the sergeant came back then she disappeared. By then, I'd had a chance to do some thinking. Unless I told the police more about my strange, even non-existent, connection with Dora Tilbury, I'd be building up serious complications for myself and others.

The sergeant suggested we should go and sit on a nearby bench. When we were settled more or less, he said there were things he needed to know for the coroner's officer and took a notebook out of his pocket.

'Can you please tell me where she lived and the name of her next of kin.'

'I know she lived at a village called Boreham in Essex, with her guardian. I suppose he'd be her next of kin. I don't know his name.'

He raised his eyebrows. I took a deep breath and explained about being an investigator who tried to trace lost people, and how Jeremy James had come to me out of the blue, a week ago, claiming to be her unofficial fiancé.

'Where does Mr James live?'

'Near her, in Essex. I haven't an address for him there, but he's staying with a friend in Islington.' I gave him the address of the friend from memory.

'How did you come to be here so early this morning?'

'I live nearby. It's part of my investigation to check sudden deaths if there's any possibility it might be my missing person. My maid told me there was a lady dead in the park.'

He looked at me, not entirely convinced by my story. I could hardly blame him.

'And you had no knowledge of Miss Tilbury's whereabouts?'

'None whatsoever. In fact, I wrote a note to Mr James just two days ago reporting my lack of success.'

He asked for my name and address and wrote them down.

'There's something the coroner's officer might want to know,' I said.

This had been the hardest decision, whether to draw the attention of the authorities to things that might be meaningless. I'd concluded that I should tell them and let them make of it what they liked.

'There seems to be a similarity with a Miss Janet Priest who went off the Monument last week,' I said.

'Oh? Were you looking for her as well?'

'No. I didn't know she existed until she was dead. I happened to be in the City that day. Miss Priest's hair was wet. I didn't see her body myself, but the police knew about it. It hadn't rained that night and it didn't rain here in the park last night. The grass is quite dry.'

The sergeant looked wearier than ever. He wasn't writing this down. I guessed that part of the problem was that the two deaths came under two different police forces. The City force was quite distinct from the Metropolitan that looked after the rest of London, with no love lost between them. Since he seemed to have no more questions for me I asked if I might go. The sergeant said yes, but I might be hearing from the coroner's officer.

Tabby appeared at my side as I was walking towards Hyde Park Corner.

'Where are you going now?'

'Islington, to look for Mr James.'

Since there was bad news to be told, I hoped I might manage it more gently than the coroner's officer. If I moved quickly, I should get there before him. But there was more to it than that. The links between the two deaths seemed to me stronger than I'd described to the sergeant. Both young women had led lives that were apparently respectable to the point of being dull. Both had been inexplicably missing before their deaths – a week in the case of Miss Priest, thirteen days for Miss Tilbury. As far as I could calculate, that meant that they'd disappeared at much the same time. Perhaps Mr James could tell me something that made sense of it.

'Can I come?' Tabby said.

'I'd prefer you to stay here around the park and talk to people you know, like the street boys. Find out if anybody saw a person of her description last night or at any time yesterday, or if anybody heard cries for help or saw a struggle. It might not have been near the statue, it could have been anywhere in the park.'

Or outside it, come to that. From the comparative lack of blood where she was lying, I was almost certain that Dora Tilbury had been killed elsewhere and her body carried to the base of the statue.

'And you might ask if anybody saw a person carrying anything near the statue late last night or very early this morning,' I said. 'Also, did anybody notice a cart or carriage stopping near it?'

Tabby would have slept out in the park many nights. Its inhabitants after dark were her people. Then I thought of what had happened to Amos, and was scared for her.

'But only ask people you know, at least by sight. If anybody seems suspicious of you or threatening in any way, go home at once and stay there until I come.'

We parted at Hyde Park Corner and I went to find the stop for the Islington omnibus.

The address Jeremy James had given me for his law student friend was in the Canonbury area of Islington. It turned out to be a terrace of brick-built houses of the last century in a muddy street with piles of rubbish strewn round. I found the number, picked my way to the faded front door, knocked and waited. No reply. Peering through a gap in sagging curtains, I saw nothing but bare floor boards and a stone fireplace from grander days. I was beginning to think I'd mistaken the address until a sash window creaked up above me and a man's voice came from the first floor.

'Tell him to stop bothering me. I said I'd have it by tomorrow.'

The face looking down on me was a young man's, but with a bad complexion and greasy-looking hair.

'I thought you were the landlord's wife,' he said.

'Is Mr James staying with you?'

'Who wants to know?'

'I'm sorry to trouble you, but I have some bad news for him. If he's there, would you kindly ask him to come down.'

A moment's hesitation. 'He's not here.'

He was about to close the window.

'Then I'd appreciate it very much if you'd come down,' I said. 'I really do need to find him at once.'

The head withdrew and the window shut. A minute or so later, the young man opened the door just enough to let himself onto the step. His bleary-eyed look might have come from too much poring over law books, but more likely he'd just got out of bed.

'Do you know when Mr James might be back?' I said.

'I don't know if he is coming back. He didn't say anything about it.'

'When did he leave?'

'Day before yesterday.'

'Where did he go?'

'Back home, I suppose.'

'I sent him a letter here. Did he get it?'

'Some letter came yesterday. He'd gone by then.'

'Did he tell you about his fiancée being missing?'

'Yes. Did they find her?'

He sounded only slightly curious. I didn't answer, apart from telling him to ask Mr James to get in touch with me urgently if he should reappear.

Something was wrong. I puzzled over it all the way home. Why should the desperate young man who'd so much needed my help have left London, with the woman he loved still not found? One possibility was that he knew very well what had happened to Miss Tilbury and that was why he'd gone. Suppose that he'd been more successful than I had in tracing her? Suppose too that my hypothesis had been right and she'd come to London to meet some other man? Two possible scenarios sprang from that. The woman is seduced, betrayed and cuts her own throat. (Having, perhaps, first tested the sharpness of the blade on her wrist.) Her true love discovers her too late. Carries her dead body to the base of the statue, with Achilles standing in for the cruel betrayer. Given the poetic nature I'd suspected in Mr James, that was just possible, though it seemed to me it would do better as an opera plot for Donizetti than a likely explanation. So suppose he finds Miss Tilbury alive, discovers she's been faithless and takes revenge? Possible, just. But would a poetic man in a jealous frenzy be cool enough to transport her to the park? Wouldn't he have murdered her and stood over her like Othello, soliloquizing and waiting to be discovered by the authorities?

It was a relief to get back to Abel Yard and find Tabby waiting there. I could tell from her face that she had news.

'Well?'

'The devil's chariot. It was driving all round here last night.'

An overreaction, probably, but I felt suddenly furious. 'Who says so?'

'Everybody. Barnabas with one leg that sleeps out in the hollow tree, Betsy the apple seller, the boy that walks the greyhounds, Simon I think his name is, and the old soldier with the hat with gold lace that begs by the barracks.'

'A great cloud of witness,' I said sarcastically, forgetting, unfairly, that I'd told her to keep to people she knew. 'And what exactly did they see?'

'Barnabas said it was going hell for leather up Park Lane at midnight. Betsy says she saw it on the Knightsbridge side, later than that but she doesn't know when. The old soldier . . . well, you can't believe everything he says . . .'

She went silent, seeing my expression.

'Go on.'

'He reckons he saw it in the sky, smelling of sulphur and trailing blue sparks.'

She looked and sounded so crestfallen that my anger melted. Still, she had to learn.

'Tabby, when you spoke to them, did they already know about the woman's body?'

'Oh yes. Everybody was talking about it.'

'It's just something people do, taking something that really happened, then adding all sorts of nonsense to it. They don't mean any harm. They probably believe it themselves.'

She listened, but looked resentful.

'Never mind,' I said. 'Only we're no nearer knowing who put her body there, or how or when.'

'Yes we are. The when anyhow.'

I stared at her. She glared back.

'You don't believe what I tell you in any case.'

'Tabby, please, just tell me when.'

'After the bugle blows at the barracks.'

I remembered, from summer with my window open, the note wavering faintly across the park. Five or half past perhaps, for early stables. Still dark at this time of year.

'How do you know?'

'The boy that walks the dogs. He sleeps by the statue sometimes. He knows when he hears the bugle it's time to get up and
fetch the dogs from the big house across the road.'

'And he slept by the statue last night?'

'Yes.'

'And left when he heard the bugle?'

'Yes.'

'And the body wasn't there then?'

'Course not, or he'd have noticed.'

'Did he tell the police about this?'

'Nah. He says the constable kicks him up the backside soon
as look at him.'

Could the girl who at least half believed in devils trailing blue
sparks be right about anything? Dealing with Tabby's reports
was like plunging a hand in a bran tub.

'If you're right, we should have been asking about things that
happened just before it was light,' I said.

Carrying Dora's body to the statue in the narrow gap between
the bugle call and daylight would have been a risky
undertaking.

'The dog boy, he didn't see anybody carrying something that
might have been her body?'

'Nah.'

'Or hear or see a vehicle?'

'Didn't ask him that. Do you want me to?'

'Yes. In fact, ask all of them. Forget the devil. Just get them
to tell you if they heard or saw anything in the early morning,
around the time of the bugle call. Try to find out if anybody
heard any carts, even handcarts.'

In my mind, I was seeing Jeremy James laying her down on
the stone slabs. Would he have risked carrying her through the
streets over his shoulder?

'Come back here before dark and get a night's sleep,' I said.
'We're going on a coach journey tomorrow.'

'Where to?'

'Boreham.'

'That's where the man that lost this girl comes from.'

'That's right.'

'Why are we going there?'

I put some pennies for a pie into her hand. 'I'll tell you on the journey.'

Upstairs, Mrs Martley was feeding her scrap book. She'd developed a fierce loyalty to little Vicky and collected every newspaper item or engraving she could find. She was reading something that pleased her, making small cooing sounds as to a baby or a kitten.

'Bless the boy, fancy him sending her his guinea pigs.'

'Hmm?'

She passed a newspaper cutting to me – *The Times* in its ponderously light-hearted vein. A small hamper had arrived from Yorkshire at Windsor coach office, addressed to 'Her Majesty Queen Victoria at Briton Palace or wherever she may Bee. A curious squeaking noise was heard to proceed from the hamper, resembling the stifled cries of a child'. The hamper was hastily opened, disclosing two live guinea pigs and a letter:

> A pressant of 2 Guinea Pigs to her Majesty from a little boy of 5 years old, that come in one day from Playing in the Street. Says Mother, I love the Queen because she is a Good queen. The child would not Rest till he had sent the Queen the only Treasure he posseses. He shed a teer over his Pigs, and told them they was Going ware they would have more plenty than he Could Have for them.

'It's preposterous,' I said, laughing. 'No five-year-old boy would give up his guinea pigs, even if the queen sent the entire Household Cavalry to take them.'

'You're very sceptical,' said Mrs Martley sadly.

I realized that I was trespassing in a sacred place and said I hoped the guinea pigs had survived.

'Oh yes. Windsor Castle wouldn't take them, but a gentleman in the town gave them a home. She read: 'The pigs, which he had christened Albert and Victoria (the latter of which will shortly be introducing some new acquaintance to his family circle) are now carefully domiciled in a spacious hutch.'

'And it's signed "Cupid",' she added, as if that clinched some argument I hadn't been following.

'A guinea pig cupid?'

'No, the proper cupid. It's *The Times*' way of letting people know they know about it, only they can't print it because it's not official yet.'

It had been a long day and my head was spinning. 'Can't print what?'

She looked at me pityingly. 'Queen Victoria being engaged to Prince Albert.'

'Is she?'

'Of course she is. Everybody knows.'

For a mad moment, I wondered what loyal Mrs Martley would say if she knew how close I'd been to prince cupid's elder brother, and why. If the contessa did manage to cause a public scandal, Prince Ernest's past might reflect on his younger and apparently more virtuous brother at a particularly delicate time.

'Is there anything about the elder brother?' I said.

'Oh no. Prince Ernest wouldn't have done, you see.'

'Why not?'

'Because he'll have to go back and rule his own country and everybody says Prince Albert is better natured and better looking.'

She turned a page in her scrap book and gazed fondly at an engraving of the two princes. 'She could have had anybody in the world. The Grand Duke Alexander of Russia, the Czar's son, he wanted to marry her too. But she's chosen Albert, a real love match.'

I bit my tongue, to stop myself saying that queen marries prince hardly added up to a Cinderella story. I said I hoped they'd all be very happy, leaving her to decide whether I meant the royals or the guinea pig family, and took myself upstairs to my room.

ANOTHER PRESENT TO HER MAJESTY

A few days since a small hamper, the contents of which were secured by a linen cloth being carefully sewn over the top, arrived at Windsor, by coach, from Yorkshire, and addressed as follows :–

"With care–To her Majesty Queen Victoria, at Briton Palace, or wherever she may Bee–With speed."

Upon the porter at Moody's coach-office taking the package (the carriage of which was 4s, 4d.) to the Castle at Windsor, it was refused to be received. The proprietor of the coach-office, however, thinking there might be some mistake, sent it a second time to the Castle, when it was again refused, by the orders (as we are informed) of the Master of the Household, the Hon. C. A. Murray. In the course of the same afternoon a curious squeaking noise (as the package was lying in the coach-office) was heard to proceed from the hamper, resembling the stifled cries of a child; and as it was clear there was something in it alive, it was judged expedient, under the circumstances, to open the package, a thousand rumours having got abroad in the mean time as to the real nature of its contents.

At length the hamper was opened, and then there were discovered, crouched beneath some hay, a couple of very beautiful guineapigs–a male and female; and a note addressed to Her Majesty, of which the following is "a true and veritable" copy :–

"Laughton-in-le-Merthom, near Rotherham.

"A Preasant of 2 Guinea Pigs to her Magesty from A little Boy 5 years old, that come in one day from Playing in the Street. Says Mother, I love the Queen because she is A Good queen. I wish to know ware she live, I would send her my two Pigs. The child would not Rest till he had sent the Queen the only Treasure he posses. He shed a tear over is Pigs, and told them they was Going ware they would have more plenty than he Could Have for them. He is Quite Happy at Parting with them. I am Afraid your Royal Highness will be displeased at a Poor woman taking the Liberty to send them to your Majesty. Your Majesty's Most Humble Servant,

"Oct. 9, 1839. Elizabeth Elridge"

The authorities at the Castle still refusing to admit the pigs, notwithstanding Master Elridge told them before they left Laughton for "Briton Palace" that "they was going ware they would have more plenty," a gentleman in Windsor paid the carriage of the hamper from Rotherham, and the pigs, which he had christened Albert and Victoria (the latter of which will shortly introduce some new acquaintance to his family circle), are now carefully domiciled in a spacious hutch in the stable attached to his residence, in Gloucester-place.

–*Cupid*. [Where, *Cupid*, did you pick up this tender piece of piggery, so complimentary to Her Majesty and Prince Albert]

The guinea pigs story from *The Times*, 24 October 1839.

NINE

The Essex coach was fully booked inside, so Tabby and I had to travel on top, along with a couple of louts who kept drinking out of hip flasks, imitating the coach horn and yelling witticisms at pedestrians. Luckily, they got down at Brentwood.

'So why's he run off, then?' Tabby asked when I told her about my visit to Islington.

'I don't know. But just because his friend was disobliging, that doesn't mean that Mr James had some bad reason for leaving.'

'Or he might have killed her himself,' Tabby said, sounding quite cheerful about it.

Yet again, I was brought up standing by her quickness. I'd decided not to share my speculation with her until I knew the result of our trip into Essex.

'So did you find out if anybody saw or heard anything just before daylight?' I said.

'Nah. Nobody saw or heard nothing.'

'No carts?'

'Only the usual ones.'

'Usual?'

As the stage jolted us eastwards, she ran through the list from that formidable memory of hers. The vagrants who slept in the park were used to the procession of tradesmen's vehicles in the early morning, glimpsed through the leaves in summer, recognized by sound in the autumn and winter darkness.

'There's only the two handcarts, a couple called William and Mary pushing them. He picks up the horses' doings for the market gardens and she does the dog dung for the tanneries. Some mornings, there's a mad old man picks up cast-off horseshoes. The rest are horse and carts.'

I took pencil and notepad out of my reticule and asked her to tell me all she'd been able to find out. At the end of the process, we had a written list, as follows: the baker's cart, making early deliveries to the clubs around St James and Piccadilly. The park vagrants waited for it, because one lucky morning a door had opened and a shower of bread rolls fallen out. Two vegetable carts, rival owners, delivering to back doorways of the big houses along Park Lane. Interesting to the vagrants, because the drivers tried to steal each other's custom and had once had a fight, using whips. The ice cart. Similar deliveries, less interesting because ice was unrewarding eating. Two builders' wagons, carrying bricks. Not on regular daily rounds, but quite frequent as a lot of rebuilding was going on around Park Lane. The night soil wagon. Carting away waste from cesspits, unmistakeable by its smell even if you didn't see it.

All of them had a good reason to be there. Discouraging news.

We changed horses at Chelmsford. A few miles further on, we climbed stiffly down outside the Cock at Boreham. A cheerful middle-aged man in a yellow waistcoat who looked as if he might be the landlord was standing in the porch, watching the coach speed away. I wished him good morning and asked if he could kindly tell us where the James family lived. He stared at me, puzzled.

'I believe they live some way outside the village,' I said. 'They have a grown-up son named Jeremy.'

'No Jameses I know of, and I've been here fifteen years. There's a widow woman called Jameson, but she's eighty or more with no sons as far as I know.'

'The son said they had a small estate.'

He shook his head. 'It was definitely Boreham, was it? You couldn't have been thinking of Basildon or Braintree?'

I was certain it was Boreham. After more head shaking, the landlord suggested we might ask the vicar, although he didn't sound hopeful. The tower of the church was visible about half a mile away. We started walking with a cold wind in our faces, between russet-coloured hedges and trees with a few yellow and red crab apples still clinging to bare branches. The vicarage stood across the road from the church, a handsome building of red brick. Two children, well-wrapped up against the wind, were playing with a white and tan terrier in the garden. When we knocked, the vicar himself came to the door, teacup in hand. He seemed a genial man, but when I introduced myself and

explained that we were looking for the James family he was as
puzzled as the landlord had been.

'Were they living here some time ago?'

'I was given to understand they're living near the village now.
In fact, the young man, Jeremy James, attends your church. He
was at a service –' I did some hasty counting back – 'two Sundays
ago, on the sixth of October.'

He frowned. 'I'm very much afraid there's been some mistake.
Have you come far?'

'From London.'

My worry must have showed in my face, because he invited
us to come and sit down in the parlour. His wife was there,
helping the maid clear up the remains of a modest lunch. He
introduced us, invited us to sit down and sent the maid to make a
fresh pot of tea.

'Has this young man, Mr James . . . er, imposed on you in
some way?'

His embarrassment showed what he suspected: Mr James had
trifled with my affections and deserted me, leaving a false address.

'I have a reputation for finding missing people,' I said. 'Mr
James came to me because an acquaintance had suggested that
I might help him trace a young woman who had disappeared.'

'And he said his family lived here?'

'Yes. He said the young woman he was trying to find also
lived here in the village. Her name was Miss Dora Tilbury.'

'I'm sorry, the name means nothing to me.' He glanced at his
wife. She shook her head.

'According to Mr James, she lived with her uncle who was
her legal guardian. He was a clergyman who'd had to resign his
living because of ill health.'

'Miss Lane, I assure you I'd have known if there were another
clergyman living in the village.'

'He said Miss Tilbury had fair hair, a pale complexion and
blue eyes. She was of average height, or a little below it, with
small and delicate hands and feet. Does that description fit any
young woman in the village, even under another name?'

The vicar glanced at his wife again. 'Not one of ours. I don't
know if among the Methodists . . .'

Another glance at his wife. She shook her head. We drank tea and made conversation, none of it to the purpose. He asked how we were going to get back to London and offered us a ride in his pony cart as far as Chelmsford, saying that he had an errand there in any case. I guessed he'd invented the errand out of kindness, still thinking that Mr James' perfidy was a serious blow to me, which it was, but not in the way he suspected. I accepted gratefully, but asked if he could kindly pick us up at the Cock, because I wanted another talk with the landlord. As we walked, there was a coldness in my head that had nothing to do with the wind at our backs. I was nearly sure what we'd hear from the landlord, and as it turned out, I was right.

'Yes, I see the coach come in every morning,' he said, polishing beer tankards in the snug. 'I have to, in case there's anybody getting off here, not that there often is.'

'What about people getting on here to go to London?' I asked.

'Once in a blue moon. We don't get many people travelling from round here.'

'A Thursday morning, second Thursday of this month it would have been, did a young woman in a blue cloak get on the coach for London?'

He gave me a sideways look. 'Nobody's got on the London coach from here since the first week in September, and that was the doctor taking his son up to school.'

The vicar's pony cart arrived outside. I thanked the landlord and we left.

Tabby and I had no chance to talk until we managed to get inside seats next to each other on the last stage into London. It was late evening by then.

'The stage coach driver reckoned he saw her getting on and getting off,' Tabby said.

'He was lying. I wasn't sure I believed him at the time. He'd been bribed to say that if anybody inquired. The question is, who bribed him?'

'Mr James,' Tabby said promptly.

'Probably. But why?'

She had no answer to that and neither did I, only more questions.

'Is he even called Jeremy James?' I said. 'Could that be as false as his home address?'

'The man out at Islington knew him, you said.'

'Knew the name and not much else. Our man could have paid simply to use his address for forwarding mail.'

'We thought there was something off-colour about him from the start,' Tabby said.

'That's flattering us, I think. We thought it odd that he didn't seem to know very much beyond the obvious about Miss Tilbury, but put that down to being absorbed in himself.'

'So was any of it true?' Tabby said.

'As far as I can see, almost nothing.'

Tabby waited for a while in case I came up with something more encouraging, then leaned back in her seat and closed her eyes. I stared out at the darkness, patched occasionally by the gleam of a lamp or candle in a cottage window, and thought of nothing – that is to say, the nothing that had been Dora Tilbury. The home at Boreham, the elderly guardian and his strict house-keeper, the quiet life with her embroidery and pet linnet, had all vanished like smoke into the wind, or even less than smoke because they'd never existed. She'd never got up early, put on her blue cloak and climbed into a stage coach. The other Miss Tilbury of my own imagining, who'd stepped out of that coach to find a different sweetheart waiting for her in the inn yard, was less than the shadow of a shadow. Both Dora Tilburys had existed only in a story told by a young man whose name was probably false and place of residence certainly so. Cinderella and Scheherazade were no more of a fiction than Dora Tilbury.

And yet, Dora Tilbury had existed enough to be dead. That was what my mind came back to time and again. I'd seen her lying there under the Achilles statue, in her scuffed black shoes and grey wool jacket, answering well enough to the description I'd been given. A very vague and general description it had been too, apart from one item: the birthmark on her left wrist. It was the only useful identification that the man who called himself Mr James had given me and the one thing that marked her out as Dora Tilbury. In my tiredness and confusion, it seemed to me that she'd been brought into existence simply to die.

The coach slowed from a trot to a walk when we encountered the traffic on the eastern outskirts of London. Tabby woke and picked up the conversation where she'd left it.

'If he killed her, he might have wanted to make out to us he was worried about her to put everybody off the track.'

'If she'd been found dead the day after he came to us, I'd entirely agree with you,' I said. 'But look at the timing. He came to us on Wednesday the sixteenth. I don't think she can have been dead for very long when they found her, or the blood wouldn't have been flowing at all. She was probably killed either this Tuesday or possibly the first few hours of Wednesday morning. That would mean he knew six days ahead he was going to kill her. In any case, it would be useless as a defence in court. The prosecution could simply say that he'd been genuinely worried when he came to us, then found her and murdered her for some reason later.'

'Because she'd gone off with another man?'

'Except we don't know there was another man. We were trying to build a house on a quicksand.'

By the time the coach reached its depot in Aldgate it was dark. We missed the last omnibus to Piccadilly and though Tabby was in favour of walking home for the sake of economy, we were both so dog-tired that I insisted on taking a cab.

'So what do we do now?' Tabby said.

'The inquest on Miss Tilbury . . .' I hesitated, because she almost certainly was not Miss Tilbury. 'The inquest should have been today. I need to know what happened.'

It had been in my mind to divert to Fleet Street on the way back and find Jimmy Cuffs, but that could wait until tomorrow's papers. I had no direct interest in the matter now and no client. But the body of the girl under that triumphing statue, with no name, no home, no history made its own claims. Besides, even if I had wanted to walk away, I'd given misleading evidence to a police officer at the scene. Even though I hadn't known it was misleading at the time, I'd have questions to answer.

I paid off the cab in Grosvenor Square. It was less complicated than trying to shout up to the box to direct the driver to the mews. The windows of the contessa's apartment were dark, curtains drawn back but not even the glimmer of one candle. It was about ten o'clock by then, so perhaps she went to bed early, though I doubted that. I wondered if Mr Clyde had already acted on my suggestion and carried her away by trickery or by force.

Quite possibly I'd lost both my clients and gained nothing but a feeling of failure. I'd been too proud of my little skills and a few early successes. Perhaps I should be in Ireland after all, being introduced to a surprised family as Mr Carmichael's fiancée. I must have sighed because Tabby was looking up at me, the light from a window falling on her worried face.

'That Mr James or whatever his name is, he's not going to be paying us any more money, is he?' she said.

'No.'

'Don't you worry,' she said. 'We'll manage somehow.'

Her small ungloved hand landed briefly on mine and flew away again. I could have cried. Here was a girl who'd never had more than a few coppers to her name, mistaking the cause of my sadness and trying to console me.

'Yes, we'll manage. Don't you worry either,' I said.

Next morning I went riding with Amos. It was a drizzly day and he was in a sombre mood. Both eyes were open now, but the bruise on his cheek was purple and yellow.

As he helped me down at the end of our ride he said he was going away for a few days.

'Again? More horse dealing?' I said. Then I looked at his expression and knew it wasn't.

'Amos, please don't take risks.'

He turned to remount his cob without replying. When he was in the saddle, with the cob's reins in his right hand and Rancie's in his left, he looked down at me.

'I've got it arranged with the governor. A boy'll ride out with you whenever you like.'

Then he wheeled both horses and went, so what I tried to say to him was lost in a clattering of hooves.

Still in my riding clothes, I went to buy newspapers, choosing two that used the services of Jimmy Cuffs. Back in my room, I searched for reports of the inquest. The fact that the dead girl had been found in such a public and dramatic place should have ensured at least half a column of coverage. Eventually, after much searching, I found a small paragraph in one paper recording only that the inquest into the death of an unknown young woman whose body was found by the Achilles statue in

Hyde Park on Wednesday morning had been opened and adjourned.

At midday, the earliest that Jimmy Cuffs welcomed callers, I was outside the Cheshire Cheese again. Jimmy appeared soon after a boy took in my message. He looked tired and less good-humoured than usual. I asked him if he had time to talk.

'The Achilles inquest?'

'Yes.'

'Shall we walk?'

We strolled in the light drizzle along Fleet Street. It seemed only half alive at this time of day without the rushing copy boys and the thump of presses.

'So what happened?' I said.

'I was hoping you might tell me that.'

'All I know is what I've read – two sentences saying it was opened and adjourned. Did you write more?'

'There was no more to write.'

'The coroner must have said something.'

'He made the jury view the body as usual, then said that circumstances had arisen which made it necessary to adjourn the inquest *sine die*. When one of the jurors tried to ask a question he cut him off pretty sharply.'

'No explanation?'

'None. I know the coroner's officer quite well and sometimes he'll give me a hint, off record, of things that don't come out in court. Not this time. He clamped the official look on his face like a portcullis coming down and wouldn't say a word.'

We turned into Chancery Lane.

'The report described her as an unknown young woman,' I said.

'Inevitably, since she wasn't named at the inquest.' Jimmy Cuffs thought he was owed an explanation. I could hardly blame him.

'I ask because I was there quite soon after the body was discovered,' I said. 'I told the police sergeant her name: Dora Tilbury.'

'You knew her?' He stopped so suddenly that a lad with a pile of legal papers chin-high cannoned into him and nearly knocked him over. The boy cursed him and whirled on, papers intact. I put out a hand to steady Jimmy.

'I didn't know her exactly. I'd had her described to me by a client who wanted to find her. There was a birthmark on her wrist.'

He started walking again, firing questions at me. 'Why weren't you called at the inquest?'

'The sergeant had my address, but I was out of town yesterday. I'd given the sergeant the name of a man who should have been able to identify her much more positively than I could.'

'A relative?'

'A young man who considered himself her fiancé – or so he said.'

'Your client?'

'Yes.'

'So why didn't he identify her?'

'I don't think the coroner's officer would have found him. He'd given me a false address, out in Essex.

Jimmy Cuffs said nothing for a long time. We came to the top of Chancery Lane, turned and started walking back down towards Fleet Street.

'What you've just told me doesn't explain what happened at the inquest,' he said at last.

'It might. The coroner's officer probably wouldn't be allowed to move as quickly as I did.'

'No, it still doesn't explain it,' Jimmy said stubbornly. 'I've attended hundreds of inquests. In those circumstances, they'd have heard evidence from the sergeant you spoke to and almost certainly demanded your attendance. There should have been a police officer on your doorstep first thing yesterday morning.'

'I told you, I was out of town.'

'In which case, they'd have informed the jury of the facts and adjourned the inquest until you attended and until the coroner's officer had a chance to go to Essex and find this client of yours.'

'But he wouldn't have found him.'

'The point I'm making is that even in these peculiar circumstances, adjourning the inquest abruptly like that was most irregular. The first point of any inquest is establishing the identity of the deceased. At the very least, the jury should have been told what steps were being taken to do that. They weren't. In my experience, that's unique.'

'So what do you conclude from that?'

'That there's something very strange going on, and you probably know more about it than I do.'

I opened my mouth to deny it, then closed it again. I'm sure Jimmy noticed, but he was too much of a philosopher to provoke an unnecessary quarrel.

'Your friend Huckerby was asking me about it too,' he said. 'He came and found me last night.'

For some reason, this worried me. I hadn't even known that Tom and Jimmy Cuffs were acquainted, but the tribe of journalists is wide. The puzzle was that Tom took very little interest in crime, only politics. As we came near the turning to the alleyway that led to the Cheshire Cheese, Jimmy Cuffs simply asked me to tell him what I could when I could. I promised. As he turned to go, I had a last question for him.

'That other inquest, the one on Miss Priest at the Monument, there was a mention of an unusual ring she was wearing. Did you happen to get a more particular description of the ring?'

He turned back. 'No. Does it matter?'

'Probably not, but if you do happen to hear, would you let me know?'

He nodded, raised his hat and turned into the alleyway.

TEN

On Saturday morning, at least I had an answer to Tabby's question of what we did now.

'We're going to City Road,' I said.

'The Monument girl?'

'Yes.'

Janet Priest had possessed an address, an occupation, a sister. At least, I hoped so. If not, then we were even deeper in the quicksands. We decided to take the omnibus from Piccadilly and walked by way of Grosvenor Square. I knocked at the contessa's door. A manservant in her sky blue livery answered it and said the contessa and her maid were out. He didn't know when they'd be back and promised to tell the contessa that I'd called. On our way down Piccadilly I remembered that I had an appointment with Madame Leman for a final fitting of the green velvet dress. I might not have bothered with anything so frivolous (although I did feel a pang at the thought of not seeing the dress again) but she might have heard gossip about the contessa. I told Tabby to wait for me outside and climbed the carpeted stairs to her fitting room.

Madame announced that she was enchanted to see me, altogether ravished with the effect of the soft green on my complexion. While she made minute adjustments to the ruching on the bosom and her seamstresses fussed around the hem with pins, she asked if I'd seen the dear contessa recently. The question seemed casual, but her fingers hesitated while she waited for my answer.

'I saw her on Tuesday,' I said. 'You know she hurt her leg?'

She nodded. It was her business to hear everything. 'She is recovering well, I hope. Is she planning to go home to recuperate?'

'Not as far as I know,' I said.

Implied questions there from Madame. Where was home for the contessa? Was there a family that might meet her bills? Madame told me that my gown would be ready that afternoon. The cost, though astronomical by my standards, would be only a small fraction of the account facing Mr Clyde if he settled the contessa's debt too.

Tabby and I caught the omnibus and got down at the western end of City Road. It's a long road, becoming poorer and shabbier as you head eastwards out of London, with terraces of narrow but respectable homes giving way to run-down lodging houses. The stationer's shop with the name Nathaniel Priest on the window in faded gilt letters was about a third of the way along, still clinging to respectability. Inside the window, a slanting shelf held sample pages of merchants' ledgers, school copy books, penholders and a variety of nibs, brown paper and red sealing wax. Everything looked tidy and freshly dusted, but there was a defeated air about it as if the shop had few customers at any time. On this Saturday morning it had none. Inside, a plump young woman in a black dress stood with her back to the counter, arranging something on a shelf. A bell on a spring twanged above the door as we walked in.

The girl turned round. Her face was pale and her eyes red. The narrow counter was bare apart from a small pile of pasteboard rectangles, like calling cards. The top one carried a religious text and a watercolour violet, inexpertly done. On the way there, I'd thought about what to say and decided to keep as close as I could to the truth. I wished her good morning and asked if we were talking to Janet Priest's sister. She nodded, tears filming her eyes.

'I am very sorry to intrude on you,' I said, 'only I know of another young lady who was found dead in circumstances something like your sister's. We're trying to find out what happened to her and it might help if you'd be kind enough to tell us something about Janet.'

'This other lady, was she pushed off the Monument too?'

The elder Miss Priest's voice was a harsh whisper. Her hands twisted together against her chest, fingernails bitten to the quick.

'No. Her throat was cut. But you said Janet was pushed?'

'Of course she was pushed. She'd never have destroyed herself. She knew she'd go to hell if she did.' Her eyes went from me to Tabby and back again, with a look of desperate challenge.

'You sister was a religious person?'

'She believed in the Holy Bible, like we all should. We'd talk about it some nights lying awake in our beds, especially Sunday nights if there'd been a powerful preacher, about what it would be like to be burning in hell and never get out of it. A few times, she scared herself so much she couldn't sleep, then we'd get out of bed and pray together on our bare knees, then I'd tuck her up in bed, tell her she was a good girl so she wouldn't go to hell and hold her hand till her eyes closed.'

It sounded a desperately sad memory to me, but as she talked about it the challenging look in Miss Priest's eyes had changed to tenderness.

'Did you say any of this at the inquest?' I said.

Her eyes dropped. 'I wanted to. I thought they'd ask me "Did your sister kill herself?" Then I'd have told them what I've just told you. But they never asked. It was just insulting things like did she have any gentleman followers. I was in a daze all the time, from when I saw her poor body. I couldn't believe it was happening. Afterwards I wished I'd told them, whether they'd asked or not. I asked a legal gentleman who comes in here sometimes whether I could go back and tell them, but he said once the inquest verdict was in, that was that. It's not right.'

The words came pouring out. Grief makes some people silent and others talkative. It seemed to be a relief to her to talk even to strangers, or perhaps especially to strangers.

'Did you ever find out what happened to your sister in that week when she was missing?' I asked her.

'Somebody was keeping her prisoner against her will.' She said it with total certainty.

'How do you know that?'

'Because otherwise she'd never have stayed away from us, worrying us like that. If she went out for a half pound of butter she'd always say where she was going. She knew how it bothered Father if he didn't know where we were.'

'But you have no other reason for believing she was being kept prisoner?'

'I don't need another reason. I know her. Knew her.'

She turned away and dabbed at her eyes with a handkerchief. Tabby looked at me and opened her mouth. I signalled to her to be quiet and we waited until Miss Priest turned back towards us.

'Have you any idea who might have kept her prisoner?' I asked.

She shook her head. I spoke as tactfully as I could, knowing that we were on dangerous ground. 'I know your sister had no gentleman followers and from what you tell me, I'm sure she wouldn't have encouraged anybody without your knowing.' (I was sure of nothing of the kind.) 'But sometimes a man will become attached to a woman, even if she gives him no encouragement at all. Were there any men who showed interest in your sister?'

'No.'

She said it as if the idea were an insult to her memory. I persisted gently. 'I believe she helped in the shop, as you do.'

'We have to. Father can't stand behind the counter because of his legs.'

'Were there any customers who seemed to take a particular interest in her, perhaps find reasons for talking to her?'

'Janet wasn't a great one for talking. She was always polite to customers, of course, but if talking was needed, she left it to me.'

As in the case of Dora Tilbury, it struck me that Janet Priest's existence had been simple to the point of unreality. But Janet had been real. She'd stood behind that counter, stacked reams of paper and canisters of ink powder on the shelves, breathed this air with its faint scents of ink and brown paper.

'I suppose most of your customers are well known to you?'

'Oh yes. The same year in, year out.'

'So if you had anybody new in the shop, you'd notice them?'

'Yes.'

'Was there anybody new in the weeks before your sister disappeared?'

Nobody had asked her that question before. She had to think about it, and the reply came slowly.

'The Brett brothers who do roofing had a new chief clerk in September. He came in to introduce himself and query an invoice for letterheads. It turned out we were right. He was quite civil about it.'

'A young man?'

'No, quite elderly. Then there's been a couple of new messenger boys since the summer, from firms we've dealt with a long time. I had to tell one of them not to whistle and stand with his hands in his pockets in the shop, apart from that there's no harm in them.'

'And that's all?'

'I think so. Oh, there was the foreign gentleman, back at the end of September.'

'What sort of foreign?'

'I don't know. I don't think he was French. German perhaps or Prussian.'

'Did he speak in a foreign language?'

'No, he spoke good English, only with an accent.'

'What did he buy?'

'A dozen pen nibs. He was quite fussy, trying them out. When he found some that suited him he said he'd send his servant in for a parcel of them, but he only bought the dozen then and there because that was all he could carry in his pocket without making a bulge.'

'Did your sister speak to him?'

'No more than a word or two. She was mostly fetching nibs and mixing ink.'

'And did the servant come back for more?'

'No.'

'A foreign gentleman, you say. Do you see many of those in the shop?'

'None hardly, apart from him.'

The bell twanged. A travelling salesman came in and tried to get her to take an interest in his samples of blotting paper. She told him they were well suited for blotting paper and sent him on his way.

'What happened the day your sister disappeared?' I said. 'Did she tell you where she was going?'

'She didn't have a chance. I was upstairs, giving Father his tea, as I always do at six o'clock.'

'And your sister?'

'Down here in the shop. We don't get much trade at that time of day, but we stay open till seven to oblige customers who work late. I gave Father his tea, came down as usual, and Janet was gone.'

'Had you heard any noise or any talking downstairs?'

'None. I thought at first she'd gone out in the street for some reason, only it wasn't like her to leave the door open and money in the drawer when anybody could have walked in. There was no sign of her, so I started asking up and down the street. No sign of her.'

'Had anybody seen a vehicle stop outside your shop?'

'Not outside the shop, no. One of our customers thought he saw a plain carriage with two horses and a coachman on the box further down the street, but that's nothing out of the way.'

'Did you go to the police?'

'Yes, straightaway. They were no use, though. They thought she'd just taken herself off. They wouldn't believe me that she wasn't like that. I went to all the police stations, tramped round the hospitals. Nothing. Until . . .' Her voice trailed away. She scooped up two of the pasteboard rectangles and thrust them at Tabby and me. 'She did those herself.'

Mine said 'A good name is rather to be chosen than great riches'. Tabby glanced at me as if asking what to do with hers.

'Thank you,' I said. 'Just one more thing, if you don't mind my asking. Had you ever seen before that ring that was on your sister's finger?'

'It was evil, evil.' The words came out more passionately than anything she'd said so far. 'How could they do it to her – a dirty animal's head on the finger where a woman wears her marriage ring. Wasn't it enough killing her without shaming her like that?'

Then she clapped her hand over her mouth and glanced upstairs, probably for fear of disturbing her father. I waited for a while but it seemed that she had nothing else to say. I gave her one of the cards I'd had printed with my name and address.

'If we find out anything about how my friend died, and if it relates in any way to your sister, I promise to come back and tell you,' I said.

We wished her goodbye. I had my hand on the door when she spoke again.

'Another thing I could have told them at the inquest: she'd never have gone all the way to the top of the Monument of her own free will. She hated heights. If anything had to go up on the top shelf, I had to do it because she couldn't even stand on those steps.'

She pointed to portable wooden steps, the topmost of them no more than waist high.

'She was taken up there by force, just as she was taken away from here by force,' she said. 'If you or anybody can tell me why or who by, perhaps I'll be able to sleep at nights because I can't. Not now.'

'So she didn't throw herself off,' Tabby said as we walked back westwards.

'No, not unless her sister was telling us lies. Was she?'

'No.'

Tabby's flat certainty matched mine. Miss Priest hadn't known we were coming. Why should she have lies ready? But more than that, my instinct too was that she was no liar.

'So was it the foreign gentleman took her away?' Tabby said.

'We can't know. He might have had nothing to do with it.'

'Seems a lot of fuss to make about pen nibs.'

'Some people are very fussy about pen nibs.'

She accepted that, although grudgingly.

'At any rate, somebody had been keeping that shop under observation,' I said. 'You heard what she said about giving her father his tea at six o'clock?'

'She said she always did.'

'Exactly. So somebody who'd been watching them would know Janet was always alone in the shop at six o'clock, probably without customers.'

'If somebody took her away, why didn't she kick up a row? I would have.'

'Perhaps she was tricked. Suppose somebody said there was a child or even a dog hurt and she went out to help.'

'Yes, then they might have pulled her inside the carriage and knocked her on the head,' Tabby said. 'After that, they carted her up the Monument and threw her off, like the old man Gaffer told me.'

'Only that happened a week later. Where did they keep her all that week, and why?'

Which brought us back to the central question. For somebody, it hadn't been enough that the two women should die: it must appear to happen in the most public manner possible and at some particular time. Why? We were no further with that by the time we arrived home.

COURT CIRCULAR

The Duchess of Gloucester visited the Princess Augusta yesterday, at Clarence-house, St. James's.

The Princess Augusta took an airing in a carriage on Saturday.

Viscount Palmerston came to town on Saturday morning. His Lordship returned to Windsor Castle in the afternoon.

The Queen, accompanied by Prince Albert of Saxe Coburg, rode in the park yesterday afternoon, attended by the whole of the Royal visitors and suite (except Viscount Palmerston).

Lord Palmerston dashes back to London
The Times 28 October 1839

ELEVEN

For once, there was a pleasant surprise waiting – a note from one of my best friends, Beatrice Talbot.

> My Dear Liberty,
>
>   I wonder if we could persuade you at such short notice to come with us to Drury Lane this evening. It's Collins and Mrs Waylett in *The Fairy Lake*. We have taken a box, and George's cousin has had to cry off at the last minute because of a cough. If you can come, don't bother to reply to this and we'll collect you in the carriage at six.
>
>   Yours affectionately, Beattie.

Beatrice Talbot's husband was a wealthy businessman from Yorkshire and they kept a hospitable house in Belgrave Square. We'd met because I taught music to their large family and even though my investigative work had taken over from most of my teaching, I kept up my visits to them for the pleasure of it. My first thought was that I could not go jaunting off to the opera when so much sadness was happening round me. Then I thought how good it would be to forget about it for a few hours. The delivery later of the green velvet dress convinced me. It deserved a carriage to Drury Lane for its first outing. Before I changed I went to let Tabby know that I was going out and found her in the mews with some of her stable lad friends, back in street-urchin mode. They were decent lads essentially and as good as a bodyguard for her, so I felt secure about leaving her.

A fourth member of our party arrived in the box just a few minutes before the overture started. He was a man of about my own age with dark curls and a smile of such open enjoyment that my spirits rose just to look at him. George Talbot introduced him as Michael Calloway, who worked at the Foreign Office.

'For my sins,' he said. 'That's the excuse for my atrocious unpunctuality. They kept their poor galley slaves working so late, I scarcely had time to go home and change.'

From his manner, I guessed he was by no means a galley slave but a young diplomat learning his trade before being sent to some foreign embassy. A man appeared in front of the curtains to explain that Mr Collins would be singing, bravely, in spite of a bad cold. It was a pleasant enough piece, but not first rate, with a rather depressed chorus of fairies who sounded as if they too were suffering from Mr Collins' cold.

At the interval, the Talbots had arranged for supper to be served to us in our box. From the way Beattie glanced at Mr Calloway and me as we were forking up our chicken in aspic, I suspected her of matchmaking. With the instant understanding of two people who like each other on sight, but without romantic complications, Mr Calloway and I exchanged our own looks, which said we were not playing that game. Once that was decided, I was free to enjoy his gossip about life at the Foreign Office.

'There we all were, a nice quiet Saturday morning with only a few messages coming in from the cipher clerks, feet up on our desks, looking forward to being out of harness by lunchtime. Then, a hawk in the dovecote. A panting messenger arrives with the news that our esteemed chief, whom we'd all assumed to be safely occupied at Windsor being bored to distraction by the happy couple, has been sighted in Whitehall. Feet off desks, novels into filing cabinets, immediate Pam alert.'

He mimed wide-eyed civil servants, straightening collars and smoothing hair. Pam was the irreverent name for our formidable Foreign Secretary, Lord Palmerston. Even heads of state would not lightly annoy him, let alone young civil servants.

'So we all sit there, shining with alertness, waiting for Pam to burst in and tell us what international crisis has brought him rushing back from Windsor to London on a weekend. Is there another revolution in Paris? Have the Ottomans insulted us? Where should we send the gunboat? So we sit and we shine and we wait and at the end of it – nothing happens.'

'So the crisis must have gone away of its own accord,' Beattie suggested.

'If so, it managed it without the help of the Foreign Office. At half past five word gets round that Pam has gone straight back to Windsor without even setting foot in the building.'

I hoped I didn't look guilty. Were the contessa and I responsible for the strange behaviour of our most senior statesmen? The letter I'd delivered to His Highness might have made the Foreign Office uneasy about a threat to the dignity of their royal visitor. George Talbot said there must surely be some reason for the Foreign Secretary's return to the capital. Calloway shrugged.

'Who knows. Perhaps he'd forgotten his dress studs. Perhaps he was attempting to escape from the Windsor treadmill and our sovereign lady had him rounded up and brought back.'

Over the dessert of raspberry ices, Beattie asked Calloway if court life at Windsor were really so boring. He admitted that he had no direct experience of it, but the head of his department had to make frequent trips to Windsor Castle when Pam was in attendance there.

'From what he says, it's the combination of Love's Young Dream and all that formality which makes it such a burden for everybody else. Can you imagine, the pair of them riding together in Windsor Great Park and about thirty assorted courtiers and statesmen of various nationalities riding at a respectful distance behind them, pretending not to be there?'

It was clear that the engagement of Victoria and Albert, although still not officially announced, was already a fact of life in Whitehall.

'They really love each other then?' Beattie said.

'Evidently. At least it's not one of those diplomatic marriages where the two parties can hardly bear to be in the same room. I'm told she looks at him as if the sun rises in his eyes.'

'What about him?' I said.

'Almost equally devoted, it's said. Though he's a young man of such impeccable breeding and virtue, it's hard to tell what he really thinks.'

'Is any man's virtue impeccable?' I asked, teasing him.

'Albert's is, I'm sure. He's unbelievably serious minded. A friend of mine met him, and within two minutes Albert was quizzing him about workers' housing in Birmingham. His Highness had more facts and figures at his fingertips than an entire committee.'

'It's no bad thing for a young man to be serious, with such burdens ahead of him,' George Talbot said.

Calloway arranged his features into diplomatic agreement. 'And perhaps we should all give thanks to Cupid that it was young Albert who won her affections and not his elder brother.'

'Is Prince Ernest not so virtuous then?' I asked.

'Not quite,' Calloway said.

He and George exchanged a look that said some things were not to be discussed in front of ladies, which annoyed me. George turned the conversation to diplomacy. 'I suppose there are some countries which won't be entirely pleased with the arrangement.'

'Quite true,' Calloway said. 'I know the prime minister had reservations on that score. The Coburgs aren't popular abroad and the Russians hate them. Some people think Albert's Uncle Leopold won't rest until there's a Saxe Coburg on every throne in Europe.'

'I thought she was going to marry the Czar's son,' Beattie said.

'That was a distinct possibility back in the spring. I'm sure there'll be some disappointment in St Petersburg. I dare say Austria will have reservations too, which is amusing since Kolowrath is actually a guest at Windsor at present.'

'Kolowrath?' I asked.

I suspected that the Talbots didn't recognize the name either but didn't want to show their ignorance by asking. I had no shame on that score.

'Count Anton Graf von Kolowrath, the Austrian minister of the interior and Prince Metternich's right-hand man, though he'd probably be quite happy to see Metternich go under the wheels of a coach.'

'Like quite a lot of other people,' Talbot commented.

In European politics, Metternich was generally regarded as the prince of darkness, capable of any kind of diplomatic double dealing.

'Yes,' Calloway said. 'I'd give quite a few guineas to be there when Count Kolowrath has to give formal congratulations to the happy couple.'

I felt sorry for little Vicky. She was only twenty years old after all, and the whole world was taking an interest in what should be the private matter of choosing a husband. If I became annoyed sometimes at my friends' matchmaking attempts, how much worse it must have been for her.

We finished our raspberry ices as the orchestra began to file back into the pit and settled to more fairies and a ballet about Mars and Venus that had probably been grafted in from some other opera. In the foyer after the performance, Mr Calloway helped me deftly into my cloak. We were halfway to the door when George Talbot spotted a friend of his who was a member of parliament with a particular interest in foreign affairs. One of the many amiable things about George was that he never missed an opportunity to advance a protégé's career, so Calloway and I had to be introduced to the MP and serious chat followed, with the crowd surging round us like the outgoing tide round a rock. I was only half listening to exchanges about some trade agreement when something in the sea of people caught my eye. It was the briefest of looks, a dark head of hair and a light-footed way of walking even in a crowd. Oddly, I had the impression that, at the moment I'd glimpsed him, he'd only just started walking and until then had been standing still, as we were. A person may stop walking for many reasons and London is full of dark-haired men, but I was immediately sure that he was the man I knew as Mr Clyde and he'd been staring at me. He went on, out of the door. You can't go running after men in public places. Then, as usually happens, I was not so sure after all. If it had been Mr Clyde, might he have paused, hoping to speak to me, then decided against it? By the time my party had got outside, there was no sign of him or anybody like him on the pavement.

We all went together to find the Talbots' carriage. Calloway handed me in, hoped we'd meet again then wished us goodnight, because his rooms weren't far away.

'Did you like him?' Beattie asked, as soon as our wheels were rolling.

'Yes. He's very entertaining.'

Beattie looked at me, trying to make out my expression from the headlamps of an oncoming carriage.

'No more than entertaining?'

'Heaven knows, that's rare enough.'

Until that possible sighting of Mr Clyde reminded me of business, I'd enjoyed the few hours' respite and friendship and was grateful. I craved warmth and kindness, like a cat hungry for cream.

'Is there somebody else?' Beattie said.

'I think so, yes. But he's away in Ireland.'

'Only think so?'

George told her to stop plaguing the poor girl with questions and turned the conversation to what I thought of the evening's performance. They dropped me off at the gateway to Abel Yard, promising that we'd meet again soon for a musical evening at their home.

The first thing I looked for was a glimmer of a candle from Tabby's cabin, but there was nothing but darkness in that direction. When I did pick up a faint light it came not from the cabin but between the closed doors of the carriage repairer's store shed by the gates. There shouldn't have been a light in there. It was after eleven o'clock and Mr Grindley never worked so late. I listened and heard low voices inside. One of them was male, the other Tabby's. I prised open the door and walked in to find a man holding a mallet. His shadow wavered over the wall in the candlelight. Tabby was bending over a bench, an odd white hat on her head that I'd never seen her wearing before. My heart turned several cartwheels before I recognized the man with the mallet.

'Tom Huckerby, what in the world are you doing now?'

He looked a little shamefaced. The mallet was the kind printers use to pack type into its frame, Tabby's strange hat a paper one that printers make fresh for themselves every day to keep ink out of their hair. Another man I'd never seen before was crouching close to a second candle sorting through type.

'Seemed a pity to have the press here and not bring out a new edition of *The Unbound Briton*,' Tom said. 'We didn't think you'd mind.'

They'd dragged the press out of its hiding place and reassembled it in an empty space between parts of carriages.

'It's not a question of whether I mind,' I said. 'It's not my storeroom.'

'I know, but Boadicea here says the man never works Saturday afternoons and Sundays and in any case he's out visiting his sister.'

I looked reproachfully at Tabby. She grinned back. It seemed to me ironic that a girl who scorned reading and writing could so easily be seduced by the glamour of the press.

'What are you printing?' I asked Tom.

'Latest edition of *The Unbound Briton*. Don't worry, we'll have every drop of ink scrubbed away and the press back under the stairs by daylight.'

I tucked away my good white evening gloves and picked up a proof page. Surrounded by columns of type was a picture of a gentleman's dress chariot. It was done from a rough woodcut,

over-inked and gleaming black. On the back, where footmen should
have been, two creatures reared up with horned heads and animal
bodies.

'Not you as well, Tom,' I said.

He was political to the bone and would not usually waste paper
and ink on horror stories to scare housemaids.

'Not really our style, I know but we had a page to fill,' he said.
'A fellow I know runs another paper, more of a penny-dreadful
than ours, but we help each other out when we're short of copy.
He takes some of our politics and I take some of his shockers.'

'More appearances of the devil's chariot, then?'

'All over the place, and half a dozen girls supposed to have
disappeared. You know how these stories grow legs.'

He sounded as sceptical as I was.

'The man you know who wrote this story, has he actually talked
to anybody who's seen it or is it all second hand?'

Tom had to think about it. 'As far as I remember, he claims he
spoke to a girl in Holborn who reckons she was dragged into the
chariot by two men with bulls' heads, only she struggled and got
away.'

Tabby gave me a 'told you so' look.

'When was this supposed to have happened?' I said.

'Last week.'

'He only *claims* to have spoken to the girl?'

'Codling's not exactly the most reliable man in journalism.'

I tried to return Tabby's look, but she was too entranced with
Tom setting up a line of type to notice.

I was about to go to bed and leave them to it, when Tom remembered something. 'I saw your friend Jimmy Cuffs. He gave me a
note for you.' He pulled it out of his pocket and handed it over,
ink-smeared. It was addressed to me in Jimmy's meticulous writing:

> Miss Lane,
> Re your inquiry about a certain ring. My informant tells me
> it was the head of a bull on a man's body, finely modelled.
> The Minotaur?

Candlelight wavered over the note as I read. But the candle flame
was burning steadily. The wavering was from my hands shaking.

'Tom?'

He looked up. 'Bad news?'

'That friend of yours, Codling, do you think he could get the woman to speak to me? The one who says she was nearly dragged off in the chariot.'

He was puzzled, both at the request and the urgency I couldn't keep from my voice.

'I could try.'

'As soon as possible.'

He hesitated, torn between curiosity and the demands of his printing, then nodded. I got his permission to take the proof page upstairs with me, took off my fine clothes and read the story by the lamplight. The black chariot worked itself into my dreams. I woke shivering from a dream of it rumbling along behind me as I ran away down an endless street of blank houses. I was not much better than all those nervous housemaids now. I was starting to believe in it.

TWELVE

Tom Huckerby was at my door around noon next morning, weary and hollow-eyed.

'The woman's name is Blade. Codling thinks he might be able to get her to talk this afternoon.'

'Where?'

'You know the Flora Tea Gardens, near the Swan Inn on the Bayswater Road? He said he'd try and get her there about three.'

I said I'd be there. He hesitated, looking worried. 'He says she's accustomed to . . . to being paid for her time. That's why she was out on the street so late on her own.'

'How much does she want?'

'Codling thought she might talk to us for five guineas.'

'Five guineas!'

I didn't know the rates for the midnight sparrows, but that seemed excessive.

'That's what he says.'

In the few hours available, the only way I could put my hand
on that sort of money was by raiding the store of guineas Mr Clyde
had left for me in the desk at Grosvenor Street. Normally that
would have troubled my conscience but I was past that by now.

Suzette opened the door less promptly than usual, looking sulky
and not pleased to see me. I took five sovereigns out of the bag
in the writing desk, knowing that I could make up the extra five
shillings from my own resources. On the way downstairs, I asked
Suzette if she'd seen Mr Clyde that day.

'No, ma'am.'

'When did you last see him?'

'Can't rightly remember, ma'am.'

I might as well have spoken to the banisters.

At two o'clock, Tabby and I were walking across the park towards
the Bayswater Road. I hadn't wanted to take her, but it turned out
that she'd been eavesdropping from under the stairs when Tom
Huckerby was talking to me. I'd given in, on the condition that
she kept her distance when I was talking to our witness.

'If she sees a whole group of us, she might turn and run,' I said.

'Not with a chance of getting her hand on five guineas.'

It struck me that my apprentice might know more than I did
about the tariff for Miss Blade's kind. The Flora Tea Gardens were
not far from the livery stables where Amos worked. They'd been
fashionable once, but on an afternoon in late October there was a
sad and faded air about them. Rosemary bushes in the sparse
borders still showed a defiant blue flower or two, but geraniums
hunched as if waiting for the first frost. Tom Huckerby was already
there sitting at a table, the only person in the gardens. I joined
him and sent Tabby into the neighbouring Swan Inn, just in case
the tea gardens still ran to providing tea. Tom was ill at ease.

'I don't know if they'll come. This Codling, I shouldn't want
you to think he's a particular friend of mine.'

A sulky girl came out with a tray, followed by Tabby. The
teacups were chipped and the milk so sour that, when I poured,
white globules floated on brown sludge. A long time after three
o'clock, two more people came into the garden. One was a man
in a low crowned hat and a black overcoat. Blue smoke and the
smell of a cheap cigar came ahead of him. He was small, in his

late twenties, with sparse fair hair, pale eyes with near-white lashes
and a protruding lower lip like a carp. A woman followed, shoulders hunched, an Indian shawl over her head. I glanced at Tabby
and she withdrew to a seat a couple of tables away.

Tom introduced Mr Codling to me. The woman was slumped
on a chair, with just a glance up at me from under the shawl.

'Miss Blade,' Codling said.

Hers was a strong face, or should have been, with high cheekbones and a good chin, arched eyebrows, dark hair waving over
a white forehead. But her eyes were as dull as bottle stoppers, her
cheeks too bright with rouge. She wore a brown wool skirt and a
dark blue jacket. The brown bodice under the jacket was fastened
unevenly with buttons in the wrong holes, glimpses of red chemise
showing through. Codling sat down and looked a question at Tom.
I'd given Tom the five guineas. He handed it over and it disappeared
into Codling's pocket like a fly down the carp's gullet. I asked the
woman if she'd care for a cup of tea.

'She'd prefer gin,' Codling said. 'With hot water and a lump of
sugar.'

He spoke with a dandyish drawl, wafting cigar smoke aside
with his hand. Tom stood up and went inside The Swan.

'I'd like to know exactly what happened to Miss Blade,' I said
to Codling.

'So what's your interest?'

I tried to make the look I gave him as insolent as his question.
'I think that's my business.'

'Are you representing somebody?'

'Yes,' I said.

'And you're not going to tell me who?'

'No.'

'That's a touch cool, isn't it?'

'Yes,' I said. 'Five guineas cool.'

He laughed, and drew on his cigar. I spoke directly to the woman.
'Miss Blade, is it correct that two masked men dragged you into
a chariot?'

She looked up at him, not at me.

'Miss Blade wants me to do the talking,' Codling said. 'She's
still shaken from what happened. She'll say if I'm getting it wrong,
won't you?'

She nodded. Tom came back, followed by the girl with a steaming glass and a pint of porter on a tray. Codling took a swallow of porter.

'You've read what I wrote?'

'I've read what Mr Huckerby published in his paper.'

'Don't read papers like mine, eh? You should.'

I reminded myself that I needed his help. 'Yes, I probably should. But since I've missed it, I wonder if you could kindly tell me the details?'

He took another swallow. 'We say in the story that she was a servant walking home, but Becky was out working, if you take my meaning.'

I couldn't tell whether the brutality in his tone was directed at me or at the woman sitting beside him. When neither of us reacted, he went on talking. 'She hears this carriage coming along slowly behind her so she glances round, sees a dress chariot with the lamps lit and a driver on the box in a three-cornered hat and a black cloak, so being in her line of business she walks on, but slower than before, thinking there's probably a gentleman inside the chariot who wishes to have a conversation with her. Is that right so far, Becky?'

A nod from the woman, as if none of this had much to do with her.

'The chariot comes level with her, then stops. She sees the blind is drawn down on her side, but that's not unusual. Some gentlemen like to get a closer look at the lady before they commit themselves, so to speak. So she puts her foot up on the step – probably taking care to show a neat ankle in case the gentleman happens to be glancing out from under the blind. That right, Becky?'

He was enjoying this too much. I told him fairly sharply to get to the point.

'We're there already. No sooner are her dainty toes on the step than the chariot lurches, and these two men jump down off the back. Of course, she wouldn't have seen them before, being at the side of it. They run at her and take hold of her by the shoulders. By the light of the carriage lamps, she sees they've got bull faces and horns where their heads should be and yells blue murder. But they bundle her into the chariot. There's two gentlemen inside. She says one was in what looked like military uniform, with gold braid. The bull men throw her down on the floor and hold her there while the gentlemen do what they want to do. She's screaming and struggling, but it's no good.'

He blew a smoke ring and watched as it rose slowly and dissolved in the damp air.

'And they try to carry her off?' I asked.

'That's right. Only the bull men have to open the door so they can get out and get back up behind. When they do, Becky here manages to throw herself out, yelling for help.'

'And she gets away?'

'Yes. A couple of Peelers come running up, shouting out and rattling their rattles for all they're worth. The bull men jump back on and off goes the chariot towards Soho at such a lick that the Peelers couldn't have caught it if they tried, and not many of them care for running unless there's somebody chasing after them.'

Codling settled back in his chair. 'Not a bad little story, is it, even if it's not the sort of things *The Times* prints,' he said. 'And she was a lucky girl, weren't you, Becky?'

The woman didn't react. It was left to me to ask him what he meant.

'A few days after that, they found the girl by the Achilles, with all the blood drained out of her. I reckon that's what they were going to go with Becky if she hadn't got away. They'd put their mark on her, all ready for sacrifice.'

'Put their mark on her. What do you mean?'

'Show her, Becky.'

Still without looking up, the woman took off her jacket and began to undo the buttons on her bodice, slow and fumbling. It fell open, revealing the red silk chemise. Tom turned away. She hesitated, looking up at Codling.

'Go on,' he said.

She froze. He stood up and drew the chemise down, baring her bosom over the top of her stays and her left shoulder. She gave a gasp of pain.

'That,' Codling said.

Just below the collar bone, the white skin was hatched with a series of shallow knife gashes, beaded with blood at the edges.

'See what it is?'

I didn't at first, too horrified. Then I made out horns and the profile of a bull's head, rough and angular as a thing must be when drawn with a knife blade, but unmistakeable.

'You're saying the men in the chariot cut that on her?'

'Yes. That right, Becky?'

She just managed a nod, trembling. As carefully as I could, I drew the chemise back over it, re-buttoned the bodice for her and put the jacket back round her shoulders.

'Miss Blade, may I ask you something?' I said.

She looked at me but I'm not sure she was seeing me.

'She's not up to talking much,' Codling said.

'Are you sure it happened inside the chariot?' I said. 'There's not much room inside one, is there? With the four men and you struggling, in the dark as well, I don't understand how they managed to do that to you.'

Her dull eyes slid away from me towards Codling.

'Perhaps they pulled her down on the pavement,' he said. 'You can't expect the poor girl to remember every detail.'

'It's quite a big detail, isn't it? What about those policemen? The story said you were too badly shocked to go to the police.'

'She was,' Codling said. 'When they couldn't get any sense out of her, they just went off and left her there. Anyway, you don't think they'd take any notice of girls like her, do you? Girls have been murdered and they don't care.'

'And when was this?' I said.

'Monday before last,' Codling said promptly.

I looked at the woman. 'Is that right?'

No answer.

'Her nerves are so torn up, she doesn't know what day of the week it is,' Codling said. 'You're just making things worse for her.'

Sharp creature, he'd picked up how much I was hating this. I couldn't bear to look at her sitting and shivering and go on coolly asking questions. I spoke to her. 'This man's got five guineas in his pocket that should belong to you. Get them off him, if you can. If you need help, ask for Miss Lane at Abel Yard.'

But I knew that even if she were hearing me, she wouldn't remember. I stood up.

'Two last questions for you, Mr Codling. How much were you paid for printing that story and who paid you?'

I waited in case there were answers, but I didn't expect them and didn't get them. So I walked away, Tom following with Tabby close behind. While we'd been talking she'd moved to the neighbouring table and had probably heard and seen everything. I looked back as we left the gardens. Codling was sitting beside the woman. He was holding what was left of the gin to her lips, but it would be cold by now.

'I'm sorry,' Tom said. 'If I'd had any idea what he was really like, I shouldn't have let you within a mile of him.'

'He made it up, didn't he?' I said. 'Or somebody else did and got him to print it.'

'Why would anybody do that? Besides, his isn't the only paper running the story. It's all round London.'

'Then perhaps other people have been paid as well.'

'I hope you don't think I was.'

'No. But the further the rumour goes, the stronger it gets, and whoever's spreading it is relying on that.'

'It was a good point you made about not much room in a chariot,' Tom said.

'Something more than that. Did you manage a close view of those cuts?'

Tom blushed. 'Enough to make out what it was.'

'According to Codling, they were done nearly two weeks ago,' I said. 'The cuts weren't much deeper than scratches. They'd have scarred over by now and they wouldn't still be bleeding.'

Tom looked puzzled. 'I reckon he was speaking the truth, for once, when he said she doesn't know what day it is,' he said. 'She looked drunk to me, and probably drugged as well.'

'I expect she was,' I said. 'She'd have needed to be when Codling was cutting her this morning.'

'What?'

The two of them stopped walking and stared at me.

'You mean *Codling* put those cuts on her?' Tom said.

'Yes, or possibly some accomplice, but certainly with his knowledge. Those cuts were made only a few hours ago, some time after he agreed to see us.'

'The red thing she was wearing,' Tabby said suddenly. 'It was red so it wouldn't show she'd been bleeding on it.'

'The chemise, yes. He'd have to agree to pay her something, I suppose, but I don't suppose she'll get more than a guinea in her hand.'

Tom started walking again. 'So if I hadn't asked to speak to him . . .'

'It was my fault, not yours. But, yes, he did it because he wanted to back up his story. I'm sure it wouldn't have mattered so much to him on his own account, so he probably got word to whoever paid him in the first place and was told what to do.'

'But why?'

'I only wish I knew.'

We walked back together to Abel Mews, where Tom parted from us. Before he left, he stared at the bundles of *The Unbound Briton*, stacked under the stairs.

'I'd like to tear off those back pages, but then the front ones would go as well and we can't afford the paper to reprint.'

I told him not to worry because his retelling of the story wouldn't make matters any worse. The devil's chariot was out and about and the important question was what it was going to do next.

Tabby sat down on a bundle of newspapers. I settled on another one, weary and sick with myself.

'It's not a coincidence,' I said.

'What's a coincidence?'

On the walk back, one of the things going round in my mind was how much to tell Tabby. I didn't understand what was happening but whoever was responsible wouldn't hesitate to kill an urchin girl who asked questions in awkward places. Then I thought she was in too deeply in any case, so the best protection was to tell her everything.

'For instance, if your birthday and mine were on the same day, that would be a coincidence,' I said.

'I don't know what day I was born.'

'When we were looking for Miss Tilbury we happened to hear about the young woman who fell off the Monument. Hearing about it wasn't really a coincidence because we were looking for a young woman so we had to find out if she happened to be our young woman. So the two things were connected. Are you following me so far?'

'Yes.' She was watching my face, concentrating hard.

'The young woman who came off the Monument had wet hair

and an unusual kind of ring that didn't fit her very well on her wedding finger. It was exactly the same with Miss Tilbury at the Achilles statue – wet hair and a ring that didn't fit, too large in her case and too small in Miss Priest's. I've found out that the two rings were the same design. It was a man with a bull's head.'

'Like the bull head on the woman's shoulder?'

'Yes.'

Like, too, the signet ring on the contessa's dressing table. I wasn't ready to tell Tabby about that yet.

'Another thing,' I said. 'Janet Priest went missing on the tenth of October. When the man who called himself Mr James came to us, he said Dora had been missing since the previous Thursday. That was the same day. Is that a coincidence?'

'So the people with the devils' heads and the chariot killed both of them,' Tabby said.

'Whoa. That's galloping on too fast. We haven't proved any connection between the two women being killed and the chariot.'

'But it was there both times. Is that a whatdycallit?'

'There are people claiming to have seen it near where the bodies were discovered, but a few hours before. And we've already proved that people are being paid to spread stories about it, so we don't know what's true and what isn't.'

Tabby thought about it for a while then took a button out of her pocket, showed it to me and rubbed it between her palms.

'Choose one.'

She held out her two clenched fists to me. I tapped the left one. She opened it. Nothing. She opened the right one. Button. She got me to try it twice more. I was wrong each time.

'So?' I said.

'I was with a cove once did the pea and thimble trick. When you know how, you can make people choose wrong.'

It struck me that it was one of the few fragments of autobiography Tabby had ever given me. Also, that I must get her to show me how, one day. For the present, the surprising thing was how closely her instincts matched mine.

'Looking at the similarities, does anything strike you about where the two women were found?' I said.

'They was both places where a lot of people would see them.'

'Exactly! The Monument and the Achilles statue are two of the best known landmarks in the whole of London. A body found in either place would attract much more attention than in a back street somewhere. So that's four similarities: the places, the rings, the day they disappeared and, yes, probably appearance of the chariot.'

'So it's the same people?'

'Yes. I think our working assumption must be that they were both killed by the same person or group of people.'

I hesitated about going on to the next thing I needed to tell her. It was so odd and dark that it seemed an unfair burden for a girl of fifteen. But a lot of her young life must have been dark and odd.

'I was thinking as we walked back, why should it be a bull's head?' I said. 'I think I've guessed.'

It had come to me as I'd glimpsed the Achilles statue in the distance and shuddered at the memory of it towering apparently in triumph over the dead girl at its base. In my imagination, the head of the statue became transformed from handsome demigod to rampaging bull, a creature from the wildest shores of myth. Jimmy Cuffs had recognized it.

'There was a story a long time ago about a monster with the body of a man and the head of a bull,' I told Tabby. 'It was called the Minotaur. It lived in the middle of an underground labyrinth—'

'A what?'

'A kind of maze, you know, lots of twisty paths where people get lost. Anyway, this bull-monster ate people. There was a city called Athens—'

'Is that further away than France?'

'Yes. Listen, every nine years Athens had to send seven young men and seven young women to the island of Crete where the bull-monster lived, as food for it.'

'Why didn't they all get together and kill it?'

'Because the old stories don't work like that. They had to wait for a hero. He turned out to be a man called Theseus. He had himself sent to Crete as one of the young men who were supposed to be eaten, found his way to the middle of the labyrinth and killed the monster.'

Tabby nodded her head in approval, but was clearly waiting for me to come to the point.

'I think there may be some wicked club,' I said. 'Like the old Hell Fire club, only worse. Those rings on their wedding fingers are the club's mark. We know about two of them, but for all we know there may be others.'

'And the bullheads on the devil's chariot are all part of that?'

'Yes.' I admitted it reluctantly. 'I don't understand how it's linked, but it's all part of the same horrible game. The people involved must have a lot of money to spend.'

Power too, I thought, if they were able to have inquests adjourned indefinitely.

'So isn't anybody trying to stop them?' Tabby said.

'I think somebody may be.'

'Who?'

'The man who doesn't exist. Our client Jeremy James.'

From her look, Tabby was wondering if I'd gone mad. 'But if he doesn't exist . . .?'

'Not in the name or address he gave us. But suppose he'd somehow found out about this club, perhaps even been a member of it, and wanted to stop it. He couldn't go to the police without accusing himself and if the other members found out, he'd be in danger. So he invents a false name for himself and a girl and gets us to investigate. But . . .'

I stopped talking, seeing a snag. Our so-called Mr James had come to see me a week before 'Dora's' body was found at the Achilles statue. Everything about this case was like trying to grasp handfuls of mist.

'It doesn't fit. Where was she all that time?'

'Perhaps they were keeping her shut up somewhere,' Tabby said. 'The other one too.'

Kept like animals, ready for killing. It fitted. If there were some foul club, with regular meetings, perhaps they did choose their victims in advance.

'What about their hair?' Tabby said.

Unerringly, she'd picked on the detail that sickened me most.

'I wonder if there's some horrible ritual involved . . . some sort of ceremony. In the old days, when people sacrificed animals, the poor creatures were supposed to be clean and perfect.'

The picture was in my mind of a scared, helpless girl being

forced to bath and wash her hair, having a ring forced on her finger. Tabby nodded again.

'So how are we going to find out who they are?'

She'd taken it for granted that we were going to do that, as simply as we might set out to find somebody's missing silverware.

'I don't know,' I admitted. 'I don't think there's any use telling the police.'

'Nah.'

Her rejection was instinctive. I decided not to tell her that I might have no choice in the matter. I'd expected to find a police officer waiting for me when I came back to Abel Yard. I'd given the sergeant Mr James's name and Islington address. Surely by now they'd have sent a man to investigate. If they were even reasonably conscientious, they'd have made the journey out to Essex and drawn the same blank as we had. At the very least, I had things to explain. The question was, how much if anything should I tell them about my theory? I had no shred of proof and it would sound like hysterical imaginings, worse than housemaids' tales. No, I didn't look forward to the arrival of a police officer, but there was a prospect that worried me even more: his non-arrival. If nobody came to question me, that would mean the police were not investigating Dora Tilbury's death. If so, this labyrinth had an even darker heart than I'd feared.

THIRTEEN

Late that afternoon, with dusk not far off and the yard sunk in Sunday quiet, apart from the low clucking of the hens, Tabby called up that there was a gentleman come to see me. I called back that he should walk up, expecting the top hat and blue coat of a police officer to rise into view. He'd taken only a few steps up the stairs before I knew I was wrong. When he was no more than a broad silhouette rising tread by tread against the dim light, I sensed that this man had the confidence of a statue come to life. The heavy and measured steps said that what he wanted was what mattered and the rest of us who did not happen to be walking on legs of stone must accept that as the order of the universe. I went out onto the landing and the evening light from the open door of my room fell on his face. He was possibly in his fifties, or older, clean-shaven with grey hair close cut, eyes pale, head like a Roman emperor's. There was somehow a public look about the face, as if it was accustomed to being recognized. The stare he gave me as our eyes met would have been impolite, if politeness or the lack of it had ever played any part in his life.

'Miss Lane?'

'Yes.'

I stood back in my doorway to let him go in. By the time I'd closed my door and joined him he was sitting in the larger chair that I usually keep for myself, leaving me no alternative but to take the one meant for clients. His clothes were expensive but unremarkable: black coat and trousers, white shirt and high stock, sleek black shoes. He'd placed his tall hat and white gloves on my note pad. I made him wait while I lit my lamp.

'You evidently know my name. May I ask yours?' I said.

'My name is not relevant.'

The voice was cultivated and resonant. He made no attempt at sounding polite and the pale eyes that met mine were as hard as cobblestones. Then they slid away from me to the door.

'There's a person listening outside.'

I stood up and opened the door. Sure enough, there was Tabby.

'My assistant,' I said.

'What I have to discuss with you is confidential.'

'Tabby, will you leave us please. I'll see you tomorrow,' I said.

Her footsteps went reluctantly downstairs.

'So you're not going to tell me your name?' I said.

He didn't even trouble himself to shake his head. I didn't insist because he could simply have given me a false name and I could see no point in adding another one to our collection.

'This is a matter of the utmost secrecy.' He spoke as if men were standing ready with chisels to record his words on marble. 'Nothing that I discuss with you is to go outside this room.'

He didn't ask for any promise or assurance from me. If he wanted something, it would happen.

'I suggest you tell me the nature of your problem, then I can decide whether I shall take it on or not,' I said.

He wasn't pleased. There was no change in his expression, but the air round us seemed a few degrees cooler.

'There is no question of your taking on anything.'

'Then perhaps you'll be kind enough to tell me why you're here,' I said.

'I want to know who's paying you.'

'How dare you?'

I didn't need to pretend indignation. I felt like standing up and slapping the man, and the slightest flicker in the cold eyes showed he knew that.

'Am I wrong, then, in suggesting that you accept money for certain services?'

He made it sound disreputable.

'I am an investigator,' I said. 'And I'm choosy about my clients.'

His hand went into his pocket and came out holding a chamois leather bag. The leather was new and clean, but he held the bag by its edge between his fingertips as if the touch might contaminate him. It clunked accurately onto the middle of the table between us.

'Fifty sovereigns,' he said.

I looked him in the eye and repeated what I'd said. 'I suggest you tell me the nature of the problem, then I can decide whether I shall take it on or not.'

Silence. From next door, I heard Mrs Martley moving around in our parlour and smelt onions frying.

'I know that you are being paid to spread some deeply unpleasant and scandalous rumours,' he said. 'I doubt if your paymasters are being as generous as I am prepared to be. I want to know their names and the details of what you have agreed to do for them.'

I began to have a suspicion where this was heading.

'I have clients, not paymasters,' I said. 'And I don't accept payment to spread rumours.'

'I believe otherwise. I know very well that you're not the only person involved. You're in very disreputable company, you know.'

'Am I? Suppose you tell me what you're talking about?'

His expression didn't change but the chair creaked under him. The man of stone was annoyed.

'You're simply wasting your time and mine in trying to keep up the pretence,' he said. 'Perhaps I'm doing you too much kindness by assuming you do not realize the dangerous nature of what you're doing. If you persist, you are heading into serious trouble, and you won't be able to rely on your friends to extricate you.'

I wondered what friends. Did he mean Disraeli? We stared at each other. His eyes were so pale that the pupils were more silver than grey.

'So are we agreed?' he said. 'Fifty pounds for the names of the people employing you?'

'My clients' confidentiality is not for sale. In any case, you've already told me I'm keeping disreputable company. That implies you know what company I keep.'

'In this case, women of no reputation, men with too much of the wrong kind and scandal-mongering journalists.'

The words were all the more offensive for being spoken in that graven-on-stone voice. His eyes went down to the chamois leather bag, then up again to my face. I knew I should have played him at his own game, to drag some information out of him, but I couldn't keep a hold on my temper for much longer. I picked up his top hat and held it by the brim.

'I suggest that you leave,' I said. I stood up. He remained seated. I turned his hat upside down, picked up the moneybag with my other hand and dropped it inside. 'I also suggest that you leave now of your own free will. The carriage repairer in the yard likes nothing better than a chance to throw people downstairs.'

This was a gross slander on peaceable Mr Grindley. Stone man stood up, his lips a sharply chiselled line. I handed him his hat. Automatically, his hand came up and took it. He now had a dilemma. Either he could place the hat on his head with the moneybag inside, or he'd have to face the distasteful business of handling it again. I watched as he took it out of the hat like a housewife holding a dead rat at arm's length by its tail and put it back in his pocket.

'I believe you will regret this, Miss Lane.'

He turned to go.

'Don't forget your gloves,' I said.

He grabbed them and put them in his other pocket, with a force that looked likely to split the lining. I followed him downstairs and watched him stride stiffly across the cobbles and through the gateway into Adam's Mews.

I didn't bother to watch whether he turned left towards Park
Lane or right towards Bond Street. There was no need. Before Mrs
Martley and I had finished our steak and onions, a high-pitched
whistle came from the yard. When I went down, Tabby was waiting
in the dark.

'There was a little carriage with a brown horse waiting for him
down the road by the church. They went off like he had a bet on
it. I kept after them as far as Park Lane, then I lost them.'

'Never mind, you did well. Was there any crest on the door?'

'Couldn't see none.'

I gave her the hunk of bread and piece of steak I'd grabbed from
my plate. She started chewing at once.

'He's trouble that one, isn't he?' she said through crumbs.

'Probably, yes.'

But then so were they all.

That night, after Mrs Martley had gone to bed, I sat by the fire
in the parlour and re-read a cheerful letter from Robert Carmichael
that had arrived the day before from Ireland.

Dear Liberty,

   Many apologies for not writing since our arrival in Dublin.
It has taken five days to travel from there to the home of the
Fitzwilliam family, a distance which I expected us to cover
in two at the most. I had not realized the magnetic attraction
of the Irish family, which transforms a journey between two
points into something like an attempt at web-spinning by a
demented spider. On the way, we have visited three separate
lots of cousins. Stephen has had to endure some heavy-handed
pleasantries about letting his younger brother marry first, so
I am glad to be here to support him but I confess I am missing
you. At least a dozen times a day I'll see some especially fine
view, or hear an amusing remark, or even pat an amiable dog
and think: how Liberty would like this. So, at long last, here
we are at the castle. Already friends and relatives are arriving,
although the wedding is still more than a week away. With
many of the bachelors having to double up, I am lucky to
have been given a small room of my own, apart from a pigeon
which seems to live in here and is cooing on top of the wardrobe as I write. I have no notion when the post goes from

here, if indeed it goes at all, so shall end this letter and make inquiries. Take good care of yourself, my dear. Your safety is more important than perhaps you realize to somebody who hopes you will permit him to describe himself as your very affectionate friend, Robert.

I tried to write an answer, in the same light-hearted vein. *'I wish you could have been with us at the opera on Saturday night, even though flat-footed and flat-toned fairies might not be to your taste . . .'*

Only, the words wouldn't come. And suppose I'd written him the truth: *'My dear friend, I am confused and so very scared. Two young women have died and it's part of something worse which I'm only just beginning to understand . . .'*

It would bring him rushing back from Ireland with, quite possibly, an invitation that was almost an ultimatum. *'For heaven's sake, Liberty, marry me now and forget all this.'*

And if he did, I might even do what he said and fall into his arms. But a hard, stubborn part of me resisted and the argument in my head wouldn't let me write one way or the other. So I gave it up and, rather than risk waking Mrs Martley, went upstairs to sleep on the daybed under the patchwork quilt in my own room.

Perhaps that cheerful letter I couldn't write worked its way into my dreams, because instead of the nightmares I'd half expected, sleep took me back to the evening at the opera, the box in the interval by soft gas light, friendly faces, Calloway's entertaining chatter. It even re-created the sharp coldness of raspberry ice on my tongue. And yet the dream wasn't entirely cheerful. There was an insistent quality about it, as if there were something important that I'd forgotten trying to nudge its way into the scene. If I'd gone on dreaming, that something might have managed to break through into consciousness, but it never had the chance. I woke, deep in darkness, smelling smoke and knowing something was wrong. Smoke itself was nothing new. Mr Grindley often fired up his forge before daylight in winter but there were always sounds first: screech of hinges as he opened the workshop door, clank of coal buckets on the stone floor. There were no sounds this time and the smell of the smoke was wrong too, not from cheerful and familiar hot coals but something harsh and acrid.

I jumped up and looked out at the darkness, but my window overlooked rooftops, not the yard where the smell was coming from. Without bothering to light the candle, I grabbed my cloak off the hook, wrapped it round me and stepped out on the landing. The smoke hurled itself straight into my lungs and backwards against the wall. It was like being hit by a dark wave. The stink of tar was part of it. I was coughing, choking, but when I opened my mouth for air more of the foul smoke forced its way in. I had just enough sense left to know that my only chance of safety was to go through the smoke and downstairs and took a step towards the cloud roiling up towards me, blacker than the darkness. Whether I'd have found the resolution to go on through it and down I don't know, but my cloak saved me. It must have fallen off my shoulder and tangled round my foot, because I slipped and went head first, with a yell that was instantly transformed into another fit of choking.

The door at the bottom of my staircase was unlatched, so I rolled all the way down the stairs, out into the air and hit the cobbles of the yard with my shoulder. Flames now, sunset-coloured among more black smoke, in the space under the stairs where the pump was, and a smell of tar like the entrance to hell. The strange thing was the silence in the yard, apart from my coughing and a *huff, huff* from the flames under the stairs, like a lion breathing between mouthfuls of meat. I scrambled to my feet, took a breath of air and yelled 'Fire'. For what seemed like a long time nothing happened, then a window opened in the Grindleys' rooms and Mr Grindley's voice asked what was happening. I shouted, 'Fire,' again. But I couldn't wait for him before doing something about Mrs Martley. The black smoke clotting my staircase must be doing exactly the same to our other staircase a few yards away. Mrs Martley, a heavy sleeper, would be snoring in her bed two floors up.

I knew that I should soak my cloak in water and wrap it round my head, but the pump was at the heart of the fire, so no hope of that. I unlatched the other door and started up the staircase, the wooden treads rough under bare feet, forcing myself back into the smoke. Thank the gods, it wasn't as thick as on my back staircase, though bad enough. When I came to the first landing, the door of the parlour opened suddenly into my face so that I stumbled backwards. I yelled again. The person who had come out of the room grabbed my arm and saved me from falling.

'Is that you, Liberty?' Tom Huckerby's voice.

'What's happening?' I said.

'I'd come up to find you.'

'Mrs Martley. She's upstairs.'

He told me to go back downstairs and wait, but I followed him at a run through the parlour. Some cinders of our fire were still glowing and giving a faint light, with the silhouette of the cat, standing with arched back on the rug. She came towards me, miaowing.

'Out, out.'

I tried to nudge her with my foot towards the stairs, then ran on and up the next stairs behind Tom towards the attic bedroom.

'Who's there?' Mrs Martley, dozily belligerent.

'There's a fire downstairs,' I said. 'Come on.'

'Is that a man with you?'

'Yes. Come on.'

'Tell him to wait outside while I light the candle and get on my clothes.'

'There's no time for that,' I shrieked it at her. 'For heaven's sake, just come.'

'In my nightdress? I'd catch my death.' But her feet padded heavily to the floor. I reached for her arm in the dark and dragged her upright.

'You'll catch it all the sooner if you stay here.'

Some heavy garment was on a chair by her bed, dressing gown possibly. I scooped it up with my free hand and flung it at her. Tom took her other arm and we hustled her sideways through the doorway. People were shouting down in the yard now, men's voices mostly.

'What have you done now?' she said to me.

If the four horsemen of the Apocalypse arrived in Abel Yard, I believe Mrs Martley would blame me. We dragged her downstairs, ignoring her bleatings about slippers. In the parlour, the cat came bounding towards us.

'We can't leave Mippy,' she said.

I flung the creature over my shoulder, willing her to hold tight with all her eighteen claws and we went on through the parlour. The smoke was thicker now and we all started coughing. Mrs Martley jibbed on the top step.

'We can't . . .'

Tom pulled, I pushed and she went sliding down the staircase.
The cat was slipping, holding on with front claws only, so I unpinned
her from my shoulder and threw her down the stairs as well.
Probably neither of them would ever forgive me. By the time I got
to the bottom of the stairs, somebody had picked up Mrs Martley.
She was making wild whooping sounds. Mrs Grindley and
Mrs Colley, the cowman's wife, were trying to comfort her. Near
them, Mr Colley and Mr Gindley were holding a small figure that
was struggling wildly and filling the air with a string of obscenities,
audible above the shouts of the men and the clank and thump of
buckets on cobbles. For a moment I thought they'd managed to lay
hands on the fire raiser, until I recognized the voice.

'It's all right, Tabby. I'm here.'

The obscenities stopped.

'She's a wildcat,' Mr Grindley said. 'Scratched my face.'

'They wouldn't let me come in and get you,' Tabby said.

'Talking of cats . . .' I said.

'She's safe over here,' Mrs Colley said. 'Trust a cat.'

All round us, men were rushing and shouting. Two bucket chains
had been set up, one from the pump at the far end of the yard, the
other longer one through the gateway and out to a pump in Adam's
Mews. Black silhouettes swayed through smoke clouds, passing
buckets from hand to hand. Not just buckets either. From the shapes,
there was a hip bath in there and some half gallon ale jugs. Nobody
in the yard or the mews was rich enough to afford fire insurance,
so we couldn't look for help from one of the hand-propelled or
horse-drawn fire engines. Because of this, our ramshackle commu-
nity had its own way of tackling fires. By daylight, those swaying,
coughing figures would be stable lads from the mews, apprentices,
even some of the ragged boys who slept rough in doorways and
loved excitement even when there was no profit in it for them. The
two men at the end of the chain flung bucketful after bucketful at
the seat of the fire under the stairs. The black and orange heart of
it was stubborn, but at least it wasn't gaining ground. The *huff huff*
sound had faded to a frustrated growl. At last, the black clouds
began to die away and wisps of white steam came up instead. Faint
cheers broke out among the chorus of coughing, but the buckets
kept coming until the fire was out.

By then, all of us not on the bucket chains were shivering in the early morning drizzle, the sky still dark. Mrs Grindley had taken Mrs Martley upstairs to her own rooms above the workshop and come down to look for me.

'I've put the kettle on.'

'Tabby and I will come in a minute,' I said. 'I want to see how much damage has been done. Besides, all my clothes are upstairs.'

'You can't go up there,' she said. 'It might start again.'

Somebody had lit a couple of lamps, showing that the fire had been pretty well confined to the understairs area. Unfortunately, the bottom part of the flight of stairs to my room and office had disappeared entirely, but it looked as if the other staircase next to it might be intact. Still, it might be wise to wait until daylight before investigating.

'They were determined to get us, one way or the other,' said a voice from out of the darkness.

Tom Huckerby stepped forward into the lamplight, face as black as a coal miner's, teeth showing white. After rescuing Mrs Martley, he'd joined one of the bucket chains.

'Who were?' I said.

'The bastards who started it. Three of them.'

'You saw them?'

He nodded towards the blackened cavern under where the stairs had been. 'I was sleeping in there.'

'Oh god. You could have been—'

'Lucky I don't sleep heavily. I heard something and went out. Couldn't see who they were. I smelt the tar and saw flames. Then one of them shouted something and another one swung the bucket and threw it straight in, where we'd left our piles of papers.'

'Bucket?'

'Tar bucket. There it is, see.'

He kicked something at out feet. It clanked on the cobbles: a metal bucket with holes pierced in the side, rust-coloured from the fire. The heat still throbbing from the metal scorched my bare foot. The anger burning off Tom Huckerby was as fierce.

'I reckon what woke me was the scrape of the flint when they lit it,' Tom said. 'The cowardly, hireling bastards.'

Usually, he wouldn't have sworn in my presence, but he was beyond thinking of that.

'Hirelings?' I said.

'Government hirelings. Our masters couldn't silence my press any other way, so they decided to burn it out. Lead type won't have survived this. God help me, I'd like to melt it all over again and pour it down the greasy, greedy gobs of those criminals at Westminster.'

I didn't argue. There might even be some consolation for Tom in thinking that this had been directed against him. But I doubted if *The Unbound Briton* was considered such a danger to the authorities that they'd go to these lengths to silence it. There were many papers like it, some of them much more vitriolic in their criticisms of the government and the royal family, and as far as I knew, none had been the victims of arson. In my mind was the stone man pacing across the cobbles and his voice: '*I believe you will regret this.*' Ten hours or so after he'd left, the men with the bucket of pitch had arrived.

'They'll pay,' Tom said. 'God knows, they'll pay.'

'Yes, they'll pay,' I said.

But I said it with less confidence than Tom, wondering who would pay, and how and when.

FOURTEEN

As soon as it was light, I went to assess the damage. The space under the stairs – or where the stairs had been – was no more than a blackened cavern with the skeleton of the printing press. Tom Huckerby was gone, probably trying to beg or borrow a replacement. The heat had cracked the cast-iron shaft of the pump so it would need replacing. More expense. Up the other staircase to the parlour, the news was better. The stairs had survived undamaged, and although the parlour floor and furniture were covered by a thin coating of greasy soot, a few hours of mopping and sponging would make the place habitable. It was only when I went through the small door to my office and sitting room that the worst of the damage hit me. The overlay of soot in both rooms looked inches thick and the smell of smoke and tar hung over everything. My daybed, the glass mermaid hanging in the window, my books and writing things, were black and sticky to the touch.

I picked up the volume of Shelley's poetry that had been a present from my father, near to tears. When I opened it at random, at least the words inside were still legible. 'To defy power that seems omnipotent/ To forgive wrongs darker than death or night . . .' Well, I had no intention of forgiving this wrong. I'd been thinking about it for hours, over endless cups of tea in the Grindleys' parlour, and was certain that this had been directed at me, with Tom's press as an accidental casualty.

'Oh, all your lovely clothes.' Tabby's voice, from the doorway behind me. The clothes hanging from pegs were ruined beyond cleaning, including the new green velvet. I opened the lid of the chest where my other good clothes were kept. Relief there, at least. The close-fitting wooden lid, designed to thwart moths, had kept out most of the soot as well. I dressed in my blue merino, not caring much about how I looked. Anger at what had been done to us was driving away tiredness from a sleepless night.

'I'd like to kill him, I would,' Tabby said.

'Who?'

'The one you was talking to yesterday. That Codling.'

'You think he did it?'

'Course. Even if he wasn't there himself, he paid them to do it.'

'Why?'

'Because you smoked him out. He knew that when you asked the girl those questions. From the look on his face, he'd have liked to kill you then and there only he didn't have the nerve.'

It made sense of a kind. Although I doubted that Codling was capable of planning or paying for such drastic revenge, he was obviously taking his orders and his money from somebody. If he'd reported back to his masters when he left the tea gardens, there'd have been time for them to organize the arson gang.

I went down to the parlour, found some writing paper and an inkwell and wrote a note to Mr Clyde with Mrs Martley's scratchy pen. 'Miss Lane presents her compliments to Mr Clyde and requires to see him as a matter of urgency. She will be at 4 Grosvenor Street from midday onwards.'

I marked it urgent and told Tabby to deliver it into Suzette's hand. Once she was gone, I sorted out some clothes for Mrs Martley and took them across to the Grindleys.

'I'm taking you to stay with the Suters for a few days,' I said to her. 'We'll have everything clean by the time you get back.'

For once she was too weary to argue, only telling me to remember to feed the cat. I knew Daniel and Jenny would be glad of her help with the baby. I walked with her over to their home in Bloomsbury, glad to be breathing air that smelt only of horse dung and of smoke untainted by tar.

Mr Clyde arrived at ten minutes past midday. He was neatly dressed in tones of grey, with light shoes and no overcoat. Either he'd been somewhere in the building or had arrived by coach.

'What's happened?'

'There was a fire where I live. Some men threw in a tar bucket. We could all have been killed.'

He stared at me, then sat down heavily on the armchair opposite. 'My god. Why?'

'I was hoping you might be able to tell me.'

He seemed genuinely shocked, his eyes not leaving my face. As calmly as I could, I told him about the visit of stone man.

'Do you recognize him from the description?' I asked.

He shook his head.

'He accused me of associating with women of no reputation,' I said. 'Did he mean the contessa?'

I thought Miss Blade was a more likely candidate, but had decided not to tell Mr Clyde about that episode.

'You suspect that this man was some kind of emissary from official circles, trying to stop the contessa causing any more embarrassment?'

'It's one possibility,' I said.

'But if so, that would put us all on the same side, wouldn't it?' he said. 'So why should he threaten you?'

'I don't know, but I think there are things I'm not being told.'

'Perhaps you should have played his game, accepted the bribe and found out what he wanted.'

'He wanted to know who my associates were,' I said. 'You surely didn't want me to name you.'

He stood up and walked over to the window. 'Believe me, Miss Lane, I know nothing that makes sense of this. In any event, the contessa is no longer a threat to the authorities. She's left London.'

'Where's she gone?'

He smiled for the first time. 'I don't know. Not exactly.'

'You mean, you took my advice and had her kidnapped?' I was amazed, having meant it at least half in joke.

'Kidnap's a harsh word. Let's say she was persuaded to leave London.'

'Was she angry?'

A nod. His smile faded.

'Why aren't you with her?'

'From what I understand, I'm the last person in the world she wants to see. At present, at any rate.'

He walked over and opened the writing desk, came back and sat in the armchair.

'I'm glad to have had the opportunity to see you, Miss Lane. I too am going away.'

'Abroad?'

A nod.

'I shall always be grateful for what you have done for her. I notice you haven't claimed your fee yet. I insist on your accepting it.' He put the bag of coins on the table.

'I took ten sovereigns out,' I said. 'I didn't do enough to earn any more.'

'For the fire damage then, whoever caused it.'

I thanked him and put the bag in my reticule. I'd have rather not have taken it, but couldn't see how we'd repair our home otherwise.

'Were you at Drury Lane on Saturday?' I said.

He smiled. 'You saw me then?'

'Yes.'

'I saw you too, with your friends. I hope you'll excuse me for not acknowledging you. Again, and from my heart, thank you Miss Lane. I shan't forget you.'

We both stood up. He took my hand and held it for a while, looking into my face.

'One last question,' I said.

He let go of my hand. 'What?'

'When I was with the contessa, she'd left some of her jewellery spread over the dressing table. There was a ring.'

He waited.

'An odd sort of ring,' I said. 'It looked like a gentleman's signet with a bull's head engraved on it. She seemed annoyed that I'd seen it.'

I was watching his face closely. A flicker of curiosity, nothing more.

'And what did you deduce from that?'

'I don't know. I just wondered if you'd seen anything like it.'

'Not that I remember. Some keepsake from a gentleman, I suppose.'

There was nothing more to be said.

I walked across the park to the livery stables. Amos had always been one of the few certain things in my life, and I'd had too much of uncertainties. Simply being in his company made the world a less threatening place. He wasn't there.

'No word from him,' the owner said. He was sitting at the battered table in his office, checking feed bills.

'Do you know when he might be back?'

'I wish I did. The man he sent in his place is doing well enough, but all the ladies are inquiring for Legge.'

'Where exactly did he go in Surrey, that weekend before he was attacked?'

I was so used to Amos's absence on horse-dealing errands that it hadn't occurred to me to ask at the time.

'Egham,' the owner said. 'It's next door to Runnymede race course so you get a lot of gentlemen down there, trying out their horses.' He hesitated, shuffling bills but not looking at them.

'Day after he went, there were two men inquiring for him.'

'Oh?'

'Little dark cove and big one with stubbly hair. Reckoned they were friends of his.'

'You don't think they were?'

'Whiff of trouble about them. Struck me, they might be bailiffs, but Amos never seems to me a man in that kind of difficulty.'

Amos wasn't extravagant and only gambled for the fun of it.

'He isn't. So what did you tell them?'

'That I didn't know where he was or when he'd be back. Don't know if they believed me, but no odds to me in any case.'

'Do you have any idea at all what he's doing?' I said.

Another hesitation. 'Him and some of the others have been getting themselves in a lather about the chariot business. Some of the lads have got sweethearts and don't like to think of people going round attacking young women.'

My heart stopped.

'You think Amos has gone off on the trail of the devil's chariot?'

'I'm not saying yes or no, because I don't know. But that's what some of the lads think.' Then, reacting to my expression: 'No need to worry if he has. I reckon Amos Legge's a match for anything, devils included.'

I asked him to send word to me at Abel Yard if there were any news of Amos. On my way out I went to say hello to Rancie and her cat Lucy, then walked back across the park, trying to make out what Amos thought he was doing. Egham was about twenty miles out of London, a day's ride for him, or three hours or so away by stage coach. If he weren't back soon I'd go and look for him, whether he liked it or not.

Tabby and I, wearing our oldest clothes, swept and scrubbed all through the rest of the afternoon, until it was time to light the lamps. By then, we had the parlour pretty well clean and the worst of the soot removed from my room and office. We bundled up curtains, books and papers that were beyond saving, carried them down to the yard and made a bonfire close to the midden. While we were raking out the ashes, Tom Huckerby arrived. He sounded subdued and, for a wonder, apologized to me.

'I wouldn't have come here if I'd known I was putting you in danger.'

I refrained from saying it was late in the day to think of that and invited him and Tabby upstairs to find something to eat. Mrs Martley would have had a conniption if she'd known. We found ham in the meat safe (Tom pointed out that since it had been smoked already, a bit more wouldn't have done it any harm), eggs in the bowl and some potatoes. I made omelettes in the Spanish style, an adequate meal for three people who hadn't eaten since the night before, washed down with tea for all of us and a glass of wine for

Tom and me. Tabby screwed up her face at the taste of it and said
she'd prefer gin if we had it. We hadn't.

When we were sitting round with out feet to the fire, I put it
to Tom that it would seem strange if government agents had
singled out his press alone for an arson attack. He surprised me
again by agreeing.

'I've been thinking about that. I don't believe it was over our
politics after all.'

'Ah. So what was it then?'

'The chariot,' he said. 'The devil's chariot. I reckon the newspapers have been making things too hot for them. This was their
way of telling us to lay off.'

'But other papers have been writing about it much more. You've
only just started.'

'Maybe we were just easy to get at and they'll go after some
others as well now.'

I asked if he could remember anything more about the three men
who threw in the tar bucket.

'I told you one of them shouted out something. I reckon he was
telling the one with the bucket where to throw it, but I couldn't
make out the words.' He hesitated. 'I don't know for sure, but
looking back, I think it might have been foreign.'

'What language? Italian? German?'

'I wouldn't know. Plain English has always been good enough
for me.'

He couldn't remember anything else to the purpose and had no
description of the men. They were just figures in the dark to him
and he'd been too occupied in trying to rescue me to run after them.

When Tabby was clearing up the plates for once, I gave Tom
five sovereigns from Mr Clyde's money bag.

'To help replace your press.'

He looked startled at the amount. 'You can't afford this.'

'It's from a fee I didn't deserve. At least, I don't think I did.'

As we shared the last of the wine, I asked him where he intended
to sleep.

'You can't stay under the stairs,' Tabby told him. 'It's all burned
and wet. There's the shed next to the cows that I had before I got
the other place.' She seemed determined to make Tom a fixture in
the yard.

'That's a good idea,' he said. 'If they come back, I'll be ready for them.'

I took one of the lamps and showed him downstairs. When I got back, Tabby was staring into the fire, a worried expression on her face.

'If it was the devil's chariot people that done it, they know where we live, don't they?'

When I said she could sleep on the parlour sofa if she wanted, she leapt at it, but with a face-saving addition. 'It'll be safer for you, having me here.'

Tabby volunteered to fetch water from the pump at the far end of the yard, since our own was out of commission. As soon as the door closed on her there was a shout, a metallic clattering and the bumping of a body all the way down the stairs.

'Tabby.'

I was on the landing, heart thumping, looking down into the dark. From the bottom of the staircase, a voice uttered curses.

'Tabby, is that you? What's happening?'

'I'm all right. Fell down the bloody stairs, that's all.'

I fetched a candle from the parlour and went down cautiously. By the time I got to the bottom, Tabby was upright, leaning on the door frame with her hand to her ribs.

'Let me see. Have you broken anything?'

By then, Tom had arrived with a stick, ready to ward off another attack.

'Just winded. Don't fuss,' Tabby said to us.

She was annoyed, pride hurt. Usually she was as sure-footed as a cat. But when she tried to take a step away from the doorpost, she nearly went over again and fell against me.

'Stuck to my bloody boot.'

Tom knelt to look. 'Soap.'

He scraped it off her boot sole and held it up into the light to show us – the remains of a cake of cheap yellow soap, soft from soaking and flattened by Tabby's tread. The soap that we'd been using to scrub the stairs. Not hostile action this time, just our own tired carelessness in leaving it there.

As relieved as I was, Tom took the bucket and filled it. I thanked him, said a second goodnight and carried the bucket upstairs, following Tabby. An inspection of the damage showed nothing worse than a tender patch on the ribs and a badly scraped elbow. I applied arnica, settled her on the sofa and finished the clearing up.

'Will you be all right there?' I said. 'I'll be just upstairs if you want me.'

She was half asleep, pride restored now she knew the reason for her fall.

'Like stepping on ice, it was. Anybody'd have fallen.'

Of course I slept fitfully, drifting in and out of panicking dreams. For some reason, Tabby's last remark kept coming back to my mind. Then, briefly, I was back under the gas lights again, in the box at Drury Lane, the sweetness and the cold tingle of raspberry ice on my tongue. Suddenly, I was broad awake.

'Oh ye gods.'

I saw again the flurried constable hurrying back from the pool in the dell with his soaked handkerchief, saw him slipping and almost falling on top of the girl's body. Why had he slipped? Not in her blood, I'd have remembered that. Not mud either. The rest of the stone area round the statue was dry and clean. I must have noticed at the time the small detail that was so clear in my mind now, but there'd been so much else going on that it had needed the coincidence of two quite different things to bring it back to me. As soon as it was light, I went down to the parlour, stirred up the fire and put the kettle on the hob to boil for tea. Tabby was still sleeping, her face younger and more childlike than when awake. I moved quietly, wanting her to have her sleep out, but the tinkle of spoon against teapot brought her eyes open. I waited until she'd had a chance to sit up and drink her tea, before asking my question.

'Tabby, do you remember that list of tradesmen's carts, from just before they found her body?'

The list I'd written down had been obliterated by soot, but her memory was as clear as ever. She went through them all, almost word for word. Just as I'd thought, it was there.

FIFTEEN

S oon after daylight, I walked down South Audley Street and Half Moon Street, across Piccadilly and into Pall Mall. Only a few hours before, gambling and drinking gentlemen would have been helped or even carried from their clubs and into their carriages by weary hall porters. Now yawning maids were scrubbing and mopping the doorsteps of those same clubs, ready for a new day. I came to one of the grandest of the clubs, went down some steps to a basement and knocked on a modest door. A middle-aged woman opened it to me and a sweet smell of baking bread billowed out.

'Miss Lane, we were just talking about you the other day. Come on in out of the cold.'

It wasn't especially cold outside, but it seemed so compared to the snugness of the Pollitts' home. Mrs Pollitt was plump and neat in a dress of mulberry-coloured wool.

I followed her along the passageway, she calling out to her husband, 'Mr Pollitt, guess who's come to see us.'

As we came into the room he was on his feet and buttoning his jacket. It would never do even for friends to find him sitting down to breakfast in his shirtsleeves. Mr Pollitt was hall porter at the club. In his way he was a much a part of club aristocracy as the gentlemen he served. His father had been a club porter too, his grandfather a head waiter who had been complimented on his skill in mixing punch by the great Dr Johnson himself and had exchanged witticisms with Richard Sheridan. Mrs Pollitt was housekeeper at the club. Even in private, they always referred to each other by their surnames. One of their sons was a musician in a small orchestra run by my friend Toby Kennedy. Through that connection, I'd been called in to deal with an unpleasantness at the club about disappearing silverware and settled it discreetly enough to please everybody, except the member who had to resign. The Pollitts had remained good friends.

'You'll have breakfast with us,' Mrs Pollitt said.

A freshly starched cloth fell on the table like snowfall and was rapidly weighed down with plates of rolls fresh from the oven, boiled eggs, preserves, potted meats, a silver coffee pot bearing the club's crest. We ate companionably, catching up on gossip, then Mrs Pollitt carried the dishes away to the kitchen. When I told Mr Pollitt why I needed to consult him, he was surprised, but asked no questions.

'Yes, we use it. Not as much this time of year as in the season but I always like to have some on hand.'

'How is it delivered?'

'From the cart, early in the morning. Would you like to come and see?'

We went into the club's kitchen, where Mr Pollitt changed his good black jacket for a brown one, took a key from a hook and lit a candle in a holder. He led the way down narrow stairs between whitewashed walls and a smell of damp stone came up to meet us. Since we were already in the basement when we started, we must have been deep under Pall Mall. A carriage rolling overhead sounded like distant thunder. We passed between cobwebbed racks containing thousands upon thousands of bottles, some of them probably laid down before our grandfathers were born, then he ducked through a low opening and held the candle so that I could follow without banging my head. We were in a smaller cellar, with bottles of champagne ranged round the walls. He went to the corner where a box had been constructed from planks and lifted off layer after layer of sacking.

'There we are.'

Candlelight glinted on a transparent cube.

'We had a delivery just last week,' Mr Pollitt said. 'In summer, when everybody's drinking champagne and hock, we have to order two or three blocks a week.'

'Are you here when it's delivered?'

'No. The ice man likes to do his rounds in the early morning when the temperature's at its coldest. So we have a system for delivery.' He unhitched a rope from the wall, tugged on it, and a big canvas tube came down. 'The tube goes up to the street. If we've ordered a delivery, we set this up the night before and whoosh, down comes the ice.'

'Where do you order it from?'

'A firm in Limehouse.'

I asked if he could let me have the firm's name and address. He led the way back upstairs to the kitchen and took a box of tradesmen's accounts out of a cupboard.

'Here we are. Nathaniel Hobbes and Sons, Limehouse Lock.'

I thanked him and called out a goodbye to Mrs Pollitt. Two hours later, Tabby and I were on an omnibus, jolting along Commercial Road towards Limehouse.

The area east of the Tower of London was new territory to Tabby and she sat wide-eyed and silent, taking in everything. There were no fashionable carriages once we'd left the City area behind. Most of the traffic was a stream of great carts being drawn westwards by heavy horses with cargoes of crates and barrels and massive squared timbers from the docks. I'd only seen the area from the river, when travelling from the Pool of London towards the sea. The Thames is broad there, crowded from bank to bank with merchant ships bringing spices from India, tea and silks from China, wood and tar from the Baltic, coal from Durham, even red-sailed barges from Essex sliding in and out with hay for London's horses. I hadn't told Tabby why we were going to Limehouse. My hunch was based on something so close to being non-existent that I didn't want to talk about it.

The driver shouted 'Limehouse' and we got down. To our left a mass of masts clustered around the West India Docks. In front of us was Limehouse Basin, also crowded with ships. On the far side, a narrow neck of water joined it to the Thames. Closer to us, barges clustered at the opening of the Regent's Canal. Tabby and I attracted some curious looks as we walked towards the water, the only women in sight. The wharves were full of dockers, unloading half a dozen ships at the same time. Cargoes swung out in nets that looked heavy enough to scatter the men like ninepins, but they seized them with hooks and guided them to the ground, then divided them into separate burdens to be carried to waiting carts. The chains of men from ship to carts were in motion all the time, the shouting, clanging and banging like the sounds of a battle. Tabby and I had to jump out of the way of three men running with crates as large as cabin trunks on their shoulders. A gang of sailors sitting on a wall whistled at us and made unmistakeable signs. Tabby made signs straight back at them, bringing ironic cheers and more whistles.

'Come on,' I said.

I'd spotted the bar of a lock gate above the cluster of barges, and anything was better than staying where we were.

The lower lock gates were open when we reached them, letting several loaded barges from the canal into the basin. We went up a flight of steps to the narrow dock wharf. A line of warehouses stood back from the wharf, with a smaller building that looked like the lock manager's office in front of them. The door was open, with several men standing inside. Most of them seemed to be bargemen, but one was dressed formally in a black suit and top hat.

'Excuse me,' I said. 'Can you tell me where to find the ice importer, Nathaniel Hobbes?'

One of the bargeman laughed. The manager turned round and seemed surprised to see us. 'He's been dead ten years, ma'am.'

'So who runs the company now?'

'His widow, Mrs Hobbes.'

The bargeman laughed again and muttered something about the old bitch having sharper teeth than the dog ever had. The manager shushed him. I asked where we might find Mrs Hobbes.

'She lives over there in Narrow Street.'

He pointed to a line of houses parallel to the river. Tabby and I picked our way back across the wharf and round the water, towards a street of straight-fronted eighteenth-century houses, where the channel from the basin joined the river. The smell of river mud hung over everything. I asked an urchin where Mrs Hobbes lived and he pointed to a house with a newly painted green front door and a polished brass knocker. The window box was planted with a double row of sempervivums, every rosette of leaves exactly the same size as its neighbours.

We paused a few steps away, while I explained to Tabby something that was troubling my conscience. 'I try not to lie, but sometimes people deserve to be lied to. I have no idea whether Mrs Hobbes deserves being lied to or not. Just keep quiet and don't look surprised.'

She nodded, looking less bothered than I was about the ethics of her new trade. We walked up to the front door and knocked.

It was opened after a short delay by a maid, neat and correct in black dress and white mob cap. I gave her my card, apologized for calling without an appointment and said I hoped Mrs Hobbes might see me on a matter of business. The maid shut the door on us and several minutes passed before she came back.

'She says you can come in.'

She led the way into a parlour facing onto the street. For an ice merchant's house, it was surprisingly snug. A fire burned in the grate behind a bright brass fender, with a tortoiseshell cat asleep on the rug and a kettle on the hob. Mrs Hobbes sat by the fire on an upright chair of carved oak, softened with embroidered cushions. She was a small woman with a round lined face that suggested she was fifty at least, but her hair, under an old-fashioned widow's cap, was dark and glossy. If she used hair dye, it was of the best quality. Her black wool dress was offset by collar and cuffs of starched white linen. More white linen swathed her left foot that was propped up on a stool. She saw my eyes going to it.

'An accident. You'll excuse me not getting up, I'm sure. Sit down.'

She had a clipped way of speaking, as if words were valuable. Her eyes were steel grey and sharp. We sat.

'Thank you for seeing us,' I said. 'I'm here on behalf of a friend. She's planning a Christmas ball and is thinking of having a large sculpture in ice as a centre piece.'

'How large?'

'Oh, more than lifesize.'

'What of?'

'A Jack Frost possibly. Or perhaps a couple dancing, on a big mirror like skating on a frozen pond.' (Perhaps I could even persuade one of my rich acquaintances to do it.)

'Dancers would be better than Jack Frost,' she said decisively. 'You want curves, not jagged bits that break off.'

The kettle hissed and spat. She gestured to Tabby to move it back from the hob.

'My ice is normally carted in twenty inch cubes,' she said. 'If your friend gives me a month's prior notice I can have larger cubes cut especially, but they're more awkward to ship so the price would be higher. She'll need to have the ice delivered at least three days before the carver starts work. For an extra charge, I can send a man to supervise.'

'Where does your ice come from?' I asked.

'A lake in Norway. There.'

She pointed to a framed map on the wall. It was mostly black and white, but near the west coast of Norway, a lake had been picked out in bright blue water colour. A blue painted line ran from the lake, across the North Sea and into the Thames estuary, ending at the Limehouse basin.

'That's amazing,' I said.

All this to cool Pall Mall's champagne.

'It's the purest ice in the world,' Mrs Hobbes said. 'The men go out with horse-drawn sledges, to cut blocks of ice from the middle of the lake. I've seen them doing it.'

'You've been all the way to Norway yourself?'

'Three times. You have to see things are done properly.'

'Did you take over the business after your husband died?'

'I had no choice. On our carts, it said Nathaniel Hobbes and Sons, but that was only for the look of it. There were no sons, only four daughters.'

This brought me back to business. 'I think I've seen your carts around town,' I said.

'If you see an ice cart, it will be one of ours.'

'Do you distribute it from the docks here?'

'No. It's unloaded from the ship here, then it goes by barge up the Regent's Canal to the dock by Regent's Park. Just by the park, in Cumberland Market, there's an ice pit eighty feet deep that will hold fifteen hundred tons.'

'I should like very much to see it,' I said.

'We don't let the public in. It can be dangerous, handling ice.'

'Dangerous?'

She glanced down at her swaddled foot.

'Did that happen at Cumberland Market?' I asked.

'No. Here when I was watching them unload. Somebody let a block slip.' Her tone suggested that the somebody had not been forgiven.

'When did that happen?'

'A month ago.'

Mrs Hobbes was tired of my curiosity and brought us back to

business. When would my friend decide? If she wanted it for Christmas, she shouldn't waste time. I put the price list she gave me in my reticule and promised to pass it on to my friend. Outside, Tabby and I walked in silence for a while.

'You're not a bad liar,' she said.

I led us inland, towards an ornate church tower in white stone. St Anne's, Limehouse, had been a landmark for ships coming up the estuary for more than a hundred years. Tabby paced along beside me.

'So it was the ice cart?' she said.

'I think so, yes.'

'Does the old woman know?'

'What do you think?'

Tabby's judgements were usually instantaneous. This time she had to think about it. 'She's a close one. She could have known, but I don't suppose she watches every cart that goes out.'

'Certainly not for the past month, with that leg. That's assuming she's telling the truth about when the accident happened.'

'You think she told a lie about that?'

'I don't know. Even if it's true, the question is why it happened. Did somebody arrange the accident to make sure she wasn't keeping as close an eye on her business as usual?'

'Could we ask somebody?' Tabby looked towards the busy dock basin.

'If we go asking around there about an accident that might have been deliberate, I think we might meet with one ourselves,' I said.

'So what are we going to do?'

'Find somebody somewhere else. That's why we're going to the church. People are more likely to have time on their hands.'

'So you're looking for some old busybody who knows about the accident.'

'Yes.'

Something besides that, too. Something so unlikely that I wouldn't mention even the possibility to Tabby, so that I shouldn't look a fool in her eyes. We walked round the side of the church and into the churchyard. An old man dozed on a bench in the cool autumn sunshine, his body twisted sideways, probably from a lifetime of labour in the docks. A thin woman in black knelt

to weed a grave plot. Neither looked likely gossips. I sat down
on a bench by the church wall and signed for Tabby to sit next
to me. She sat, but fidgeted.

'What are we waiting for?'

'Somebody who's alert enough to notice two strangers and
inquisitive enough to want to know what we're doing here.'

A curate passed, in a hurry and muttering to himself, not
noticing us. The thin woman straightened up painfully from the
grave, wrapped the kitchen fork that she'd been using to weed
in a piece of brown paper and put it in the pocket of her coat.
She walked slowly past us, eyes downcast. For twenty minutes
or so nothing happened, except that Tabby got up and walked
round the graves, frowning at their inscriptions as if they'd been
chiselled to annoy her.

A woman came out of the side door of the church. She was
middle-aged and comfortable looking, dressed in a cape of navy
blue wool, with a basket on her arm. As she came alongside our
bench she smiled and wished me good morning. I smiled back
and said it was a fine day for the end of October.

'Yes, but we're getting the mists in the morning, aren't we?'

'It's not so bad back in town,' I said. 'I suppose it's always
mistier by the river.'

Tabby was back, standing within listening distance.

'You're not from round here then?' the woman said, as if she
didn't know.

'No. We've just come from calling on Mrs Hobbes.'

She smiled, with a mouthful of teeth so even and white they
must be false. 'Oh, how is the poor soul?'

I moved aside in an invitation to sit with me on the bench.
She took it.

'Pretty well in the circumstances,' I said.

'She must be finding it so hard not being able to get about.
She was such an active body. I don't suppose she'll ever be quite
the same again, will she?'

I thought the pleasure in her voice was not from somebody
else's misfortune, but rather a liking for drama.

'It seems to be taking its time to heal,' I said.

'Oh, they do. A niece of mine was off her feet for two months,
though that was only a sprain, and she always walked with a

limp afterwards, but it turned out not to matter because she married a very nice man from Southwark and he didn't mind her limp at all.'

'Is it two months for Mrs Hobbes then?' I said, pretending to have misunderstood.

'No, a month almost to the day. I remember because we were taking down our summer curtains and putting up the winter ones, which we always do the last Monday in September and that's when I heard she'd had the accident. Of course, some people said that served her right for being down at the docks in the first place because it wasn't the place for a woman, but everybody has to admit that she never puts up with disrespectful behaviour from anybody. Even the bargees don't say anything worse than "botheration" when she's there.'

Tabby caught my eye and tapped her palms together in soundless applause. There was our main question answered, or so she thought. It turned out that our good busybody kept house for two of the curates. She'd lived in Limehouse all her life and was defensive of its reputation.

'It's been given a bad name, but there are good and bad people here just as anywhere else. I'm sure if the truth were known there are as many sinners in Mayfair as in Limehouse.'

'Probably more,' I said, not letting on that was where we came from.

We chatted in a general way about London crime, none of it much to the purpose. She was shifting on her seat, saying regretfully that she must get on and fetch the curate's shoes from the cobbler, when I slipped in the question I really wanted to ask.

'By the by, did they ever find that girl who went missing?'

Our woman stopped in the act of getting to her feet, haunches hitched on the bench. She was puzzled, then it came to her. 'Oh, you mean Mrs Bitty's kitchen maid? No, she didn't come back. Mrs Bitty thinks she went off with a sailor.'

She pushed herself to her feet, smiling. 'They do go off, don't they?' Tolerance in her voice for the unpredictable ways of kitchen maids. 'Well, it's been pleasant talking to you. I hope you have a good journey back.'

Tabby and I stood watching as she walked away.

'What girl?' Tabby said.

'I don't know. We're going to find out.'

I started walking back towards the river. When Tabby fell into step beside me, I tried to explain one of the mysteries of our strange craft. 'Most people like to talk,' I said. 'It's just a matter of asking the right questions and, above all, listening.'

'I thought we just wanted to know about the accident.'

'Yes, and we have our answer. Whether it was a real accident or deliberate, Mrs Hobbes hasn't been able to move from her parlour for a month. That's around the time that all this started. Either way, she's probably not involved in whatever's happening. But when you find things are running your way, always ask that extra question. It's like a carpenter working with the grain.'

We came alongside a small row of shops, an ironmonger, a greengrocer with nothing but cabbages on the shelf, a butcher.

'We'll ask for Mrs Bitty's address in there,' I said. 'Any household prosperous enough to have a kitchen maid will have an account with the butcher.'

'Let me ask,' Tabby said.

I waited across the road as she went into the shop. She was away for a surprisingly long time and came back looking pleased with herself.

'She lives at number eight, facing the ropemakers' works, that's just off where we were this morning. She's a cussed old curmudgeon with a face like the backside of a sow and when she buys a couple of lamb chops she expects the head and tongue thrown in for free.'

'The butcher told you all that?'

'I thought of what you said about people liking to talk.'

Number eight was a narrow house standing apart from its neighbours on either side by the slightest of gaps, as if drawing in its shoulders to avoid contact with them. Here by the rope walk, the smell of damp hemp was stronger even than river mud and small fibres of it hazed the sunlight. I knocked on the door and waited. A maid who looked no more than twelve years old answered, looking apprehensive. I gave her my card and said I'd like to talk to Mrs Bitty. The woman who appeared at the door a few minutes later proved that the butcher's description had been pretty accurate.

'Well?'

'I'm sorry to trouble you, but I understand that your kitchen maid has gone missing,' I said.

I was going to add that I specialized in tracing missing people. Her scowl was like volcanic lava.

'I suppose you're from the orphans' home. If you're trying to palm another of them off on me, I don't want her,' she said. 'They're more trouble than they're worth and no gratitude.' Her glare transferred from me to Tabby. 'So you can take that one back where she came from and tell them not to send me any more. Good day to you.'

She slammed the door in our faces with a force that juddered my teeth. We stood for a moment, stunned.

Tabby was the first to speak. 'What was that you said about asking the right questions and listening?'

'It doesn't always work,' I said.

SIXTEEN

Nothing could be gained from standing there staring at a closed door so we turned back towards Commercial Road.

'I'd have left the old bitch too,' Tabby said.

'I'm sorry I've wasted our time on her,' I said. 'All the same, we've learned two important things here at Limehouse.'

She frowned, trying so hard to see what I meant that she reverted to her old scuffy-toed way of walking. It's right to be a few jumps ahead of one's apprentice.

'Ice,' I prompted. 'What happens to it.'

'They take it off a boat and put it on a barge.'

'That's right. And the barge takes it up the canal, right to the edge of Regent's Park.'

My brother Tom, as a boy, had been obsessed with canals, from the building of the new Caledonian canal in the north down to the Hythe Military in the south. I tried to bring to mind his map of the course of the Regent's Canal. From the Thames at Limehouse it ran north to Mile End, then made a long curve round the east of London, through Haggerston and Islington to King's Cross and Paddington. It really wasn't fair to expect Tabby to follow me without giving her the essential part of the puzzle.

'There's something I haven't told you yet,' I said. 'Last Wednesday, when they found Dora Tilbury's body, one of the policeman slipped on a piece of ice. He didn't know it was ice and it didn't come to me until later, but it must have been dropped when her body was brought there.'

It had come back to my mind suddenly and clearly: a small disc of something as bright as a diamond, skittering out from under the constable's boot. He'd slipped because he'd trodden on a piece of ice.

'So that's how you knew it was the ice cart.'

Tabby spoke in the tone of a person who's seen how the magician does his trick and is unimpressed. My brother's drawing was growing clearer in my memory. At some point, before it reached King's Cross, the Regent's canal had a rectangular opening at right angles to it, a place where barges could moor or turn, close to the heart of the City.

'City Road,' I said. 'There's a canal basin at City Road.'

I was about to explain to Tabby why it mattered when running footsteps sounded behind us. They were small, light footsteps. The voice calling to us was small too, almost inaudible.

'Excuse me . . . can you tell me? . . . Excuse me.'

We turned round. The maid who'd opened Mrs Bitty's door to us was a few yards behind, gasping from running and pale-faced. The hem of her black skirt had come unstitched where she'd trodden on it in her haste. Her hand was pressed to her side. We stopped and she stopped too, as if scared to come too close. Any idea that Mrs Bitty might have relented and sent her after us disappeared at her next words.

'You won't tell her, will you? She'd be so mad at me. She doesn't know I'm gone and there'll be hell to pay when I get back.'

'Mrs Bitty? No, of course we won't tell her,' I said. 'What do you want?'

She came a couple of steps closer, still gasping and glanced over her shoulder as if fearful of seeing her employer. 'It's about Peggy, ma'am. You were asking about Peggy. Do you know what's become of her?'

'Is Peggy the maid that went away?' I said.

'Yes. Only she wouldn't go away, not of her own free will. Not without telling me. I think something's happened to her, only Mrs Bitty snaps me up if I even say her name.'

'I heard Mrs Bitty thinks she went away with a sailor,' I said.

Her pale face flushed. 'It's a lie. Beg pardon, ma'am, but Peggy never would. She never even liked sailors. If she liked anybody it was the boy from the fish shop and even that wasn't anything, apart from a few words every Friday.'

She stood staring at us from damp, dark-ringed eyes. Tabby and I looked at each other.

'When did you last see Peggy?' I asked.

'Two weeks ago last Thursday. Mrs Bitty sent her out to get the bread and she never came back. Mrs Bitty tried to get the policeman to go and find her. She said she didn't want Peggy back but she wanted her basket and the threepence. She nearly went mad when the policeman said he couldn't do anything about it.'

'Does Peggy have any friends or relations she might have gone to?' I said.

'No, she's from the orphans' home, like me.'

'What does she look like?'

The girl's scared face broke into a smile. 'Oh, she's pretty. I think that was what Mrs Bitty didn't like about her. She's got lovely yellow hair and blue eyes. Her hands are as white as a lady's, even with all that scrubbing.'

A weight of sadness came down on me. I didn't want to ask the next question. 'Did she have a pale brown birthmark on the inside of her left wrist?'

The girl's mouth fell open. She stared at me, terrified. 'How did you know that?'

'She did, then?'

'Yes, but you wouldn't notice it unless you were looking. It didn't spoil her. But how . . .?'

She must have seen from our faces that the news was bad. She put her hands to her mouth and made retching noises. I walked up and put my arm round her, but she was as rigid as a metal rod.

'I'm so very sorry,' I said. 'I'm afraid your friend has had an accident.'

She took her hands away from her mouth just long enough to gasp out, 'Dead?'

'Yes, I'm afraid so.'

She slipped out of my arm and was sick in the road. Between us, Tabby and I got her to sit down on the edge of a horse trough. I dipped my handkerchief in the water and cleaned up her face.

'There should be somebody to look after you,' I said. 'We'll go back with you to Mrs Bitty's.'

'No. If you do that, she'll know I've been talking to you.'

The idea terrified her so much that we didn't persist. I felt like forcing my way into Mrs Bitty's house and telling her what I thought of her, for her callousness about her missing maid and her cruelty to this one. But it would only mean trouble for the poor girl when we'd gone. We went with the girl as far as the corner, then she asked us to go before we came within sight of the house.

'What was Peggy's second name?' I asked, as we parted company.

'Brown. It was the orphans' home name. We were all Brown, Green, Black or White. She never had another one.'

Tabby and I watched as her small figure walked unsteadily round the corner.

'I hate letting her go like this,' I said.

'No choice,' Tabby said.

But even she sounded shaken. We walked on, hardly knowing where we were going. The Dora Tilbury who had brought us into this had already been stripped of her false identity until only her name was left to us. Now even that had gone. Dora Tilbury, found dead under the Achilles statue in Hyde Park, and Peggy Brown, who'd walked out to buy bread in Limehouse sixteen days before that, were one and the same person.

The small pleasure of keeping Tabby guessing had gone. I told her outright what I suspected. 'Both the girls were killed some time before the bodies were found, and kept in an ice store. That accounts for the wet hair. The people who did it could thaw out a body and dress it in dry clothes, but they couldn't do anything about the hair.'

'Why would they do that?' Tabby said.

'I don't know. Even if there is some hideous, perverted club that murders young women, why do it that way? Did it matter that they were supposed to have died on a particular date?'

Janet Priest's body had been flung off the Monument – I was sure of that now – on Thursday the seventeenth. The body of the girl we know knew as Peggy Brown had been discovered six days later on Wednesday the twenty-third. I couldn't see any special significance in either date.

'They're both connected with the canal,' I said. 'Peggy disappeared from this end in Limehouse, Janet near the City Road basin. Alive or dead, it would be easier to carry them by water than by road.'

We went back down to the dock basin, then up the steps to the lock manager's office. I apologized for troubling him again, and asked if he could kindly tell us the date of the last shipment of ice up the canal from Limehouse basin. He didn't even have to consult his ledger.

'It's always a Thursday. The last one would have been the tenth of this month.'

I thanked him and we went back down the steps. 'I want to see inside that ice store,' I said.

Tabby and I discussed it while we waited for the coach back to the centre of town. We knew pretty well where it was, but not how to get into it. Then we thought that the ice carts would have to be loaded for their rounds, so it was simply a matter of watching for an empty one near Cumberland Market and seeing where it went. Tabby said that was a job for her. Normally, I would have accepted that. She was much more skilful at passing unnoticed in the early morning streets, especially in her urchin clothes. Now I was too scared for her.

'We'll both watch,' I said.

'Tonight?'

'Yes, tonight.'

Before another girl was spirited away. Before another death in a public place.

When we arrived back in Mayfair, the light was going. I'd planned to walk across the park to the livery stables to see if there was any news of Amos. He'd been away for four days and normally he'd have managed to send some kind of message to me, even if only a few words on the back of a bill for horse-feed. In my heart, though, I was scared of walking across the park. The trees were silhouetted against a thin bar of sunset in the west, the colour of a burn on skin and nobody was walking under them. At the corner of Adam's Mews, a lad jumped at us with a hollowed out mangel-wurzel on a pole, a candle inside to show gaping eye sockets and mouth with pointed teeth. An ordinary boy's trick in the days leading up to Halloween, but Tabby gasped and caught at my cloak and it was all I could do not to scream.

With Mrs Martley still away in Bloomsbury, the coast was clear for Tabby to join me upstairs. We didn't talk much over our supper of beef pie from the bakers on the corner and potatoes baked in the fire. When we'd cleared up, I insisted that she should wrap herself in a blanket and catch a few hours' sleep on the sofa in front of the fire.

'When are we going?'

'Two o'clock. I'll wake you.'

I tried to read by lamplight, but mostly stared at the fire as it collapsed into cinders, going over things in my mind. The dates mattered, only I couldn't see why. The workhouse clock struck two. Tabby woke as soon as I stood up.

'We going?'

'Yes. Go and put on your warm jacket and your boots. Take the candle.'

I watched the small flame crossing the yard to her cabin, then went upstairs to sort out my own clothes and find a spare pair of gloves for Tabby. At that time of night, October was as cold as mid winter. I dressed for it in a thick woollen gown and stockings, a shawl under my cloak. Tabby and I walked along the mews and through Grosvenor Square, heading towards Oxford Street. Occasionally a figure walked towards us out of the darkness, then passed us without a look or word, no more anxious to be noticed than we were. In Oxford Street, two policemen patrolling the opposite pavement gave us curious looks, but decided not to ask questions. Further along, two drunk gentlemen were shouting at each other about welshing on a bet. A very few of the midnight sparrows and their customers were out and about, but it was too late for most of them, so we attracted less attention than I feared. It was past three o'clock by then and we were in the sunken hours when one day is over and daylight still a long time away.

We went on, up Portland Place, with no more than two or three lamplit windows showing on either side, the road between as dark as a river. Tabby had gone quiet. We crossed the Marylebone Road and walked with the railings of Regent's Park on our left. I knew where Cumberland Market was because I'd ridden out there one summer day with Amos when the owner of the livery stables had sent him to choose some loads of hay. He'd taken his time, walking from heap to heap, sometimes just looking, sometimes drawing out a handful and sniffing at it like a connoisseur. A couple of times he'd even chewed a blade or two, looking thoughtful. Once he'd simply kicked at a heap and shook his head.

'What can you tell from kicking it,' I'd asked him.

'Listen.'

He'd kicked again. A faint rustling came from the hay.

'Thistles in there, look. You can hear them. Now listen to this one.' Another kick. This time the sound had been as soft as a breeze over standing grass. 'That's what good hay sounds like.'

I remembered that, just as the smell of damp hay came into the cold air round us.

'Nearly there,' I said to Tabby.

Cumberland Square was deserted with no lamp showing anywhere. A dark bulk that we bumped into turned out to be an empty haycart. We clambered up and sat on the end of it.

'What do we do now?' Tabby said.

'Wait for the ice cart.'

Something else happened first. Heavy steps sounded and a man walked past us. He was smoking strong tobacco. We followed his progress across the square by the red glow of his pipe. A door opened and closed and the scrape of a flint came clearly to where we were sitting. Gradually the outline of a building took shape from the lamplight inside it, an odd shape, like a stubby dome. Beside it was a smaller building, a workman's hut from the look of it, with more lamplight spilling from a half open door. Ten minutes or so after that, the sound of slow plodding hooves came from the direction of town. Eventually a cart appeared, drawn by a heavy cob, and lurched past us over the

cobbles towards the building. The man with the pipe appeared
from the hut and said something to the driver. I couldn't make
out the words, but from the tone of it, he was grumbling.

The driver got down and the two men opened what sounded
like a heavy door in the dome. Sure that nobody would hear our
steps above the noise of it, I slid down off the haycart and signed
to Tabby to follow. By the time we got to the dome, the horse
and cart had gone through the door and disappeared inside. The
hooves had a hollow sound, as if on a platform. The grumbling
man swore and told the other man to make the horse stand.

'He'll be down the pit cart and all otherwise.'

The next sound was a clanking of iron and rattle of a heavy
chain.

'Right, when I give the word, you turn that handle and winch
'em up,' the grumbling man said to the driver, who was evidently
new to the job. 'Then when you've got 'em up, swing it round
and land them in the cart nice and gentle. Got that?'

I was near the door by then, and heard clearly the ringing
sound as a pair of nailed boots went down what sounded like a
long iron ladder. Soon after that, an echoing shout came up from
the depths and the winch handle started grinding.

Knowing that both men were well occupied, I risked a glance
round the door. The lamplight seemed very bright after the dark
outside. The horse was standing on a wooden platform with a
patience that suggested he at least was not new to the work. That
was just as well, because a dark opening gaped a few feet away.
As the winch ground on, a gleaming cube rose into the light,
gripped in the jaws of a huge pair of pinchers. A twenty inch
block of ice, just as Mrs Hobbes had said. The driver shoved the
winch round so that it was above the cart and lowered it not
quite carefully enough, so that the boards rattled and the horse
twitched. Another grumble came up from the depths. The cart
driver sent the giant pincers back down the shaft on their chain.
They went rattling down a long way.

As they got into the rhythm of it, the gleaming cubes came
up faster. There was a strange beauty to the process, with the ice
blocks rising into the air against the dark silhouette of the man
manouevring them, like a slow juggling act. As the cart filled
up, I drew Tabby back from the doorway so that we could talk.

'I want to get inside there. There may be a chance when the cart leaves.'

She nodded. It was too dark to see her face, but I could sense the tension in her. Tabby was afraid, and so was I. The last thing I wanted was to go down into that pit of ice, but having come so far, I had to try at least.

'If I'm not out by daylight, I want you to go and tell—'

'I'm coming with you.'

I'd been about to say 'Mr Legge at the livery stables' until I remembered that Amos was not there. It made the hollow feeling inside me even worse, so I didn't argue.

Four o'clock had struck before they finished. We stayed outside, taking a glimpse now and then to see how things were going. The boots came ringing back up the ladder. By then it had struck me that there wasn't room to turn the horse and cart on the platform, so there must be another door on the opposite side. I watched as the driver shook the horse's bridle to wake it up. The other man, still grumbling about the time it had taken, stamped across the wooden platform and, just as I'd hoped, opened a door on the far side. Under cover of the trampling and creaking, we dashed inside. The cold struck like a blow. There was no concealment on the wooden platform, under the lantern light. I touched Tabby's hand and pointed down the shaft. The rungs of the iron ladder rose from what looked like a bottomless pit of glowing pearl. Forcing myself to grasp the top rung and lower my feet down was one of the worst things I'd ever done. My skirt and petticoats bunched round me and my knee grazed against cold iron as I fought for a foothold. As soon as I was as secure as possible and far enough down, I called to Tabby to follow me.

By now, the cart had gone and the iron door it had left by was closing. Any second now, the grumbling man would turn away from it and cross the platform to the other door. Tabby's boot came down heavily on my finger. I bit my lip and moved cautiously a couple of rungs further down. The man walked across the platform above us. The other door ground on its hinges and shut. He'd left the lamp burning, so that must mean he expected more trade before daylight. I took a deep breath and made myself look down. The steps went down and down, through the ice blocks and into darkness. I couldn't see the bottom of the pit, but guessed it must be fifty feet deep or more. At least there were stopping places on the way down. As my eyes adjusted to the half-light, I saw that the ice blocks were stacked in layers, with floors of rough planking in between. The first of those floors was only ten feet or so below us. I climbed down to it, slowly and cautiously, making as little sound as possible. Tabby followed me into a gleaming cave of ice.

SEVENTEEN

We crouched against a wall of ice blocks. More layers of ice glinted through gaps in the planks, far down. The cold was like being struck in the chest and my fingers felt immediately numb. There was no sound from the top platform, so the man must have gone back to his hut to wait for the next customer. I stood up cautiously and walked along a board, trying not to slip down the gap on either side. Sand scrunched under foot. I supposed the ice man had sprinkled it to give a better footing. The ice picked up and multiplied the lamplight from above, so we could see clearly enough. Tabby and I walked close to each other, peering into the blocks. Most of them were as clear as diamonds. A few had air bubbles and even leaves from their birthplace in the Norwegian lake. A childish and fearful part of my mind more than half expected to find a woman lying entombed, like Snow White in her glass coffin. Nothing.

By the far wall, we came to a gap in the ice, with nothing but sand-scuffed planks. There were marks on the sand as if several people had walked there. It seemed odd that there should be a space here, some way from the bottom of the winch. You'd have expected them to load the nearer blocks first. Tabby gave a gasp and went down on her knees. I thought she'd fallen, but she stood up holding something out to me. She mouthed, 'Look'. I had to move nearer the light to see what it was. Of all things, violets. A spray of artificial violets, made not very skilfully of felt and wire, smelling of damp wool, the kind of cheap ornament a girl might wear on a hat or a belt. My mind went to the painted violets on the prayer card that Janet Priest's sister had given us. I was sure beyond reason that both had been made by the same hand. Janet and the girl we'd known as Dora had both lain in this gleaming cave.

I took another step and stumbled over something lying across the planks, pitched forward, dropping the violets through a gap, only just stopping myself from crying out. Tabby caught me by the coat sleeve. The smell of damp hessian was rising round us. The thing that had made me stumble was loosely wrapped in sacking dark with moisture. I waited until my heart steadied then kneeled down and put out a hand to touch the sacking, trying to find the resolution to pull it away from whatever was inside. Before I could manage it, wheels rumbled from outside and above us, echoing like thunder from wall to wall of the pit. Two horses, stepping more quickly than the first ice cart horse. With both doors shut, there was no chance of hearing what was being said, but it was a certainty that any minute now the door above us would slide back and the ice man come climbing down. Tabby caught my eye and pointed that we should climb down to a lower level. I nodded, but there was something that must be done first. I started folding the sacking back then pulled my hand away. I'd touched hair. Damp hair, just as my own felt after washing it. Damp, thick woman's hair.

When Tabby saw my face she kneeled down beside me. Her hand, more resolute than mine, pulled the sacking down further. When the pressure of it was released, something white surged out, so white that it seemed to carry a light of its own. When I touched it, it felt soft but springy, like the pelt of a healthy animal. My mind went back to a fitting room in Piccadilly. *This is what it must have. See.* The contessa, eyes bright, holding the fur of the Arctic fox against her cheek. My hand slid away from fur onto velvet, mulberry-coloured velvet, rich and new. When I drew velvet and fox fur aside, her skin was stretched tight over her cheekbones, pale as paper. The lids closed over her eyes looked so tight and thin that I half expected the amazing colour of them to shine through. I made myself touch her face, as if against all sense and reason there might be life there. It was colder than the ice itself. I folded the cloak hood back over her.

'Another one,' Tabby said. Her voice was level and sounded calmer than I felt, but then she'd never met the contessa.

Above us, the door was grinding open. The ice man still had his pipe in his mouth and the whiff of tobacco hung round him as he began climbing down the steps. By then, I'd gripped Tabby's shoulder and pushed her towards the ladder, down to the second layer of ice. I went after her. Another set of footsteps followed the ice man down to the tier above us. They were making straight for the cleared space where the hessian bundle was lying. I let go of the ladder and moved towards the same space, but ten feet or so below.

'Well, are you waiting for something? Pick it up.'

The voice came from the newcomer. He spoke drawlingly, like a man accustomed to giving orders. He had a foreign accent, but I couldn't place it in those few words. Looking up through a gap, I saw the jowly face of the ice man as he bent down, then straightened up. The woman in the sacking was a light weight and he carried her easily on his shoulders up the steps. The other man followed him, not hurrying. The horses above were less patient than the cart horse had been, trampling on the boards and snickering uneasily. They weren't used to this, any more than we were.

'Up,' I said in Tabby's ear.

I went first, moving fast. It wouldn't take long to load that bundle and drive away. I hoped we could get ourselves outside when the ice man opened the opposite door and the noise of the vehicle departing hid our rush in the other direction. Up we went through the top layer of ice blocks, blinking as the pearly light changed to the glare of the oil lamp on the loading platform. I'd mistimed it. The vehicle was still there. Not an ice cart or anything like it. I was looking at the back of a gentleman's travelling chariot. As soon as I set eyes on it, it started moving. Knowing we might have no more than a second or two, I scrambled onto the platform, landing on my knees. Tabby was so close behind me that her head banged against my shoe soles. The chariot started moving, at a walk. I straightened up. We could do it, just. While the ice man was closing the exit door, we could get out the way we'd come in and . . .

And nothing. I was at the door but where Tabby's footsteps should have been behind me, there was silence. I turned, to see what was keeping her, and found the worst thing I could have imagined in the circumstances. She was there, on the back of the departing chariot, in the footman's place, if there'd been a footman, standing there wide-eyed, holding onto the strap with one hand. The other hand gestured to me to join her, urgently and impatiently as if I were the one who'd taken the wrong turning. In her terrier mind, there'd been nothing for it but to stick to a hot trail and she thought the same thing was in my mind. A terrier's human being goes where the terrier goes. I picked up my skirts, sprinted across the echoing boards, jumped up and joined her on the footmen's platform just as the chariot cleared the doors. Her hand closed round my wrist, steadying me. The ice man had turned away, to close and bolt the door. Alerted by my rush past him he turned, shouted something. Too late. As soon as we cleared the surrounds of the ice pit, the horses broke into a trot and we turned sharply into Cumberland Market and out towards Albany Street. The ice man was shouting behind us, but the shouts faded. Either he lacked the energy to follow, or whatever he'd been paid didn't cover the extra effort. Tabby kept hold of my wrist and guided my hand towards the second footman's strap.

'Bleeding hell, what were you waiting for?'

Fine language from an apprentice to employer, but I said nothing, not having the breath.

Tabby was used to this. As soon as she could toddle, probably, she'd joined the urchins in the park, daring each other to cling to the backs of carriages. If I'd been able to speak, I'd have asked her why she'd thought it was a sound idea to cling like flies to a chariot, driven by somebody unknown but probably murderous with a dead body on board.

We were going at a fast trot, heading southwards towards the centre of town. No sooner had I worked that out than we turned right without slackening speed, going along the south side of Regent's Park. I cannoned against Tabby as we swung out to the left, but she kept her footing and nudged me back upright. The roads and pavements were deserted, so no reason for the chariot to slow down and no chance for us to jump off without serious injury. With that decided for the moment, I began to think that Tabby's reckless decision was not necessarily a bad thing. If the murderer were following the same pattern as with the Achilles statue, his intention would be to leave the body in some very public place, where she'd be found at daylight. What better proof could we have than to see him in the act of doing it? All we'd need to do was cling on to the end of the journey and stay there while the man, or men, unloaded the body and arranged it as required. He, or they, would be intent on their task and have no reason to look behind the chariot. The question was, how we'd get away once we'd seen what happened. An idea began to form.

'We'll stay here until it stops,' I said to Tabby, not even bothering to whisper because of the noise of the chariot. 'We'll watch what they do, then run out, get on the box and I'll drive us away.'

I'd driven various carts and carriages so had no doubt of my ability to manage this one. There was piquancy in the idea of arriving at some police station, not only with the case practically solved but in possession of the murderer's own vehicle. It would take a lot of influence in high places for the guilty ones to explain that away. Tabby simply nodded, as if I'd proposed a walk to the shops.

We turned sharp left into the New Road, then left again at Lisson Grove and down to Bayswater Road, past the Flora Tea Gardens, heading westwards at a canter. This area was familiar to me from rides on Rancie and I considered where they were likely to leave the body. We were well past the Achilles statue by now, heading for Kensington. If they intended to leave it in a place as prominent as the first two, there weren't many choices left. Only Kensington Gardens and Kensington Palace lay ahead before we were out into the country, heading for Kew and Richmond. Still at a canter, we passed Kensington Palace. A few lights were gleaming in its top windows. The working day had started, with the early servants getting out of bed in the attics to rake out grates, clean boots, set water to boil. It was cold, so cold that I felt as if my hand were frozen to the strap.

Once or twice we sped past slow carts creaking from the other direction. They were no more than shapes moving in the darkness, except for one pale, astonished face of a rustic carter who had just escaped being hit by us, head on. Farm carts, probably, with potatoes and cabbages for Covent Garden. We sped out of Kensington, towards Chiswick. A breeze blowing from the Thames brought the smell of water and mud. Could Kew Gardens be their chosen place? I doubted it. The previous two bodies had been left in places where all London would know and talk about them. At this time of year, a body might lie undiscovered in Kew Gardens for days. They wouldn't want that. There was a pattern to all this, and although I couldn't guess what it was, it depended on the bodies being found at a particular place and time. Besides, if we were making for Kew we'd have to cross the river. Our driver gave no sign of doing that and went on westwards, back to a trot now, but a fast one.

We were well outside London now, on the old coach road heading towards Hounslow. If we kept up this pace, we'd be in Hounslow before it was light. I began to think I was wrong about our driver planning to leave the body in a public place. Perhaps it was being taken to some house these people owned, in Hounslow or beyond. If so, Tabby and I were letting ourselves be carried into a trap. We should jump off after all, only not at this pace. Somewhere surely the driver would have to slow down. Even the best of horses couldn't keep up this pace for long. In the end, fate in the shape of another farm cart decided it for us. I only saw it after our near-accident had happened. The first thing we knew, the chariot's speed checked suddenly then it swerved violently to the right. Shouts and a splintering of wood sounded from the dark. When it happened, Tabby had taken her hand off the strap to push her hair out of her eyes. The change from a fast trot to a near halt was too much even for her sure-footedness. Without a word or a sound she plunged sideways onto the road. One moment she was beside me – the next moment, nothing but emptiness. Before the chariot could pick up speed again, I jumped off on the other side, landing on hands and knees in the dirt. The farm cart that had caused the trouble was in the middle of the road, one wheel hanging at an angle and the driver waving his whip in the direction the chariot had gone and cursing.

I ignored him and started looking for Tabby, no easy task in the darkness and dirt with the cart driver making such a racket. A low sound, like a hoarse cock crow, was coming from

somewhere behind me. I followed it and found Tabby curled in
a ditch. Dreading that she was badly injured, I knelt down beside
her.

'What's wrong? Can you tell me where you're hurt?'

No answer, except more harsh crowing. She was clasping her
hands to her chest, head bent over them. I didn't dare try to move
her for fear of making things worse. As far as I could make out
in the darkness, there was nothing but fields on both sides of the
road and no gleam of light anywhere. Certainly no help was to
be expected from the cart driver, still cursing and, by the sound
of it, freeing his horse from a tangle of harness.

The crowing sound grew fainter so that I feared Tabby was
going to die here in the ditch, with me helpless to do anything
about it. I put my hand gently on her shoulder. She was trying
to say something.

'Can't . . . can't . . .'

'Don't try to talk. Lie still.'

Another long drawn-out crow, then a shuddering intake of
breath and her whole body was trembling. Thinking it could
hardly make things worse, I got my arms round her.

'All right, Tabby. It's all right.'

Even though I feared it was anything but. Her head came up
and her eyes opened.

'Couldn't get my breath, that's all. Got it now.'

Her voice was shaky, but the tone matter-of-fact. I kept my arms
round her until she stopped trembling then helped her sit up.

'So what are we going to do now?' she said.

'Never mind that. Are you hurt?'

'Think I've done something to me wrist.'

'Can you stand up?'

She could, so I got her out of the ditch. The carter and his
horse were gone by then, though the disabled cart was still in
the middle of the road. I guided her over to it so that she could
lean against it and tried to make out how badly she was hurt.
Her left wrist was swelling already but we decided it was sprained,
not broken. I clambered up on the cart tail and tore strips from
my petticoat for bandages. I had to tear pretty high up, because
the bottom of it was soaked with mud from the ditch.

By the time we'd finished, there was that slight change in the texture of the darkness that means morning isn't far away. I sat on the cart tail and considered. We'd have to walk, no doubt about that. We were on a coach route out of London, so there must be an inn or a tollgate before long, whether we went back or forward. My first instinct was to go back towards London. At least there'd be safety there, and clean clothes. Then I could report what had happened to the police. But the more I thought about that, the less I liked it. We had no chariot now, no body, no evidence. We were simply two women with a very unlikely story. If there was indeed a determination in high places to hide what was happening, we were wasting our time, or even putting ourselves in danger.

The alternative was to walk on westwards. On the face of it, that made very little sense and yet I liked it better. That was, after all, the direction the chariot had gone with the contessa's body on board. But something stronger drew me westwards, and that was the thought of Amos Legge. The last thing I knew about him was the guess of the livery stable owner that he was heading for Egham in Surrey. Egham was in the same direction as Hounslow, only about half a day's ride further on. Amos had gone there for revenge on the men who had attacked him. I was certain now that his quarry and mine were the same. I slid down from the cart and asked Tabby if she felt capable of walking, if we took it slowly.

'Doesn't need to be slow,' she said. 'It's me feet I walk on, not me hands.' She was clearly recovering, so we set off at a good pace along the road towards Hounslow.

EIGHTEEN

When you're tired, muddy and draggle-petticoated, it's no time to be humble. At the first inn we came to at Hounslow, I played the fine lady and explained that my maid and I had suffered an accident on the road. Our driver was dealing with the carriage and we'd decided to go on by stage coach. It was not so far from the truth and luckily I'd a few sovereigns in my pocket for emergencies, so we could pay for

a room with a fire and several jugs of hot water. Once we'd made
ourselves as respectable as we could, I ordered a breakfast of
eggs, bacon and tea to be sent up to us. Tabby sat in a chair by
the fire and set to with ravenous appetite, eating one-handed.
Remembering the feel of that damp hair under my hand in the
ice pit, I thought I'd never be hungry again, but gradually
the smell of the bacon and the look of plump slices of white
bread and butter twitched at my appetite and in the end I was
eating as eagerly as Tabby.

When we'd eaten, I explained my plans, such as they were.
We'd inquire at this inn and any other in Hounslow if a gentleman's chariot had stopped or changed horses at some time around
five o'clock in the morning, or if anybody had seen such a
vehicle. Supposing that we drew a blank there – which was
likely – we'd take a stage coach on to Egham and hope to find
Amos Legge.

The landlord was ready to be helpful, especially since I'd tipped
him well, but had seen or heard nothing of my friend and his
chariot in the early hours. We met with the same result at three
other inns, including the main coaching establishment. When the
Alpha coach drew into the yard, heading for Southampton via
Staines and Egham, I bought tickets for us, travelling on the
outside. Even after our wash, we were hardly fit company for
inside travel and it helped conserve our small store of money.
The day was overcast and drizzling. We were both so tired by
then that, in spite of the jolting and the chatter of the other outside
passengers, we dozed, leaning against each other, for most of
the journey and only woke up when we arrived at the Red Lion
in Egham soon after midday.

It was a prosperous looking inn, red brick and thickly thatched.
The landlord came out smiling a welcome, even for two bedraggled passengers climbing stiffly down from the top of the coach.
The smile was tilted to one side because a shiny pink burn scar the
shape of a horseshoe covered most of the right side of his face. I
decided there was no need to produce my story of a carriage
accident and simply asked if we might engage a room. He looked
puzzled at our lack of luggage and the fact that I hadn't requested
separate accommodation for my maid, but he offered a comfortable
room at the back.

'The bed needs making up, ma'am, but if you care to wait in the parlour I'll have tea sent in while the girl's seeing to it.'

He brought the tea in himself, probably out of curiosity. I didn't mind that because it gave me a chance to talk to him.

'I wonder if you've met a friend of mine, a Mr Legge. He was in Egham a few days ago and I think he might have stayed here.'

A simple assumption. The Red Lion, as the coaching inn, would have more horses than any of the other establishments in town. If looking for Amos, always head where the horses were.

The landlord smiled his lopsided smile. 'Mr Legge, yes he stayed here twice. Ten days or so ago, the first time, then last Friday, turned up just when I needed him.'

'Needed him?'

'Saved one of my best horses, Toby. He'd got lockjaw from a cut. Some woodenhead had hired him and not noticed he was hurt. By the time we knew, it was set in so bad I thought there was nothing for it but to put him out of his misery. I was just going inside for my pistol when Mr Legge arrives from London. I tell him what's happening and he says to let him look at Toby. So he looks, then he says to fetch him the clippers and all the mustard I've got in the house. "Mustard?" I says. He says, "Yes, dry or mixed, no odds." So I fetch them and he clips that horse as close as a billiard ball, so you could see the skin. Before he arrived, the poor beast was in too much pain to let anyone put a hand on him, but Mr Legge says something to him and he stands still enough. Then when he's got him clipped, he rubs in the mustard all over him, then tells me to bring two good thick horse rugs and he straps them both on Toby, one over the other. Then he fetches in a couple of buckets of water and says to leave Toby quiet for two or three hours, either he'll do or he won't. "If he pulls through," I says, "you can have all the beer you can drink any time you like." He says, "I'll hold you to that." So we have a drink and a pipe or two, and when we look in a few hours later, there's the horse standing there, rugs soaked through with sweat, but right as rain. "Where did you learn that trick?" I says. So he says he learned it off a gypsy back home and sometimes it works and sometimes it doesn't, so now what about that beer?'

Even hearing him tell the story made me feel better, it was so like Amos. Amos's first visit, ten days ago, must have been the one where he discovered something that led to the attack on him in Hyde Park. Then there'd been the second visit five days ago.

'He's gone then?' I said.

'Yes, went off early Monday morning.'

'Do you know where?'

'I know where he went first. There's a friend of mine down near the race track, breeds horses.'

'And he didn't come back? Were you expecting him?'

'Well, I was and I wasn't. He didn't have any luggage with him, apart from what he carried in a little saddle bag, and he took that with him.'

'And you had no idea where he might be going after the horse breeder?'

'No.'

But this time, there was a hint of doubt in the no. I looked him in the eye.

'I didn't ask him,' he said. 'He was friendly enough, but when it came to asking him questions, it was so far and no further. For instance, when he came here on Friday, I couldn't help noticing he'd got a shiner of a black eye. "You've been in the wars then?" I said. He didn't answer, just drank his beer. But I'll leave you ladies to your tea, then.'

He went as far as the door, then hesitated. 'Mr Legge isn't in any kind of trouble, I hope.'

'I'm sure he's not,' I said. 'I'd just like to talk to him, that's all.'

He might have said more, but coach wheels sounded outside. 'You'll excuse me. I'll get the girl to show you up to your room.'

The room was small and clean, most of the space taken up by an enormous feather bed. Tabby gazed at it longingly. Her face was pale and pinched and I guessed she was in more pain from her wrist than she'd admitted.

'Rest,' I said. 'Just take off your dress and shoes and lie down.'

'What will you do?'

'Go out for a walk. Don't worry, I won't be away long.'

I turned onto a field footpath. Across the river, a white house stood among the trees on Magna Carta Island, where the barons had made King John sign the great charter more than six hundred years ago. When I was ten years old, my father had brought me and my brother Tom there from London on a summer day. It was a sacred spot, he told us, the foundation of our freedom from arbitrary power and false imprisonment. The barons, to be sure, were no friends to the common people, being concerned only with their own rights, therefore not such good men as Tom Paine or William Cobbett. Still, we should stand quietly and remember that this was where the idea of liberty, for England and therefore all the world, began.

At the time, I had tried hard to keep my mind on what my father was saying, because I knew it was important to him, and why he and my late mother had named me as they had. But I'm afraid my attention had wandered to the race course alongside the river, where men were exercising horses that gleamed bright bay against the close-cropped grass. Quite likely, my father had to struggle to keep his own attention from straying because he dearly loved a good horse.

On this autumn afternoon there were no horses out on the race course and my father's words came back to me with more force than when he spoke them. For three young women at least, life had been cut short. If somebody could kill them and not face justice, then what was the point of the barons and their charter? I stayed beside the river until the sun was almost down and walked back to the Red Lion.

Our landlord's name was Mr Webster. The horseshoe burn came from when he'd been apprentice to a blacksmith and a touchy pony had kicked out, driving the red-hot shoe onto his cheek. Tabby and I learned this after our dinner, when I invited him into the parlour where we'd had our meal served, to take a glass of claret with me. (I'd relented and let Tabby have gin and water.) I think he found me a puzzle. Here I was, unescorted by a gentleman, sharing bed and board with my maid, sovereigns in my pocket but not so much as a saddlebag with a change of linen. Luckily, he'd decided that a friend of Amos Legge was entitled to the benefit of the doubt. I repeated what I'd said about Mr Legge not being in trouble, but admitted I was concerned about him.

'He was attacked by several men in London ten days ago,' I

said. 'That's when he got the black eye he didn't want to talk
about. I think he might have met the men who attacked him on
that first visit here and come back to find them last Friday.'

He drank some wine and nodded. 'He had something on his
mind, I know that much.'

'That first visit, did you notice who he talked to?'

'No. We were that busy, with everybody coming and going
from the castle. I noticed him, of course, because of his height
and his appetite. Ate two platefuls of rabbit stew and a loaf of
bread straight off. I remember he said he'd come down from
London to deliver a horse.'

'You didn't see him taking a particular interest in anybody?'

'No.'

'Or arguing or being threatened?'

'No. He didn't strike me as an argumentative kind of a man.
As to threats, who in his right mind would try to threaten a man
who looks as if he could pick up a fair-sized pony and carry it
half a mile?'

'The second time he came here, last Friday, did you notice
anything different about him?'

'I'd say he was keyed-up. When we were drinking in the snug,
he kept looking around, as if he expected to see somebody he
recognized. He was asking me questions, too.'

'What about?'

He jerked his chin over his shoulder, towards a room next
door. As far as I remembered, it was a parlour much like the one
we were sitting in, only larger. It was a place where respectable
coach travellers, male or female, might take their twenty minutes'
rest while the horses were changed without venturing into the
more rustic public room.

'Them, mostly.'

He seemed to take it for granted that I'd know what he meant.
I didn't. 'Any questions in particular?'

'He wanted to know if there were any gentlemen who drove
a black chariot. None this side of the park, I told him. Plenty
the other side.'

I'd nearly jumped out of my chair at the mention of a black
chariot, but our landlord didn't notice because his professional
ear had caught a sound he was expecting.

'Here come the next lot. Just in time to pick up the Bristol to London. You'll excuse me, ladies.'

He drained his glass, put it down on the table and left hurriedly. Tabby looked at me.

'What lot's he talking about?'

'I don't know.'

I stood up and half-opened the door onto the passage. People were walking into the larger parlour. A couple of what looked like ladies' maids were chattering together, carrying hat boxes, followed by a kindly-faced older woman who might have been a housekeeper. Then two middle-aged men, wearing a blue uniform and a grey-haired gentleman with a discontented expression, annoyed to find himself in servants' company. Before they were settled, the wheels of the vehicle that had brought them rolled away. By now, it was pitch dark outside.

'So was it our ice people Mr Legge was looking for?' Tabby said.

'I think so, yes.'

The thought of it terrified me. Amos was simply out for revenge, not knowing about the bodies and the ice store, but that wouldn't save him. We sat and waited, Tabby sipping her gin and water. A gentle hum of conversation came from the parlour next door, none of it loud enough to make out. Who were they? About twenty minutes after their arrival, a coach horn sounded outside and the stage coach from Bristol to London clattered into the yard. We watched from the window as the people from the parlour came filing out and took their places inside and on top. It left looking dangerously overloaded.

As the sound of its wheels died away, Mr Webster came back to us. 'May I get you anything, ladies?'

By then, I'd decided to admit my ignorance. 'Who are they?'

He looked surprised. 'From over there.' Another jerk of the chin.

'Over there?'

'Castle staff.' Then, probably because of the amazed look on my face: 'With the castle staff, if they have to go up to town for anything, it's easier to bring them across the park to here, then they can go on the regular services to London.'

I'd been a fool. With everything else on my mind, I'd forgotten

my geography. To the west of Egham and Runnymede was the
open space of Windsor Great Park, and several miles beyond
the park, the castle.

'So those people were all castle servants?'

'Yes, or servants of the ladies and gentlemen staying there. A
lot of them at present, up and down from London all the time.'

'And the blue uniforms, are they some kind of local militia?'

He smiled. 'That's the Windsor uniform. The higher sort of
the men servants wear it. Then there's the grand version that her
majesty's regular visitors wear to dinner.'

'So it was the household servants Mr Legge was asking
questions about?'

'Anything to do with them, but the horses and carriages mainly.
I wondered if he was hoping to do a bit of business with them.
"No chance here," I told him. "They're a close lot, keep themselves
to themselves."'

A lad's head came round the door. They needed a new barrel
in the public room and Mr Webster had the keys to the cellar.

'Just one more thing,' I said. 'What was the name of the
breeder Mr Legge went to see on Monday?'

'Jack Dunn. Used to work at the Royal Mews, but came into
a bit of money and set up on his own. I'll tell the girl to take a
warming pan up to your bed.'

We slept, exhausted. I woke in the dark and lit the candle,
shielding the flame from Tabby who was still asleep, curled up
like a puppy. Without the workhouse clock to wake her, she'd have
no idea of time. I dressed as quietly as I could. We'd tried to brush
the worst of the mud off our clothes the night before, but my skirt
and petticoats were still stiff with it, the leather of my shoes cold
and damp. Downstairs, a girl was raking out the ashes in the parlour
grate and looked surprised to see a guest up so early. I told her
I'd be back and unlatched a side door to the stable yard. Outside
the yard there was just enough light to avoid the flooded ruts in the
road as I walked towards the race course. Horse people are early
risers, and I didn't want to waste another minute in looking for
Amos. The stable buildings looked ramshackle from a distance
but the yard was neat, with water buckets ranged by the pump and
a couple of lads filling hay nets in an open barn. A terrier came
rushing up to me, with the high-pitched barks of its kind.

'Shut your noise, Caesar.'

A man carrying a curry comb came out of one of the boxes. He was too big and broad-shouldered to have been a jockey, but had that sceptical, seen-it-all look of a man who'd spent all his life with horses and horsemen. He didn't seem surprised to see a woman on her own at this hour, or even particularly curious.

'Mr Dunn?'

'That's me.'

'I believe you've met a friend of mine, Amos Legge. I wondered if you knew where he went after you saw him.'

He looked at me, sizing me up. 'Is he in some kind of trouble, then?'

It worried me that both he and Mr Webster had the same thought.

'Not as far as we know, only he's been away from his work longer than is usual with him.'

'He came to try a horse.'

It wasn't an answer. Mr Dunn was still trying to judge whether I meant trouble for Amos or not.

'What did he think of it?' I said.

He wouldn't be rushed into anything. He turned, went into a box and came out leading a rangy looking dark bay gelding by the halter rope.

'You know him. What do you think he thought of him?' he said.

The horse was rolling his eyes and pressing his ears back in a fine show of bad temper. He looked a shade lacking in bone to me, and too narrow in the chest. Yet his length of body and his bearing, like an arrow waiting to be loosed from a bow, told another story.

'Outrun most things over half a mile, but not a stayer,' I said.

He grinned a slow grin. I'd passed some kind of test. 'Pretty much what he said. He told me if I hadn't sold him by the time he came back this way, we might have a deal.'

Hope flared.

'He's coming back soon, then?'

'Said it might be a while,' Mr Dunn said.

Hope sank again. He led the gelding back into his box and came out looking thoughtful.

I tried again. 'So do you have any idea where he was going when he left here?'

For answer, I got that over-the-shoulder nod, as from the landlord at the Red Lion. This time I knew how to interpret it.

'The castle? Why was he going there?'

'Thought he might get work. I reckon that was why he came to see me. He was interested in the horse, right enough, but he'd found out from Mr Webster I used to work there.'

'At the mews?'

'Yes. He wanted to know what his chances were if he turned up asking for work. Not good usually, I told him. They like to keep it in the family, so no chance of a regular post unless you've got a brother or a father in there. But now and then, if they're short-handed, they might take on a man casual for a few days if he looks useful, for the rough jobs like buckets and mucking out. You wouldn't want that, I told him.'

'But he did?'

'Seemed to. That surprised me, because a man who knows horses like he knows them could do better for himself. Then I thought maybe he'd had some falling out with his employer and was down on his luck.'

He looked at me, obviously wondering whether I was that employer, had sacked my groom and now regretted it. I decided to let him go on suspecting it.

'So Mr Legge went from here to ask for a job in the Royal Mews?'

'Yes. I gave him the name of a man he could try asking. Last I saw of him, he was walking across the park there.'

Another nod towards the castle. A big park and a walk of miles and miles.

'I wonder if you have a horse you'd hire me,' I said.

NINETEEN

The only side-saddle horse in his stable was a docile grey mare with a rocking-horse canter. I rode her westwards into Windsor Great Park on a morning of low grey cloud, threatening rain. Damp had changed the autumn gold of the oak trees to tarnished bronze. For the first part of the ride we saw no other riders, only deer that galloped away from us. This early, it wasn't surprising that we had the park to ourselves. After two miles or so we came to our first horseman, standing high on a hill, a gigantic figure against the grey sky. He was no flesh and blood creature. The Copper Horse was what they called him locally, a huge equestrian statue of George III. When I'd last been in the park as a child, the statue had not been there but I'd seen engravings of it. The king himself, looking infinitely more noble than was likely in real life, was dressed in the approximate fashion of a Roman emperor, riding a magnificent horse with flowing mane and tail. The engraving had not prepared me for the sheer size of it, or the way it dominated this part of the park. It stood on a high and rocky plinth, looking down on Windsor Castle, as if prepared to trample anything that challenged it under its lordly hooves.

I admired it from a distance, but as we came closer it started to trouble me. It reminded me too much of the Achilles statue – the same immense size, the same harking back to classical times, but above all the flaunting arrogance of it. The mare and I trotted towards the base of the hill. There was a path going towards the statue, but we had no reason to ride up to it. We could simply skirt the base of the hill to come on to the Long Walk. From there, a good canter on the grass between an avenue of old elm trees would bring us to Windsor town. In spite of that, I found I'd shortened the rein and turned the mare up the path towards the statue. We'd only taken a few steps before two men on bay cobs came riding down it. They were wearing dark uniforms and looked like park rangers. The first one turned his horse across the path, barring our way.

'Sorry ma'am, you can't go up there.'

The apology was perfunctory, his face grim.

'Why not?'

'Stones falling off,' said his companion from behind him, in a voice that suggested he didn't care whether he was believed or not.

From what I could see, the stone plinth looked as solid as Snowdon. I didn't argue with them. It would have been no use, and in any case I was gripped by a cold and shivery feeling that made me want to get away from there. I was sure I knew now where the chariot had taken the contessa's body. These men might be part of it, keeping strangers away while others arranged her under those arrogant hooves. If they thought I was a threat to them, there was no chance that my mare could outrun their cobs.

'Where were you going, ma'am?' said the first man. English. His voice sounded hoarse from a cold.

'Windsor.'

'Just on that way.'

He pointed down the Long Walk with his whip. I turned the mare downhill and onto the flat grass between the lines of elms. At first we walked. When I looked back, the three of them were still there, the giant horse on its hill and the two men near the foot of the hill, watching us go. I put the mare into a canter, wishing I were on the arrow-swift sprinter rather than this gentle rocking horse, anything to get away from what I dreaded.

The mare was labouring hard long before we covered the three miles or so to town, so I slowed to a walk. By then, I'd got back some measure of calm. I might be wrong. After all that had happened, it wasn't surprising if I started imagining things. At first, the feeling of normality in the little town under the great walls of the castle helped to convince me that my nerves had got the better of my brain. Shops were open, people going about their business, fashionable carriages jamming the narrow streets. I asked a group of lads if they could direct me to the Royal Mews and they pointed down a side street. A few spectators stood on either side of a pair of closed doors. I waited with them. After a while, the doors were opened from the inside and a carriage drawn by two finely-matched greys came out. The spectators pressed forward.

'Is it them?' a woman said.

The carriage rolled past, the driver on the box and the footman at the back as impassive as waxworks. There was nobody inside.

'Just out for the exercise,' another spectator said, disappointed.

By then the great doors had been closed from the inside. A brass bell knob gleamed on one of the doorposts, but I guessed it was no use pulling it and asking if they'd recently engaged a casual worker named Amos Legge. If he'd succeeded in being taken on, he'd probably be too low in the hierarchy to be known by name, let alone allowed callers.

I sat there on the grey mare and considered. The other spectators were talking amongst themselves, wondering whether it was worth waiting. What they hoped to see, of course, was the happy royal couple. I caught scraps of their conversation.

' . . . out shooting yesterday. Just him, not her.'

'We came to see them last week, when they were supposed to have a military review in the park here, only they postponed it because of the rain. It's tomorrow now.'

'They have a band on the terrace on Sundays. She almost always walks there.'

Some of them decided they were waiting in the wrong place and drifted away. A stubborn few stayed, to have their hopes briefly raised when a two-horse barouche turned into the narrow street. But the only occupant was a stern-faced elderly gentleman whom not even the most hopeful could mistake for young Prince Albert. Somebody inside the doors must have been expecting it, because when the barouche was halfway down the street, they opened as if by magic. The barouche turned into the doorway. Without thinking about it, I pressed my heel into the mare's flank, picked up the rein and followed as if I were meant to be there. The doors closed behind us.

Instantly, grooms and boys appeared to take charge of the barouche. Every buckle on the harness seemed to have its own attendant. Within a minute, the horses were unharnessed and being led into an inner yard and the stern-faced man had disappeared through a doorway. The mare and I followed the carriage horses. Any second, somebody would want to know what a bedraggled young woman on an undistinguished hack was doing in such a well ordered yard, so there was no time to waste.

I rode her into the middle of the yard, stopped by the water trough and called as loudly as I could,

'Amos Legge.' Silence for a moment, then from inside a loose box, a bucket clanked. A man appeared, ducking his head so as not to hit it on the loose box lintel.

'Hello, Miss Lane.'

He didn't sound particularly surprised to see me, but not best pleased either. He was looking less than his usual dapper self, in rough corduroy breeches and a navy blue jacket that strained across his broad shoulders. The bruises had faded to a light lemon colour with streaks of purple.

'Amos, I need to speak to you.'

'You there, what do you think you're doing?'

A man with side-whiskers, red face and a brass-buttoned jacket had appeared from a doorway and was shouting at Amos.

'Talking to the lady,' Amos said.

He wasn't used to being shouted at or called 'you there' and let the man know by his tone that he didn't like it.

'You're supposed to be doing buckets. Get back to it. As for what you think you're doing, madam . . .'

The 'madam' was entirely contemptuous. Amos didn't move a step, simply seemed to grow six inches taller and broader in the shoulders.

'The lady is doing me the kindness to call and ask after my health,' he said, in his broadest Herefordshire accent. 'I'll see her out, so you needn't be bothering yourself.'

He took hold of the grey's rein and led us through the archway into the outer yard, dignified as an ambassador at a foreign court. A couple of lads were standing by the closed doors to the street. At a nod from Amos they jumped forward and pulled them open, surrendering to his natural authority. He kept up his ambassador act, not turning or saying a word to me, until we'd turned the corner and were out of sight of the mews. Once he'd led us into another side street away from the traffic, he stopped and turned round at last.

'What's the trouble, then?' he said.

I was so relieved at finding him that I didn't try to explain and just said what was in my head. 'Did they find a woman's body at the Copper Horse this morning?'

He looked up at me, then nodded. 'Round the town already then, is it? They were trying to keep it quiet.'

'I was riding past it, and there were two men there, keeping people away. I knew they were bringing her here, you see. That is, I didn't know, but . . .' I wasn't making sense, more shocked and tired than I'd realized. I started to dismount and Amos caught me as I slid out of the saddle. Standing there, hand on the mare's shoulder, I told him about the ice cellar, the contessa and the chariot driving westwards.

'I'd guessed they were going to leave her in a public place somewhere, like the other two, only I hadn't guessed it would be outside London. But I knew somehow this morning, even before I met the men. They looked like rangers, but they might have been anybody.'

'What time was it you saw them?' Amos said.

I had to think back. 'It was nearly nine before I left the stables. Say around ten o'clock at the Copper Horse.'

'They'd have been rangers, then. It was earlier than that they found her, just after it got light. Some officers from the barracks had gone riding up there. There's a military review going on in the park tomorrow and they were getting ready for it.'

'How did you hear?'

'The men were talking about it at the Mews. Not outright though, and I wasn't meant to hear. But I knew something was going on – people all buttoned up and shocked-looking, carriages coming in and out. Then they had to get a chariot harnessed up to go to Downing Street sharpish.'

'Who was in it?'

'Somebody from the castle. Didn't know him, only they put two of their fastest horses and one of their best drivers on, so it must have been important.'

'Taking the news to the prime minister?'

'Could be.'

We stared at each other.

'So you knew the lady?' he said.

'She came out riding with me on Bella. How did she die?'

He looked down at the grey's large hooves. 'Throat cut.'

'Where have they taken her?'

He gestured over his shoulder. 'Into the barracks, from what I heard.'

'Why in the world did they take a woman's body into the barracks?'

He shrugged. 'It was the soldiers who found her.'

But I thought he guessed the real answer, as I did. She'd been whisked away from public sight and, more than that, from the workings of the law. The discovery of her body was news that had to be carried to Downing Street by the fastest horses in the royal stables.

A cart was turning into the street where we were standing, the driver making signs that we should get out of the way.

'Need somewhere quieter than this,' Amos said.

He led the mare down the street, through a small gateway and back into the park. Three miles or so in the distance, the horse and rider were still celebrating a triumph on their hilltop. After a first glance, I didn't look at them. Amos found a tree trunk and, in spite of my protests, spread his jacket for me to sit.

'You haven't told me why you're working at the mews,' I said. 'Or can I guess?'

He held the mare's reins while she ate grass and told me the story in his usual won't-be-hurried way. 'I couldn't leave things as they were, not after the way they set on me. If it had been one man, even two men and I'd got the worst of it, then I'd have had to own they'd bettered me and that would have been that. But a whole gang on one man's not fair dealing and I won't stand for it. So I went looking for them, and I thought I knew where it started.'

'Down here, that first weekend you came down to Egham?'

'Yes. That Saturday night, I was in one of the other public houses further along the street, the White Lion. It's a bit of a run-down place and the beer's nowhere near as good as the Red Lion, but a man who had a horse he thought I might be interested in was going to meet me there. So I was sitting there waiting for him, drinking my beer, when the door opens and this gang of men comes in as if they owned the place. Pleased with themselves, they were, already half cut. There were five of them, two foreigners. Two of the ones who weren't foreigners were wearing some sort of uniform I didn't recognize, though I know it now.'

'What?'

'Windsor uniform. What the people from the castle wear. The others were dressed like sporting gentlemen, only they weren't gentleman, more the neither one thing nor the other riff-raff you get hanging round race courses. Any road, they heard me asking the landlord for another beer and one of them, little runt of a man, started trying to imitate the way I talk, only he didn't hit it off right. They never do. So I stood it for a while, then I just went across, picked him up by his collar and the seat of his pants and hung him on a beam.'

'Hung him!'

'Not by the neck. There was this low beam across the room. I just put him over it, quite gentle, stomach down, his legs threshing away on one side and his arms the other, making little peeping noises like a puppy dog. I thought one of his friends would take him down, but they were laughing fit to do themselves a mischief, making fun of him. In the end, I had to put him back on his feet myself. So after that, one of the foreign ones buys me a drink and they all start acting as if we were bosom friends.'

A line of cavalry went by us and away up the Long Walk, helmets and harness buckles glinting even on this sunless day. The rocking horse mare raised her head for a few seconds to watch them, then went back to her grazing. Amos went on with his story.

'By then, I'd got the measure of them and I thought if there was summut dirty going on, they'd be just the types to know about it. So we talk about racing for a while, then I turn the conversation to gentlemen's sporting clubs and of course they know every gambling hell and what have you from one side of London to the other. So then I slip in a word about the devil's chariot and the air changes as if a fox had walked up to a hen run. One of the foreign ones steps in quickly and says they haven't heard about anything like that. Not likely, was it, with everybody in London going on about it? After that, the same man keeps looking at me sideways on, then starts trying to draw me out about who I am and where I come from. I say that's my business. The way the foreigner's looking at me, I'm thinking I'm going to have to have him up over the beam as well, but then the man I'm supposed to be meeting walks in. I tell him we'll have our talk at the Red Lion instead because the company's better, wish them all good evening and go.'

He paused for breath.

'Did they come after you?' I said.

'Not that I noticed, not then any road. But when we got outside, there was this chariot parked, reins hitched round a post, slovenly-like. It was standing near the lamplight from the door, so I had a good look at it. A black laquered dress chariot, hammercloth and wheels black as well. Two dock-tailed dark bay cobs in the shafts, well matched except the near one had a white sock on the off hind where most people wouldn't notice on account of it being on the inside. I knew it must be what some of the gang in the White Lion had arrived in and it was just their style to leave a nice outfit like that without anyone to hold it and no water bucket for the horses. Anyway, I went back to the Red Lion and settled the business with my man. When he'd gone, about an hour later, I strolled back down the street and there was the chariot, still hitched outside. And bother me, nobody had thought even then to bring a bucket of water for those horses and by then they were so desperate to get to the trough they'd got the reins all tangled round and one of them had a leg over the traces and could have broken it. I felt like putting my head inside and yelling for the crew of them to come out and see to it, but it was quicker to do it myself. So I got them sorted, found a couple of buckets and scooped some water out of the trough. They each sucked down two bucketfuls so quick you didn't see it go. Nearly died of thirst while those galumphuses were pouring beer down their throats inside.'

Cruelty to horses was one of the few things that could disturb Amos's calm. But I guessed this wasn't the point of the story and waited. After a while, he went on in his usual tone.

'So I stayed with them a bit, making sure they'd calmed down. The reins and traces were all cut up, where I'd had to take a knife to them to get the horse untangled, but that served them right. Still, from habit, I tidied up as best I could. In the ruckus, the hammer-cloth from the top of the driver's box had slipped a bit. You know there's a space under the box where the driver can keep a few things? Anyroad, there was this horn sticking out of the box.'

'Horn?'

'First sight, I thought it was a hunting horn, so I gave it a tug, thinking I'd blow a good loud "Gone away" on it, to wake the lot inside up to their duties. But I tugged at it and it wouldn't come. By then, the idea had got in my head, so I opened up the box, still holding on to the end of that horn. Only it wasn't a hunting horn at all, just the other kind. And there was a head attached to it.'

The sky and park seemed to swing round us.

'A bull's head,' I said.

Amos nodded, face grave. 'Two of them.'

'So what did you do?'

'First thought was, I'd go in there and have it out with the pack of them. Then it struck me that wasn't so sensible, look.'

'Thank goodness for that.'

'If I could've got them somewhere with proper sporting men about, I could take on any one of them in a fair fight, one after the other if they liked. But there was more to this. So I thought about it a bit, then I took out my knife and put a couple of little nicks in the hoof of the one with the sock on the off hind – nothing to hurt the horse or that anyone would notice, just so I'd know for sure when I saw it again.'

'Clever.'

And yet he looked shamefaced and hesitated before going on. 'Well, maybe what I did after that wasn't so clever.'

I waited. He didn't look at me.

'I suppose I wanted to unsettle them,' he said. 'I couldn't stand them swaggering, thinking they were getting clean away with it.'

'So what did you do?'

'Picked up the bulls' heads and put them inside on the seat of the chariot. Give them something to think about when they went to sit down in the dark.'

'Oh Amos.'

'Waste of breath oh Amosing me. It's done now.'

The cavalry were just a line of glinting helmets in the distance by now, going towards the Copper Horse. I wondered if they knew what had happened there this morning. Probably. It was only a matter of time before all the town heard.

'And were these the same men who attacked you in Hyde Park?' I said.

'Yes. Two of them I recognized the voices, one foreign and one the runt I'd put over the beam. But they'd brought in some others as well, big bruisers.'

'How did they know where to find you?'

'They might have followed me back. Traffic's heavy once you're past Staines, and I was in a hurry so I might not have noticed. Otherwise they might have found out where I worked from the Red Lion. I didn't make a secret of it. You want people to be able to find you in case they've got a good horse to sell, look.'

'They must have wanted to kill you.'

'Very likely, but they found this cock wouldn't let his neck be wrung easy.'

'There were two men asking for you round the livery stables,' I said.

'Thought there would be. That's why I didn't let on to anyone where I was going.'

'So you came down here again to look for men and the horse with the nick in its hoof?' I said.

'That's right. From the uniforms and they way they were acting, I guessed they were something to do with over there.' He jerked his shoulder back towards the castle.

'So that's why you took work at the Royal Mews?'

He nodded.

'And did you find it?'

I knew the answer before it came, because of the angry and baffled air about him.

'Not hide or hair of them. And the horses don't come from there either. One thing about being on bucket duty, you get a good look at their legs. No dark bay dock-tailed cob with that particular shape of white stocking on its off hind, let alone nicks in its hoof.'

Which settled it. Amos might, just possibly, be wrong about a man, but never a horse.

'It was a chariot they carried the contessa's body in,' I said. 'I wish I'd thought to look at the horses' legs.'

'You shouldn't have done what you did.' The words burst out of Amos so violently that the placid mare raised her head, looking startled. 'Going down in that pit, knowing what you knew, that was asking for trouble.'

'I didn't know. I was guessing. What else did you expect me to do?'

'You should have waited for me.'

I could have pointed out that I didn't know where he was or when he was likely to be back, but he was so hurt and angry I decided against it.

'When did the news that the woman's body had been found start spreading round the mews?' I said.

'Early, soon after they found her.'

'Did people seem shocked?'

'Hard to tell, seeing I wasn't supposed to know about it.' He thought for a while, staring down at the ground, then said slowly, 'I'd say they were shocked, but not surprised, if you know what I mean. Some of them go up and down from London and they knew about the other girl, the one they found by the statue.'

'So people were connecting them at once?'

'Yes. I heard somebody saying something about coming close to home, then he went quiet when he saw me. Then there's the date, of course.'

'Date?'

'Last day of October today. Halloween.'

I hadn't thought of that. It was all part of the pattern, the bodies discovered in ways likely to cause superstitious fear, the way they were kept until the moment for them to take their place in some pattern I still didn't understand.

'If somebody wanted it to be connected with Halloween, wouldn't he have waited until tonight?' I said.

Amos shrugged and I could see why. The question shouldn't have mattered, but it was part of something larger nagging at my mind.

'Did anybody say anything about the police being called?' I said.

'No.'

I guessed that in royal parks, the police would rank some way below the soldiers and even the rangers.

'So what do we do now?' Amos said.

'I must go back to London.'

'Why?'

'I think – I hope – I may make sense of this.'

A faint hope, but all there was.

'We'll go together, then,' Amos said.

'But Tabby's still at the Red Lion. Anyway, what about her?' I looked at the rocking horse mare.

Amos considered. 'There's a London stage leaves in half an hour,' he said. 'If I put you on that you'll be safe enough, as long as you go straight home.'

'I will.'

What happened after that was something I wasn't ready to discuss, even with Amos. Just as well he didn't know about the fire.

'When will you be back?' he said.

'Tomorrow, I hope. Where will you be? I don't suppose you'll be welcome at the mews after walking out on them.'

'I've taken no money from them, so I don't owe them anything. We'll get you on the stage, then I'll take the mare back and see the lass is all right.'

At an inn yard, he found a man he knew and organized a place for me in the London stage. Once he'd seen me into my seat, he gave a wave of his hand and swung himself up onto the mare's back. A lesser man might have hesitated at riding across Windsor Great Park side-saddle, but anything with horses came naturally to Amos. He waved to me as the stage coach wheeled out of the yard. I'd have liked to take him with me, but back in London I'd be in places where even Amos's writ did not run.

COURT CIRCULAR

Prince Albert of Saxe Coburg, Sir H. Seymour, and the Hon. C. A. Murray, enjoyed the sport of shooting this morning. Prince Ernest was too unwell to leave the Castle.

Prince Ernest is officially unwell.

The Times 31 October 1839.

TWENTY

Two letters were waiting for me back at Abel Yard, one from Paris and the other from Ireland. I took them upstairs unopened and, without even taking off my bedraggled bonnet and cape, found Mrs Martley's cherished Little Vicky scrapbook in its place on the shelf. The cover was grimed with soot, but the cuttings from newspapers and magazines inside as good as new. Luckily, she'd recorded every detail of the visit of the two Saxe Coburg princes, every entry in the court circular pasted in proper order. Her Majesty and Their Highnesses rode and dined and listened to the band, rode and walked on the terrace and dined again through what looked like three weeks of regal tedium.

I read through it twice over in the failing light, then lit the lamp and made notes. It fitted all too well. I went upstairs and through the connecting door into my own room, washed and changed into clean petticoat and stockings and a woollen dress that had escaped the worst of the smoke and walked to the Talbots' house in Belgrave Square. Several times in the walk, shrieking urchins jumped out at me with turnip lanterns on poles demanding pennies: a waste of their time because I was beyond being scared by Halloween tricks. Carriage wheels grinding behind me didn't even make me turn my head. I knew the devil's chariot wasn't here in Belgravia.

Beatrice Talbot came downstairs as soon as she heard my voice at the door. Her butler had been looking down his nose at my undistinguished appearance in the lamplight and asking if I were expected, in a voice that doubted it. She stepped past him and took my hand.

'Liberty, my dear. Is something wrong?'

'Yes. No . . . that is, there's something I'd like you to do for me.'

She was already changed for dinner, in rose velvet and ivory lace. Clearly, company were expected. Without hesitation, she led me through to the drawing room. The children were there, the younger ones sleepy-eyed, a board game spread out on the carpet. I'd interrupted the precious hour with them before guests arrived.

'I'm sorry, I'll come back after dinner,' I said. 'I don't suppose you could do it before tomorrow in any case, only . . .'

Something seemed to have gone wrong with the connection between my brain and my tongue. The concern on Beattie's face told me that I was looking strange as well. She undid my cape, threw it over a chair and made me sit down on a sofa. Sinking against the cushions felt like falling through clouds, down and down.

'My dear, you're ill. I'm going to send out for the doctor.'

'No. Please no.'

'What, then?'

'I need to speak to the young man who was at the opera with us, Mr Calloway. Early tomorrow, if possible, before he goes in to the office.'

She looked startled, fingertips flying to her lips to check a gasp. I could read what she was thinking. Poor Liberty, struck unexpectedly with love, struggling against it, surrendering at last and rushing to her friends' house in the dark like a madwoman, pleading for a meeting with the object of her passion. I laughed, a jagged sound that brought an alarmed look from the children.

'It's not what you're thinking, I promise you. But I do need to speak to him urgently on a matter of business.'

'Your . . . your profession?' It had always puzzled Beattie, though she tried loyally to understand.

'Yes. I have a problem and I hope Mr Calloway may be able to advise me.'

'Then I shall get George to send him round a note. He's in the dining room, seeing the wine's properly decanted. Keep an eye on the children for me.'

I slumped on the sofa. The children watched me and whispered among themselves. They knew me from many music lessons, but not in this mood. I was sorry, in a cloudy way. I'd have played with them if I could. Beatrice was back in a few minutes.

'George is writing a note now and he'll tell the boy he's to wait for a reply. Now, will you join us for dinner?'

That was downright heroic. No other hostess in London would have countenanced a semi-articulate scarecrow.

'Thank you, but no. I must get back.'

'You'll do nothing of the kind. The guest room's made up, and if you prefer not to sit down with us I shall have a tray sent up to you.'

I hardly tried to argue. Beatrice clinched the matter by saying that George's note would ask Mr Calloway to come here as soon as possible in the morning. Within minutes I was upstairs in one of their beautifully furnished bedrooms. Soon afterwards a lad appeared carrying a folding table, followed by a maid with a tureen of soup, cutlets, a glass of wine. I ate hungrily and finished the wine to the last drop. The lad took the table away and the maid returned, bringing warm water, soap, soft towels, a night-dress. I got into bed and dozed, to the sound in the background of guests arriving and being greeted downstairs. At some time in the evening, Beatrice knocked gently on the door and put her head round.

'George has had an answer already. Mr Calloway will be calling at half past eight in the morning.'

I slept, deeply and dreamlessly for half the night at least, then watched the light come back and went over everything again in my head. I knew I was right. The question was whether anybody would believe me.

Mr Calloway arrived five minutes before half-past eight, bright-eyed, neatly dressed and looking as if an inexplicable summons by an acquaintance, at an hour that scarcely existed by the normal standards of the diplomatic corps, were an invitation he'd desired above all things. In spite of that, my heart sank on seeing his cheerful face as he was shown into the drawing room. He looked so much younger and newly fledged than when I'd seen him in evening dress that I doubted if he'd be able to do what I needed. George Talbot had decided to sit in on our meeting, possibly for the sake of my reputation but more probably from curiosity. I could hardly blame him in either case. Once coffee had been offered and accepted, I launched into business.

'I need to speak to somebody in the Foreign Office about a

serious matter concerning relations between Britain and Saxe Coburg. It's so delicate that I must ask you to forgive me for not going into more details, even to you. It's so urgent that the meeting should take place in the next few hours. I don't suppose my name will mean anything to your office. All I can say is that Mr and Mrs Talbot can assure them that I am not mad. If Mr Disraeli were back in the country, I believe he would vouch for me. Apart from that, I can only rely on your judgement.'

Mr Calloway heard me out, with very little change of expression. His shapely eyebrows lifted just a fraction at the reference to Disraeli. He was more influential than most backbench MPs, but so unpredictable that the Foreign Office would probably sniff sulphur around him. Still, it was the best I could do. For a second or two after I'd finished speaking, Mr Calloway considered. One of the Talbot children shouted in the corridor outside and was shushed by her nursemaid.

'Is there anything else at all you can tell me?' Mr Calloway said. The voice and the question were both reasonable.

'One thing. Whoever you speak to, please tell him that it concerns the maze and the Minotaur. If I'm right, he'll understand.'

'That's all?'

'Yes, I'm afraid that's all.'

'Very well, I'll try to do what you ask. Where may we find you?'

'Miss Lane will be staying with us,' George Talbot said.

'Thank you. I'm truly grateful for what you've done, but I must go home,' I said to him. Then, to Mr Calloway: 'I live at Abel Yard, off Adam's Mews. I shall wait there until somebody comes to me, but please ask them to make it soon.'

He nodded, looking more serious than when he'd arrived. When George came back from showing him out, I promised to let him know what was happening as soon as I could.

'You'll say goodbye to Beattie at least?'

She was in the kitchen, discussing the day's menu with their cook. When she saw me, she ran to me and took my hand.

'George says you won't stay.'

'I wish I could.'

With all my heart. Their kind, well-ordered life had never

looked more enticing. Beatrice wanted to call the carriage out to take me home, but I said the walk across the park would clear my head.

Under a grey sky, I walked to Grosvenor Square and knocked on the contessa's door. After a long wait, it was answered by a maid I hadn't seen before, in a rusty black dress with her hair tied up in a scarf.

'They've all gone away. The landlord's sent me in to clean.'

I asked if I might go up to look. She wasn't sure, but two shillings settled the question. She showed me upstairs into what had been the contessa's salon. Bare chairs and tables awaited the next tenant in a room blank as a stubble field. The contessa's soft rainbow of shawls and cushions, the servants in their blue and silver liveries, had vanished as if the backcloth of a panto-mime had been rolled away. I thought that the people responsible for it must have spent thousands on the contessa's household alone, probably multiplied ten times over by other parts of the same network. There'd have been the simple bribes to hack journalists like Codling, more complicated ones to gentlemen and ladies primed to whisper gossip at society dinner tables. Considering the stakes, tens of thousands were probably small change to them. I'd been small change too.

Back at Abel Yard, I found Mr Colley's idle son-in-law and gave him a shilling to stand at the bottom of my staircase and shout up if any gentleman arrived. The parlour still smelled of soot and felt cold and empty. I wondered whether to make up the fire to boil a kettle for tea, but couldn't summon the energy. After a while I remembered the bottle of port wine that Mrs Martley kept in the cupboard because she said it was good for her blood and drank two glasses of it straight off. That made me feel well enough to open my two letters. The cover of the thinner one, from Paris, was addressed in Disraeli's handwriting.

Dear Miss Lane,

A propos of the gentleman you mention, I cannot recall meeting anybody of that description in Stuttgart, in fact I am positively sure I did not. It is one of the perils of being a man in the public eye that half the rogues in the world will claim acquaintanceship – a category to which I suspect your Mr Clyde may belong. We shall return to London shortly, when I look forward to hearing if my suspicions were correct.

Yours in haste, Benjamin Disraeli.

It was only what I'd expected, but I was angry with the man for lingering so long on the Continent and being out of London when I needed him. I hesitated before opening the other, much fatter letter from Robert Carmichael. I wanted so much to hear his kind, clever voice – even if only in my imagination as I read. But so much had happened in the short time he'd been away that I was scared it would make a gulf between us. I walked up and down the room, listening all the time for a call from the yard to let me know I had a visitor. After a while I sat down, opened the packet and started reading.

My dear Liberty,

How I wish you were here with me. With six days to go to the wedding, and the castle filling up, cousins two or three times removed are being stowed even in the semi-ruinous parts of it. The womenfolk are entirely involved with the forthcoming festivities. The sisters (it is three by the way) are all to be bridesmaids and much of our evenings here after dinner are devoted to the quizzing and teasing of them as to which one is to be next married. All of the bachelors are considered fair game. As a man mostly unknown, I am considered as a suitable stalking horse for a young lady with somebody else in her sights. As a sample:

Sister Two: Is not my sister Alice a beauty?

Self: (knowing the rules by now) To be sure, you are a family of beauties.

Sister Two: But some more beautiful than others?

Sister Three: (hitting Sister Two's arm with fan) Vanny, you're fishing. Stop it.

Sister Two: (hand fluttering to the sleeve of my jacket and away again) I am not, so. Besides, it's Sarah he really likes, isn't it? Confess it now.

And all the while, the men they want to notice them watch, listen and wonder whether to quarrel with me.

While I was reading, I'd even forgotten to listen for a shout from the yard. I opened the window and looked down. Nobody. The next pages in Robert's packet were written in a darker ink with a better pen nib.

> If the truth be told, we men are feeling a little bored. We fish in the lake. We ride over the tussocky moorland around the castle on some remarkably good horses. We shoot snipe in the marshy area around the lake. Or some of us do. The fact is, I have disgraced myself. You know the snipe? What a ridiculous bird, with its round body, long bill and complacent look as it roots in the mud for its food. This morning, there I was with my boots up to the ankles in mud, my borrowed gun ready, and up go the snipe, crying chicka chicka chick. I'm about to squeeze the trigger and other men's guns are popping all round me, when the contrast strikes me of all our powder and gunnery against such a silly bird and I laugh out loud. A quotation from Shakespeare comes into my head: 'O! It is excellent/To have a giant's strength, but it is tyrannous/To use it like a giant.' The surprising thing is, it comes to me in your voice, my dear, although I'm sure you never in reality spoke it to me. So I put my gun down and the snipe that should have fallen to it fly free.
>
> 'So you're not much of a shot then,' says Rosa's brother Michael to me.
>
> He can't make out what manner of man I am. I'd help him, if I could, but I'm not sure myself.

I was unreasonably pleased that my voice might have spared the snipe, but sorry that this hint of self-doubt had crept back into his mind. I'd been right not to let him tie himself down to an impulsive decision he might have regretted. I went all the way down the stairs to check that there was nobody waiting, then back upstairs to my letter.

> Three days later.
> Oh my dear, I wish even more that you were here so you could tell me I'm a fool. This evening, after dinner:
> Alice: Sarah's going to lose a guinea over you.

Self: I'm very sorry for it. Was she backing me at bringing home the biggest bag of snipe?

Alice: Michael's bet her a guinea you won't ride in the race tomorrow.

Self: What race would that be?

Alice: The gentlemen are having a race to Kibble End. They're going to draw for horses.

Self: So why should Sarah lose her guinea?

Alice: You mean you'll ride?

Self: Indeed I'll ride.

So two idiocies in one. First, I committed myself to a race over a couple of miles of rough country against a dozen or so Irish centaurs. Second, I confirmed Alice's belief that I was romantically attracted to sister Sarah, to the extent that I was prepared to risk my neck to save her a slight injury to the purse.

I sat with the page unturned, annoyed with myself for being so annoyed. Silly girls, with nothing to fill their time but gossip and matchmaking. I imagined them, with their beautiful dark hair and laughing eyes. I turned the page and read on.

The horse I drew was one Bucephalus, stable name Boozy. When his name came out of the punch bowl I was congratulated by the other gentlemen on having a possible winner with 'a mouth like a granite tombstone, but won't stop this side of Kilkenny.' They didn't add that he was getting on for eighteen hands high, a fact I found out for myself in the stable yard in the grey drizzle next morning. Our starting line-up was far from regular and Boozy, spinning like a top from excitement, was facing the wrong way when the order was given. He whirled round and caught up with the rest in two or three giant strides, over the first fence before I saw it coming then across ploughland with the air so full of flying clods that I don't suppose any of us could see where we were going. After the first two or three fences, something struck me – that Boozy and I were up with the leaders and I was enjoying this. Of course, I'd ridden over fences before, but not banks. Have you jumped a bank? If so, you know that amazing feeling when your horse touches down on the top then flies off the other side as if he'd abandoned the earth entirely.

Yes, I have. I know it. I'm aching to be there riding with you. I'm laughing too, out loud with a release from tension, as if I really were galloping beside you, with clods of ploughland flying round us.

'Visitors.'

The call of the son-in-law, coming up from the yard. Then a knock on the door and Mr Calloway's voice.

'Miss Lane? May we come up please?'

We. So he'd brought somebody with him as I'd asked, the person of importance. And that person's introduction to me, as he came into the yard, would have been the sound of a woman's laughter through the open window. He'd take me for a lunatic, if the thought weren't in his mind already. I looked out on Calloway's upturned face and the top of the hat of a man standing beside him.

'Come up,' I said. 'The door's unlatched.'

Mr Calloway came into the room first. 'Miss Lane, may I introduce . . .'

The other man had taken off his hat and was looking at me, his face giving nothing away. I needn't have worried about the impression my laughter had made on him because this wasn't our first encounter after all. Mr Calloway's senior colleague from the Foreign Office had visited my house before to try to bribe or bully me and I strongly suspected he'd had a hand in trying to burn it down. I was looking at Stone Man.

TWENTY-ONE

Calloway probably expected us to shake hands. He repeated the introduction, which was just as well because, in my surprise, I hadn't caught the name.

'May I introduce Sir Francis Downton.'

'Thank you, Calloway. We have met before. You may leave us now,' Stone Man said.

Calloway showed a spark of rebellion in insisting on civil manners. 'Will you excuse me then, Miss Lane?'

'Not yet,' I said. 'Can you confirm that Sir Francis is known to you and is from the Foreign Office?'

The other man made an impatient noise. Calloway flushed but stood his ground.

'Yes. Sir Francis holds a senior position in the foreign secretary's private office.'

So, Lord Palmerston's right-hand man. From the expression on Stone Man's face, he thought Calloway was giving me too much information.

'Thank you,' I said to Calloway. 'If you need to go, of course you must. But I'm grateful to you.'

Calloway walked to the door, then turned. 'I shall wait for you downstairs, Miss Lane.'

Which was downright heroic and I guessed he was waving away any chance of standing high in Sir Francis' favour.

'Sit down, if you like,' I said to Sir Francis. 'I'd apologize for the smell of soot, except it's probably your fault.'

'My fault!' He seemed genuinely astonished. 'How am I to blame for the deficiencies of your chimney sweep?'

'Somebody tried to burn this building down soon after your last visit.'

He sat down heavily in a chair by the cold fireplace. He looked more strained than I'd seen him five days ago, with a nervous twitch of the left eyebrow.

'I assure you, it had nothing to do with me. I tried to warn you that you were playing a dangerous game.'

'You accused me of spreading scandalous rumours,' I said. 'I didn't know what you meant then, but I do now. That's why I asked Mr Calloway to introduce me to somebody senior from the Foreign Office. He knows nothing about any of this. He's simply an acquaintance doing me a favour.'

I took the chair on the opposite side of the fireplace. Sir Francis sat, buttoned up in his overcoat, staring at me. Then he sighed as if he'd come to an unhappy decision.

'Miss Lane, I assume you've summoned me because you want to tell me something you believe you've discovered.'

'Yes.'

'Then I'll spare you the trouble of telling me the story. You have evidence, or believe you have, that a certain very distinguished visitor to this country is involved in a series of unlawful incidents.'

'That Prince Ernest of Saxe Coburg and members of his household are responsible for at least three murders of young women and possibly more?' I said.

He'd been expecting that, and didn't blink. 'But that's hardly a great discovery on your part is it, Miss Lane, seeing that several grubby scandal sheets have been hinting at it for a week or more.'

'But they only have part of the story. Do they know the girl found by the Achilles was a housemaid from Limehouse? Do they know about the ice barges? Do they know that the devil's chariot has been spotted outside the White Lion at Egham, by Windsor Great Park?'

The outside edge of his left eyebrow went into uncontrollable spasm. All this was new to him.

'Another thing the scandal sheets don't know yet,' I said. 'The woman found dead by the Copper Horse yesterday morning claimed to be an intimate acquaintance of Prince Ernest.'

'Who are you working for?' He'd asked the same question on his first visit, trying to bully and bribe. Now he was simply weary, so I told him.

'He said his name was Mr Clyde – a false name of course. I'm not working for him any more. He had the contessa killed, probably the others as well.'

I told Sir Francis about Mr Clyde's approach to me, to his story of the contessa's mission, and what followed.

'I honestly believed he was trying to prevent a scandal,' I said. 'Either he or the contessa knew about the prince's plans in advance. She knew he'd be making a private visit that night in Kensington when I gave him her letter.'

His look made me hesitate.

'Or are you going to tell me that it wasn't really Prince Ernest I saw?'

'Yes, it was the prince.'

Some kind of barrier had been crossed. He didn't trust me, but he wasn't insulting me any more. I was glad about that because I'd decided to tell him most of what I knew or guessed.

'I think this business of delivering a letter to him was so that I could see the prince and identify him as being in London that day,' I said. 'The man who called himself Clyde kept insisting on secrecy, but I was really meant to tell people all about it.'

A nod from Sir Francis.

'I suppose I was credulous,' I said. 'I believed that Clyde was trying to prevent a scandal. But it was quite the reverse. He wanted to create one. What he thought he'd found in me was a woman who had contacts in society, whose services might be hired. Perhaps he'd found out enough about me to know I had friends in the press as well.'

Another nod.

'Whoever's employing Clyde, it's somebody who doesn't wish the Saxe Coburgs well,' I said. 'They're determined to prevent that engagement becoming official. They'd do anything, spend anything to stop that.'

'Yes.'

He'd committed himself. I pressed for more.

'The contessa – did she really know Prince Ernest?'

'She was not a contessa.'

'But she knew him?'

'Yes.'

'In the way she implied?'

'They had met.'

'More than met?'

'Yes.'

'So who was she?'

'An actress, from a theatre in Dresden. Part German, part Italian. The prince's circle in Dresden did associate with theatre people and such. It's quite possible she had convinced herself that her association with His Highness was of a more lasting nature than was likely in reality.'

'In other words, she was just another discarded mistress and the man who called himself Mr Clyde was making use of her,' I said. He'd made use of me as well, and I'd admired his fine, sad eyes and pitied him. But I didn't intend to admit that to the man from the Foreign Office.

Sir Francis stirred in his chair. 'Do you know where the man who calls himself Clyde is now?'

'No. If the Foreign Office knew so much, why weren't you having him followed?'

No answer but an annoyed look.

'Does that mean you were, and you've lost him?'

'I'm not at liberty to discuss operations with you.'

I assumed that meant yes.

'So there were at least two strands to this plot to discredit the Saxe Coburgs,' I said. 'One was to have Prince Ernest embarrassed by a discarded mistress. Then there was another that was much more serious. At some point, they came together. Perhaps their contessa wasn't proving as useful as they'd hoped. So they disposed of her.'

The false contessa, with her injured ankle, was handicapped in making public scenes. In that case, simply use her for other purposes.

'People had to know that Prince Ernest was in London the night before the bodies were discovered by the Monument and the Apollo statue,' I said. 'My seeing him was only a small part of that. They'll have made sure there are plenty of others who notice the coincidence. It's probably only a matter of time before hints start appearing in papers or being whispered around the clubs.'

'They've started already. This Copper Horse business can't be kept quiet.' He said it in a half tone, sounding weary.

'You mean not like Janet Priest or Peggy Brown?' I said.

He looked puzzled. 'Peggy Brown?'

'That was the real name of the girl at the Achilles statue,' I said. 'At least, the nearest thing she ever had to a real name. She was the housemaid from Limehouse, though I don't suppose you care one way or the other about that.'

Even though he wasn't to blame for her death, he lived in a world where the likes of Janet Priest and Peggy Brown were of little account.

'You talked about ice barges,' he said.

'You didn't know then, you and your men? Peggy Brown from Limehouse and Janet Priest from the City Road died because they lived near the route of the canal barges that bring ice into London. Mr Clyde and his friends had them killed and stored them at the ice house in Cumberland Market till they were needed, as if they were no more than the carcasses of animals.'

'How did you find that out?' He was sitting forward in his chair, surprised into near humanity.

'Because Mr Clyde or the men controlling him were too clever. Two clients came to me at much the same time: Mr Clyde with his worries about the contessa and another man looking for his fiancée. At first, they seemed unconnected. They might even have stayed unconnected, except Mr Clyde saw an opportunity to weave two strands of the plot together. Even when the body found by the Achilles statue matched the description of the missing fiancée, I thought at first it might be a coincidence. But it was too much of a coincidence. Somebody wanted the world to know about that body, whatever steps the authorities might take to hide it. The decision to adjourn the inquest on the Achilles body must have been taken at a high level. I'm sure you knew about it.'

At least he didn't waste time in denying it.

'I dare say the government were in quite a panic by then,' I said. 'The public were talking about the devil's chariot and somebody was dropping hints that it involved Prince Ernest's household. The press were hinting at it – the foreign voices, the uniforms. It was only a matter of time before the rumours came out openly, and meanwhile the queen was becoming more and more attached to Prince Ernest's brother.'

'The whole thing is a nightmare.' He spoke with heavy simplicity, the statue sagging into a human being aware of his age. 'Try to imagine it from the other side, Miss Lane. We hear that these rumours are circulating. We know very well that they are untrue, but any attempt to deny them officially would make some people more ready to believe them. Worse than that, any convincing attempt at denial would involve a grave insult to interests that must not under any circumstances be insulted. Do you understand what I'm saying?'

'Diplomatic interests?'

A nod. 'It was obvious, from the expense and complexity of the deception, that more than individual interests were involved,' he said.

'So are we talking about Austria or Russia?' I said.

His shoulders went back and he glared at me. 'Did you expect me to answer that?'

'Probably not. But we can say that these are people who'd do anything to prevent a marriage between the Saxe Coburg family and the Queen of England?'

His silence, and the slightest nod of the head said that yes, we could. I waited. The next thing he said was entirely unexpected.

'You know, I have a daughter about your age.'

How in the world was I supposed to interpret that? As a rebuke to me for meddling in things that shouldn't concern young women? As a remark to himself, trying to place me and decide how much to trust me? Perhaps that, because he seemed to come to a decision and started talking again.

'It's hardly surprising if other countries are nervous. Look at the facts: the Saxe Coburgs' uncle Leopold is already king of the Belgians, has said a polite no thank-you to the offer of the Greek throne because he was waiting for bigger fish, and ever since his nephews were born he's been scheming how best to place them. He's planning that Ernest shall marry King Louis Philippe's daughter, which takes care of France but naturally England's the great prize. That needed luck as well as scheming. We have a situation in which the wealth and influence of the greatest empire in the world will come into the Saxe Coburg web because of a twenty-year-old girl's liking for a pair of blue eyes.'

And Peggy and Janet, who'd probably never given a thought to foreign politics in their young lives, had been killed by them.

'You sound as if you're justifying whoever's been plotting this,' I said.

'Of course I'm not. I'm only trying to make you understand what you've become involved in.'

I was about to say that it wasn't my fault I'd become involved, then I thought it probably was. In any case, I did not need to defend myself to this man.

'I understand some things better than the Foreign Office,' I said. 'You had no idea about the ice barge or the poor girls' bodies being kept in store, had you?' I opened the table drawer and took out the notes I'd made. 'These are the dates that matter.' I picked up one of Mrs Martley's knitting needles and used the blunt end of it as a pointer to guide him down my list.

10 October Prince Ernest and Prince Albert arrive in London.
10 October Ice shipment arrives in Limehouse basin, for transfer
by canal.
10 October Janet Priest goes missing from her home near the
City Road canal basin.
10 October 'Dora Tilbury' disappears from her home in Essex.

Sir Francis wrinkled his forehead.

'That was pure fiction,' I explained to him. 'There never was a Dora Tilbury. She was no more than a device by the plotters to recruit me as one of their rumour-spreaders. The man who pretended to be her fiancé said she'd vanished on the 10th, possibly because that was a significant date for them. So-called Dora Tilbury was Peggy Brown, who'd been seized and killed that day in Limehouse. I dare say she was loaded straight onto the ice barge, then they picked up Janet Priest's body further up the canal.'

I pointed out the next dates on my list.

16 October Prince Ernest and Prince Albert visit the Gloucesters
in London, Park Lane.
17 October Janet Priest is found dead by the Monument.

'I suppose everybody in court circles will have known about that visit well in advance?' I said.

'Oh yes. These things are not done on impulse.'

'And some of them will have known that Prince Ernest stayed on in London that evening for a private visit when most of the others went back to Windsor?'

Sir Francis jumped in his chair. 'How did you know that?'

'I guessed. But it's true, isn't it?

'That visit was entirely innocent,' he said. 'His Highness simply wished to have dinner with some friends in London without the formality of a royal occasion.' He sounded rattled now, as if wondering what else I intended to throw at him.

'As it happens, I believe you,' I said. 'But you'd have to be somebody close to court to know about that.'

Another nod, then he tried to recover ground by changing the subject.

'I still don't understand why these people consulted you about a fictitious girl.'

'They could hardly consult me about the real Peggy. Limehouse was too close to the centre of the plot. Besides, my clients tend to come from the professional and upper classes.'

'So the man who called himself Mr Clyde was just in your line?'

A shrewd question. Did he guess that the man had interested me for his own sake? I tried not to let anything show on my face.

'Yes, as I was just in his line. It was all very well spreading rumours among journalists on the penny papers. They needed them to be talked about at dinner tables, not just in the servants' quarters, and they believed that I might be useful. As I said, I don't suppose I was the only one.'

'Far from it. You might be surprised how far the fire's been spreading.'

I waited, hoping he'd give more details. None.

'Once Mr Clyde had met me, I think he decided that I could be more useful than most,' I said. (Or had he guessed my interest and exploited it? Quite possibly.) 'So he used me as one of his key witnesses. He arranged things so that I saw for myself that Prince Ernest was making a private visit to Kensington on the evening of Tuesday 22nd October.'

'Again, an entirely innocent one.'

'And again, one known only to those close to court circles. But Mr Clyde knew about it. He made sure I was there to set eyes on the prince and hoped I'd remember that when the so-called Dora Tilbury's body was discovered on the other side of the park early the next morning. With that ring on her finger.'

'Ah yes, that ring,' he said.

Again, the silence drew out. This man hadn't risen to eminence in the Foreign Office by being chatty.

'The woman I knew as the contessa had a bull's head ring,' I said.

He saw he'd have to respond before he got anything else from me and spoke reluctantly. 'At Dresden, Prince Ernest belonged to a club of young military officers and the more aristocratic sort of student. They called themselves the Cretans. It was a drinking club, a little rowdy perhaps but no worse than others of its kind. Certainly not of the appalling and perverted nature that the authors of this plot would have people believe.'

'And yet somebody among them knew enough about the prince's background to have heard about the Cretans?'

'Evidently.'

'So why did the contessa have the ring?' I said.

'It's not impossible that she had it from the prince. Or perhaps she didn't, and you were intended to notice it.'

'But she was angry when I saw it.'

'Or had been told to seem angry.'

It was like fighting with mist. I went back to my list of dates. At least I could be certain of those.

'So you see, two visits to London by Prince Ernest, and two bodies wearing that ring found early the next morning. Who's to say that Prince Ernest didn't stay in London and meet some of his bloodthirsty old friends from the Cretan Club?'

'I've told you that the Cretan Club was only . . . oh, I see.'

'Yes. It's not a matter of the facts, is it? It's what people could be made to believe. When I began to see the connections, I was more than halfway to believing it myself. It was the ice that made me see what was happening.'

'I still don't understand entirely.' For once, he sounded almost humble.

'They had to have the girls' bodies available for when they were needed,' I said. 'Clearly, the plotters couldn't influence the prince's programme, but they were close enough to court circles to know about it some time in advance. To exploit that, they needed to keep the victims on ice, quite literally. If there really had been a Cretan Club picking up girls in the devil's chariot and killing them, there'd be no reason for storing them. The logic was that the murderers wanted the bodies to be discovered on particular dates.'

'Of yes, we'd got that far,' he said.

'But not the rest?'

'No.'

Now he'd admitted that, I could afford to be generous.

'It wasn't entirely my own work. I have a friend who was trying to track the devil's chariot for his own reasons. He nearly got killed.'

I was scared for Amos, still at Windsor and following his clue of the nicked hoof. I wanted to be back with him.

'So now they've shifted the game to Windsor,' I said. 'As you say, the body at the Copper Horse can't be kept quiet. The word was already going round town when I left there yesterday.'

He nodded. This time it came close to being an admission of defeat. 'I take it that you haven't seen the latest court circular,' he said.

'No.'

'Prince Ernest has been taken ill. He will not be leaving the castle for some days.'

I stared at him. 'Because you're worried that there may be some public demonstration against him?'

'Possibly that. But until we know where so-called Mr Clyde is and what they're planning next, we can't take any risks. They know that time's running out for them so they'll want to bring things to a head.'

'Why is time running out?'

'Because if they are to have a hope of preventing this engagement, they have to do it before it's publicly announced.'

I thought of Mrs Martley and the guinea pigs.

'But it's as good as announced anyway. The whole country seems to know about it.'

'A royal engagement's not official until the queen announces it to her privy councillors. Until that happens, it's no more than a rumour that can be denied.'

'So you're implying that if the rumours about Prince Ernest are fixed in the public mind, even if they're not true, his brother's engagement might be called off?' I said.

'I'm sure the queen would know her duty.' A pause, then in more human tones, almost pleading: 'And you're sure you don't know where the man Clyde has gone?'

'No, but in your place I'd ask some questions around the White Lion at Egham.'

He stood up. 'I hope you'll understand, Miss Lane, that you're to say nothing to anybody about this?'

'Why not? I'd have thought you wanted the true story known. Wouldn't that be the simplest way?'

He actually shuddered, as if the idea of a simple way offended him. 'Because you wouldn't be believed. If what you've told me is to be of any use, then we must use it in our own way.'

'Because you'll be believed and I won't be?'

Another nod. The human, weary man I'd glimpsed was turning back to stone.

'So what am I to do in the meantime?' I said.

'I understand that you have an invitation to stay with Mr and Mrs Talbot. I'm sure that would be best.'

'Until when?'

'Until you hear from me. Until then, I'll wish you good day.'

I led the way downstairs. Mr Calloway was waiting by the yard gate.

'You'll see Miss Lane safely back to her friends,' Sir Francis said to him.

'Thank you, but I shall stay here,' I said.

He gave a glance at Calloway, as if to ask him if he couldn't control this woman. Calloway risked another downward step on the ladder of promotion by giving me a droll sideways look.

'Is there anything at all I can do for you, Miss Lane?'

'Thank you, no.'

'I hope we may meet again.'

They walked together through the gateway. Calloway raised his hat to me as they went. Sir Francis didn't. When they'd gone, I went upstairs, collected some sovereigns from my reserve and put on my cloak and bonnet. A coach back to Egham was leaving at three o'clock from Water Street, off Fleet Street. If I hurried and found a cab, I could just catch it. All I wanted now was to get to Amos.

TWENTY-TWO

I got down from the stage in the yard of the Red Lion just after five o'clock in the rainy dusk. The landlord greeted me in the doorway.

'Your maid's upstairs in your room. We've kept the fire going.'

I asked him to have tea sent up. Tabby was hunched in an armchair by the fire.

'Thought you were never coming.'

She seemed unusually depressed in spirits. My bonnet and

cloak were wet because the only place I'd been able to get on
the coach at the last minute was an outside one. I spread them
on a chair by the fire.

'Didn't Mr Legge tell you I was going to London?'

'Oh, he told me all right. Didn't say when you'd be back,
though.'

'That was because he didn't know. Where is he?'

'Dunno.'

'He must have said.'

'He was in too much of a hurry. He came yesterday and said
I was to stay here and wait for you. Anything I wanted, I was
to send down for and he'd settle up when he got back.'

'Back from where?'

'He didn't say.'

She was in a resentful mood and I felt like shaking her.

'So what *did* he say?'

'Only that I was to be sure not to go out at night. Wasn't likely
I would, was it, on Halloween with the devils and ghosts about?
They say there's a giant in the park with horns and blue lightning
all round him. He comes out of a hollow tree and if you see him,
you're dead.'

I remembered Windsor Park was supposed to have its own
ghost in the shape of Herne the Hunter.

'Then there was the devil's chariot, up and down the park all
night, just like in London,' Tabby said.

'How do you know that if you didn't go out?'

'The girl that cleans the stairs told me. She knows someone
who saw it, great flaming torches on the front of it, smelling of
brimstone.'

'It's an ordinary chariot, Tabby. You know that. We rode on
the back of it.'

'Yes, with a dead body inside it. The girl said it was probably
carrying away the soul of the woman who got murdered yesterday.'

Sir Francis and his diplomat friends could spirit the contessa
away into the barracks and silence the coroner, but gossip was
stronger than all of them. And the chariot had been out and about
in its diabolical role to make sure that gossip stayed at fever
pitch. It looked as if the diplomatic illness of Prince Ernest would
have to continue for some time.

The tea arrived. We drank it.

'The landlord says there's been a man round looking for you,' Tabby said. 'Dunn his name was.'

'That's the man from the livery stables. What did he want?'

'Dunno. Didn't see him myself.'

I was sure that Amos would have returned the grey mare to the stables at the first opportunity. This must be something else. I stood up and started putting on my damp cloak and bonnet.

'I'll be back in about an hour.'

'I'm coming with you,' Tabby said. 'I've had enough being left on my own here.'

I helped her lace her boots because her injured wrist was still painful and we walked together to the stables. It was entirely dark now, still raining, and we slipped and slid in cart ruts. The stables seemed all in darkness, until we spotted a line of light under a door and the smell of frying bacon drifted out on the wet air. I knocked on the door and Jack Dunn's voice shouted to us to come in. He blinked and stood up when he saw us, mug of tea in one hand, hunk of bread in another.

'Come in. I've been looking out for you all day.'

We walked into a snug cabin, not much larger than a horse's loose box. He had a fire going in the grate, a frying pan on the trivet over it. A chipped brown teapot stood on the hearth.

'Sit yourself down.'

There was only one chair, chintz upholstered, that had seen better days but it looked so warm and comfortable that I collapsed into it. Tabby hunkered down by the fire.

'Did Mr Legge bring your mare back yesterday?' I said.

'Oh yes, he brought her back all right.'

'Then?'

He took a gulp of tea, nodded towards the pot and gave me a questioning look. Tea and bad news went together.

'No thank you. What happened after that?'

'He bought a horse,' Dunn said.

'Yesterday?'

Horse trading was second nature to Amos, but surely he'd had other things to think about.

'The bay, the one you saw. Cash down and didn't even try to cheapen the asking price.'

Dunn sounded shocked by that and so was I. Haggling over a horse was only common politeness.

'The race horse. Did he take it away with him?'

'Rode it away just like that.'

'Did he say where he was going?'

'Not a word.'

'And you haven't seen them since?'

I expected a 'no' but he took another gulp of tea. 'Saw the two of them this morning. Early, just after it got light. I was riding across the park to Windsor to pick up some bits and buckles. I was halfway down the Long Walk when I saw this file of cavalry soldiers, ten or twelve of them, going the same direction as me at a slow trot. Nothing peculiar about that of itself, you usually see cavalry out somewhere. Only there was something a bit out of the way about these. They were keeping on the far side of a row of trees and they had a chariot with them.'

I must have jumped at the word, because he looked at me and nodded.

'Not usual for soldiers, is it? And they were going on the grass, not on the carriage drive, so the wheels were bumping and whoever was inside must have been getting a rough ride. Two dock-tailed cobs drawing it, an officer and four soldiers riding in front, the rest at the back. In between the chariot and the back lot of soldiers, there he was.'

'Amos Legge?'

He nodded. 'Mr Legge, on the bay he'd bought off me. The bay looked pretty well done-in, plastered with mud up the legs and on the belly, though still enough spirit left to be in a tearing bad temper. The cavalry horses were crowding him behind and he was rolling his eyes and showing his teeth, trying to whirl round and get at them. Still, Mr Legge was controlling him, even though he looked nearly tired enough to drop out of the saddle. And he didn't look any more pleased with the company of the cavalry men than they looked with him.'

'Did you speak to him?'

'Yes. I cantered up and fell in alongside him. He cheered up a bit when he saw who it was. "I was right," he said to me. "He's no stayer, still he did the business in the end." I was just asking him what they'd been doing when the officer rode back to us and said, "Don't talk to this man. He's under arrest."'

I nearly fell out of the chair.

'Amos under arrest. Why?'

'That was what I asked him. The officer didn't like it. He was jigging up and down in the saddle, trying to interrupt. He was just out of the egg, pink face and whiskers like peach fluff, so we didn't pay much account to him. Mr Legge nodded towards the chariot and said, "I found it for them, and the three fellows I've got trussed up inside it, only they don't seem very grateful like." So I said, what did he mean, found it? He said it was the devil's chariot they'd all been looking for and these gentlemen, meaning the cavalry, had got the wrong end of the stick and thought he was part of it all, but he supposed they'd get it fettled when they got to Windsor.'

'Did he tell you anything else?'

'He didn't have much chance. The officer was fair rattled at being made to look a fool in front of his men, so he tried to barge his horse between Mr Legge and me. Mr Legge slackened the rein just enough to give the bay the chance to writhe its neck round and nip the officer's horse on the shoulder. It squealed and reared up and the officer's helmet slipped down over his eyes. Mr Legge looked at me and grinned and I think for a minute it was in his mind to make a run for it. Only he knew the bay was too tuckered up for that. So he said to me to get word to Miss Lane at the Red Lion, but tell her not to worry. By then, the officer had got them sorted out and off they went.'

My head was sunk in my hands, the fire glowing red between my fingers. Anger with Amos for going off on his own turned quickly to panic. In spite of what I'd told him, he still hadn't realized the depths and dangers of what was happening. When I raised my head, Tabby was looking at me, her expression asking what we should do.

'Do you think they've taken him to the barracks, or even into the castle?' I said.

'Even if they have, not much you could do about it till morning.'

He was right. Hammering on barrack or castle doors in the dark would only get me arrested too. I tried to think.

'What time does the London mail coach go through Egham?'

With luck, I might get to London in the early hours. I'd call on poor Calloway's good services again, talk to Sir Francis Downton and make him give the order to release Amos. Dunn found a tattered timetable and started consulting it.

'Don't know if they run differently on Fridays.'

Of course. This was a Friday night, so even if I could catch a mail coach, I'd arrive in London on Saturday morning. The merest child in the gutter knew that nobody of importance stayed in London over the weekend. The Foreign Secretary would be close to the centre of the crisis at Windsor and it was more than likely that his right-hand man (or more sinister left-hand man) Downton was there with him. I asked Dunn if he'd be kind enough to bring the mare round to the Red Lion first thing in the morning.

'Not London, then?'

'No, Windsor.'

Dunn wanted to see us back to the Red Lion, but I felt guilty at interrupting his supper and knew Tabby would want to talk. We started trudging back together through the mud.

'What's Mr Legge done, then?'

'Gone galloping after the devil and found him.'

He'd been determined to hunt them down and guessed that they'd be out and active on Halloween of all nights. That was why he'd needed a fast horse. I guessed that he'd waited in Windsor Park for the appearance of the chariot, then followed it back to its home. Not the White Lion this time. He'd scared them away from there. Then he'd found the chariot and some of its crew and dealt with it in the only way he knew – the direct way. I tried to explain this to Tabby.

'So what was he doing with it when the soldiers arrested him?' she said.

'Driving it to Windsor to hand over to the police, I suppose. Or even coming to show it to us at the Red Lion.'

'They'll have to let him go. Won't they?'

The last two words were heavy with Tabby's instinctive distrust of authority.

'I hope so.' But I didn't feel much more optimistic myself.

We ate supper in our room, beef stew. Once the maid had taken the plates away, we took off our wet clothes and put them to dry in front of the fire. The night was long, choked with the smell of damp wool. By daylight we were waiting in the stable yard of the inn. Dunn arrived soon afterwards on a cob, leading the mare. He offered to escort us across the park, but I said there was no need. We went at a walk, Tabby riding pillion. Our combined weight was no great burden for the mare. The day was dull, mist rising slowly. When we went past the hill of the Copper Horse, the great statue was no more than a darker blur against the greyness. No rangers there this morning, but even at this early hour a little group of people was strolling up the path towards it. I imagined the ladylike shudders, the walking canes pointing at stains that might be blood. Mr Clyde and his employers were still winning. At this rate, Prince Ernest's diplomatic ill-health would confine him to castles forever and Little Vicky would have to transfer her affections from his brother to some other pair of bright royal eyes.

I cursed the endless honeymoon tour of Mr Disraeli, who knew everybody. If Amos had simply been arrested by the police, I'd have made straight for a barrister and demanded a writ of *habeas corpus*. My radical father had thought highly of *habeas corpus* as one of the cornerstones of an Englishman's freedom, so my brother and I had learned about it practically along with our nursery rhymes. Soldiers were different. Their loyalty was to the sovereign, not the law. When we reached the town, I resisted the temptation to ride straight to the barracks and hammer on the doors. Instead, I found an inn in a side street that was willing to stable the mare, then paid a shilling for the use of a corner of a table in the parlour, along with notepaper, a scratchy pen and an inkwell. I wrote two notes, one to Sir Francis Downton saying I needed to see him urgently. I would wait outside the main gate of the castle, every hour on the hour, from midday until four o'clock. Even less hopefully, I addressed another to the foreign secretary, Lord Palmerston.

My Lord,
Excuse this informal approach to you, but I have important information regarding the affair of the chariot. Sir Francis Downton is aware of my involvement.

And, since I had no better plan, I added the line about waiting at the castle gate. Of course, I never expected the most important politician in the country to come down and meet me, but perhaps he might send some minion. I walked to the castle gate with my two letters and joined a queue. Tabby had offered to come with me, but given her habit of glaring at any figure of authority, I thought I was better without her. I gave her a shilling and told her to see what gossip she could pick up in the town.

There were about a dozen of us, standing on the cobbles by the gate lodge in the drizzle. At the head of the line, a one-legged soldier on crutches, a line of medals pinned to his faded greatcoat. After him, a plump woman with a grizzling child clinging to her skirts. Then a thin man with an enormous wolfhound on a lead and a Union Jack kerchief round its shaggy neck. They were all clutching letters. When it came to my turn, I handed in my two notes and tried to impress on the porter that they were genuinely urgent and important.

'Don't you worry, miss. They all get read.'

But he said it in just the same patient tone he'd used to the petitioners in front of me. My hopes, not high in the first place, dwindled to nothing. Still, I did what I'd promised in the notes and came back to the gate lodge at midday, one o'clock, two o'clock, three o'clock. In between times I walked in the park or around the streets, listening to what people were saying. They dropped their voices when they were talking about the devil's chariot or the woman's body found at the Copper Horse, but I caught snatches.

'. . . throat ripped right out, like a wild beast . . .'

'. . . don't want us to know, but my cousin's lad works at the castle and he says . . .'

And once, louder than the rest: 'Be glad when they've gone, the whole German pack of them.'

At four o'clock, still nothing apart from another queue of petitioners in the drizzle. I waited for half an hour, but knew that if my notes had reached their targets, there would have been some response by now. Back at the inn, Tabby was waiting in the stableyard, looking as tired and cast down as I felt.

'Have you got him out?'

I believe she'd expected me to storm the castle or barracks and drag Amos out by force. I shook my head.

'So what are we going to do then?' she said.

'We'll have to stay here tonight. There's no point in going back to Egham.'

It infuriated me that the people who might help us were probably lounging in armchairs or gossiping over billiard tables no more than a few hundred yards away inside the castle walls, but as unreachable as if in a different country. I went inside and negotiated with a surly landlord for accommodation for Tabby, myself and the mare. Although it was only a back street inn and none too clean, Windsor prices were high. I had to pay most of our remaining store of money for a small back room, a scuttle of coals for the fire and a bread and cheese supper. The bread was stale and the cheese tasted as if mice had tried and rejected it. When we'd finished all we could eat, we put the plates on the landing, stirred up the reluctant fire and I asked Tabby about her day. As usual, she had every detail in her head.

'I went to the barracks first. There were guards outside but they wouldn't talk to nobody. I found some boys who kept hanging about the gates there, and asked if they'd seen a carriage and prisoners going in. They hadn't.'

'This was the main gate, I suppose?'

She nodded. 'That's right. I thought there must be a back gate and there was. It's where deliveries go in, bread and hay and so on. There was a guard on that gate too and he wasn't talking either. So I just stood there until a big brewer's dray came along with barrels on it and I thought if I could hang on the back of it, I might get in without the guard noticing.'

'For pity's sake, Tabby, haven't you had enough of hanging on the back of things?'

'Anyway, it didn't work. The guard let out a holler and made a grab at my skirt. If I'd had two good hands, I might have hung on anyway, but as it was I came off.'

'Have you hurt yourself again?'

'Nah. Nothing to bother about. Anyway, that's not the point. When I was on the ground before they got the gates closed, I got a look inside and there was a gentleman's chariot on its own in the yard, no horses, and a soldier standing guard over it. So

I thought that was the chariot Mr Legge got hold of and they'd got him in there somewhere as well.'

She was right, I was sure. Sir Francis and his men would keep the devil's chariot and its crew under guard, along with Amos as a suspected part of the crew. How much would he tell them about what he and I knew? Very little, I guessed. He'd see that information as our property and would want to discuss it with me first. So he'd just shut his mouth, jut his jaw and keep quiet. His questioners might as well bluster at the castle walls. Tabby went on with her story.

'The guard got it into his head that I was the sweetheart of one of the soldiers and that was why I wanted to get in. Not likely, I said. If I had a sweetheart it wouldn't be a stupid boiled lobster like them. So he got mad and told me to go away or he'd call the sergeant. I said he could call the bleeding Duke of Wellington for all I cared. But I knew there was no chance now of getting in that way, so I stood across the road for a bit just to annoy him, then I went.'

I thought that was the end of the story, but there was more to come.

'I got a bit lost on the way back from the barracks,' she said. 'It's all over the place, this town.'

As if the town were to blame, for not being London.

'I worried you might be back here, wondering where I'd got to. I was in this back street when I saw a gentleman coming out of a doorway, so I thought I'd go up and ask him the way back to the castle, then I could start from there.'

From her face, this was more than a simple matter of being lost.

'He had his back to me, so I said "Excuse me, sir", being polite. Then he turned round, and I knew him.'

'Who?'

'You know the morning after the fire, you gave me a note to take round to the maid at Grosvenor Street. When the maid came to the door, I noticed there was a gentleman standing behind her in the passageway. He took your note off her as soon as I put it into her hand. It was the same man as I saw this afternoon.'

I didn't bother asking if she were sure. Tabby's eye for a face was as infallible as her memory.

'Tall, early forties, dark hair and eyes?'

'Yes.'

Mr Clyde. It had been a shock when she said it, but when I thought about it, where would he be but at Windsor? He'd lost a piece on his chessboard with the capture of the chariot, but the game wasn't over. More than that, with rumours running wild and Prince Ernest holed up in the castle, he could still win.

'Did he recognize you?'

'Don't know. He looked angry when he turned round, but I don't think that was because of me. I think he was angry anyway.'

Perhaps because he'd just had news that the chariot had been captured, from whatever accomplices he'd been visiting in the back street.

'Did he say anything?'

'No. He just pointed and walked off quick. I was waiting for him to get round the corner then I was going to follow him and see where he went, only these two men started following him as well.'

'What two men?'

'Ordinary looking men. They came out of an alleyway opposite the house he'd come out of, then they waited until he'd turned the corner and went walking after him.'

'Definitely following him?'

'Yes. I think they were trying to look as if they weren't, only they weren't much good at it.'

Sir Francis Downton's men, I guessed. I hoped that Mr Clyde would have had too much on his mind to recognize Tabby as my messenger after one brief glimpse of her in London, but we couldn't count on it.

'Could you take me to the house you saw him coming out of?'

'Now?'

'Not now, no.'

'Tomorrow morning?'

'No. We've got something else to do tomorrow morning.'

'About getting Mr Legge set free?'

'Yes.'

'How?'

So I told her. It seemed quite a sensible scheme to her. That made me even more worried.

TWENTY-THREE

My time at the castle entrance had not been entirely wasted. From the gossip of sightseers and my fellow petitioners, I'd learned so much about the royal routine that Mrs Martley would have been proud of me. The habits of Little Vicky, her household and her visitors were as predictable as a clockwork toy. On Sunday mornings the Queen, visitors and courtiers walked together from the royal apartments to service in the chapel. The sightseers agreed that this was one of the best times to see the queen and her all-but-official fiancé at close quarters because St George's chapel is inside the first castle courtyard, near the gate where'd I'd waited. Anybody could walk into the courtyard. There'd be guards present, standing to attention, but this would be no more than a formality because nobody anticipated an attack on the queen.

All eyes would be on the young couple, with nobody much interested in the crowd of courtiers and assembled dignitaries walking at a respectful distance behind them. Nobody except Tabby and me. She'd been disappointed at first when she found I didn't intend to fling myself bodily on Her Majesty and demand Amos's immediate release, but soon took the point that the man we needed was Sir Francis Downton. I was depending on my hunch that he'd be at Windsor, watching developments. The plan was to pick him out in the procession and, if necessary, follow him all the way in the chapel. All I needed was a word or two with him and I hoped I could rely on a gentleman's horror of anything like a public fuss to make him listen.

'What if he's not there?' Tabby said, as we walked towards the castle on a grey Sunday morning.

'Then it will have to be Lord Palmerston himself.'

The Foreign Secretary would, for a certainty, be in attendance at Windsor. I didn't look forward to confronting the terror of the Foreign Office, but if all else failed, that's what I'd have to do. At least I shouldn't have to waste much time in explanations. I was sure that he knew more than most people about what was going on. More than likely, that procession walking piously to church would include an ambassador from the country that had started all this, and Palmerston would be very well aware of it. I was so sick of their diplomatic games that anger saved me from feeling nervous. Almost.

Fewer spectators than I expected were waiting in the courtyard in front of the chapel, maybe thirty or so. Perhaps other people were waiting until the afternoon, when the queen and her party walked on the terrace and a military band played. After a while, a party of guardsmen marched up and lined the route from the royal apartments to the chapel. From inside, an organ started playing. Then a murmur ran through the small crowd. The party had appeared from the royal apartments and was walking towards the chapel. They came at quite a brisk pace. A small woman in a grey cloak and bonnet walked in front, a tall man beside her. After that, a gap of a few yards and a group of women, probably the ladies-in-waiting. Then the rest of the party, mostly gentlemen, twenty or so of them.

'That's him,' somebody near me said. 'Second from the left.'

He was a young man, good looking but pale of face, walking rather stiffly as if not quite at ease in an occasion that was part public, part domestic. A pleased murmur went through the little crowd. Any rumours about the behaviour of elder brother Ernest didn't seem to have reflected on Prince Albert so far, but then this crowd were loyal people. The queen passed close to us, so close that we could almost have reached out and touched her. Somebody murmured, 'God bless her.' She reached the porch, where a clergyman, the dean probably, was waiting to welcome her. She said something to him then turned back to the party behind her. For a moment, she smiled directly at Albert, an open-hearted, mischievous smile like any girl to her lover. He caught the smile and his pale face and serious expression were suddenly transformed in a beam of pride and happiness. I registered to myself, Well, perhaps a love match after all. But I hadn't much attention to spare as I was too busy looking at the gentlemen now crossing the courtyard.

No sign of Sir Francis in the sober ranks of black coats, top hats and fixed expressions of important men about to make a routine courtesy call on their deity. One man stood out for his air of scarcely contained impatience as if he'd have liked to be walking faster and get the affair over. He was tall, with bushy sideburns, hair waving out from under his hat, his jaw and forehead like squared-off timbers. I recognized him from dozens of political cartoons as Lord Palmerston and got ready to make a move.

'Look.'

Tabby was tugging at my cloak. I tried to brush her off, angry at being distracted, but she was insistent, trying to get me to look at something behind us. I turned and there, no more than half a dozen steps away, was the man I knew as Mr Clyde. I'm sure he didn't see Tabby or me. His eyes were on somebody in the ranks of important men. Then somebody jostled him from behind and he turned quickly and walked away, across the courtyard, heading for the street outside. The man who'd jostled him walked closely beside him, with a second man falling in behind.

Tabby was saying something. '. . . ones I saw yesterday.'

Then, before I could say anything, she was off, trailing them. I was furious with her, because by then Lord Palmerston and the men round him had gone past us towards the chapel entrance. I started to go after them and found myself blocked by one of the soldiers.

'Sorry, miss, royal party only.'

I think he took me for no more than an overenthusiastic spectator, but the damage was done. I was wasting my breath, trying to tell him that I had to speak to the Foreign Secretary, when the shot sounded.

It came from outside the castle walls, but not far away. The queen had disappeared inside the chapel by then and probably wouldn't have heard it. A few of the gentlemen, Palmerston included, turned their heads then walked on. Some of them must have recognized it as a gunshot and possibly concluded that it was a soldier accidentally discharging a weapon. At any event, not near enough to be any threat to the royal party. The gentlemen took off their top hats and went into the chapel. By then, I was pushing my way back through the spectators who'd bunched behind the soldier and me. Nobody else seemed worried, but then nobody else knew that Tabby had just walked out of the courtyard following a murderer. Once I was clear of the small crowd I started to run, stumbling on cobbles, out of the gateway and into the street. Signs of panic here, wide-eyed people asking each other what was happening, a group of spectators forming round something a few dozen yards from the gate. They were all looking down.

A man in shirtsleeves was kneeling on the pavement. Another man seemed to be trying to persuade the spectators to go back. As I came up to them he was saying, '. . . can't do anything in any case.' A figure lay flat on the ground, head and chest covered with a jacket that probably belonged to the man in shirtsleeves. The swathed head and chest were all I could see. I had to punch one of the spectators on the back to make him turn round.

'Who is it? What's happened?'

He goggled at me for long seconds, resenting having to turn. 'Fellow's gone and shot himself, that's what.'

'Fellow? You're sure it's a man?'

For answer, he stood fractionally aside, revealing that the person was wearing black trousers and shoes. Neat, narrow shoes in highly polished leather. An elegant gentleman's shoes. Not far away from them, a pistol on its side as if it had been dropped. From behind, a hand came round my wrist, trying to pull me away. I resisted, thinking it was some officious do-gooder.

'Come on, before they do it to us.' Tabby's voice. I let her take me to the other side of the street.

'It's the same man, isn't it?' I said. 'Mr Clyde?'

She nodded, looking at me sideways on, as if surprised by something in my voice.

'And he shot himself?'

The sound she made was a growl of disbelief.

'He didn't?'

'Nah. It was one of the men following him. The one that's kneeling down there.'

She nodded towards the man in shirtsleeves. As we watched, a mixed party of soldiers and civilians came out of the castle gate. There were about a dozen of them and they made for the group round the dead man. Two soldiers were carrying a rolled-up stretcher. One of the civilians was giving the orders. They made the crowd stand back while the two soldiers unrolled the stretcher and lifted the body onto it, face still covered. A hand flopped down, blood dripping from the limp fingers. Another order, then the hand was tucked tidily inside the jacket and the stretcher lifted. As the party went towards the castle gateway, the man in the shirtsleeves and the other man who'd been trying to keep back the crowd fell in behind them.

'Are those two the ones you saw following him?' I asked Tabby.

'That's right.'

The stretcher party reached the gateway and turned inside. All except the man in the shirtsleeves and his colleague. They simply walked away and round the corner, like any other Sunday morning strollers. The sound of the organ and voices raised in the first hymn drifted out of the chapel.

'They're just letting them get away,' I said.

I couldn't have gone after the two men even if I'd wanted to. My feet felt as if they were welded to the pavement.

'Do you want me to follow them?' Tabby said, sounding unconcerned.

'For heaven's sake, no. But did you really see one of them shoot him?'

She nodded. 'I was right behind them. I knew you'd want to know where they were going. They didn't see me because they were too set on going after him and he was too set on running away from them.'

'Running?'

'When they came out of the castle, he was just walking fast but they were walking faster and catching up with him. Then he turned round and saw them and started running. Only he didn't get far. They started running too and one of them shouted something at him. Then they got up close, the one who'd shouted grabbed him by the shoulder and pulled him round and the other one shot him right in the heart. They were so close the gun must have been nearly touching him.'

'Didn't anybody else see?'

'Nobody to see. Everybody was inside, watching the queen and the others. He might of, only I think he's probably a waxwork.'

She gave a nod towards the unblinking sentry at the castle gate. I thought he might as well have been.

'What happened then?'

'The one who'd done the shooting got down on his knees, so when people started coming up to see what was happening, it looked as if he was trying to help. I suppose he must have told them the man had killed himself. I didn't get close enough to hear. I thought I'd just wait until you got here.'

Silence. Even without looking, I could feel her staring at me. 'You all right?'

She sounded both concerned and puzzled. I nodded.

'You didn't . . . *like* him did you?'

Something worse than puzzlement there, panic almost. I couldn't find words to deal with it. Did I like a man who'd killed innocent girls, or had them killed, on the instructions of some unknown paymaster? No. Did I like a man who'd used me so ruthlessly? No. But a part of my mind that was still refusing to catch up with things clung to the thought of a sad and civilized gentleman who'd walked lightly, enjoyed good music and been gallantly in love with his beautiful contessa. He'd never existed and I was in the first rank of fools – the fools who fool themselves. Even if I could have said it, why burden Tabby with that?

'No,' I said.

She sighed with relief. 'He was a bad'un, wasn't he?' Then, inevitably: 'So what do we do about Mr Legge?'

I dragged my feet into motion and we went towards the castle gate. With anybody but Tabby, the fact that she was sole witness to a murder would have complicated things even more. But I knew without thinking about it that she was no more likely to describe what she'd seen to any person in authority than the castle sentry to jump out of his box and dance a jig on the cobbles. We walked past him, under the archway that led to the courtyard. In half an hour or so the royal party would leave the chapel and walk back to their own part of the castle. There were still a few people waiting in the courtyard to see them. This time, I'd talk to Lord Palmerston even if I had to throw myself in his path. It never came to that. Tabby and I had only taken a few steps under the arch when a man appeared out of the shadows. Or not appeared, exactly. It was as if he'd always been there, growing out of the stonework like a statue in a niche. Stone man himself. Sir Francis Downton.

'Good morning, Miss Lane. I've got your note. This may be a convenient time to talk.'

He didn't wait for a response. A door opened behind him and we were inside the castle.

TWENTY-FOUR

Sir Francis led the way along a corridor to a small room with a bare table and four or five upright chairs. The walls were plain white distemper, the only decoration a framed engraving of some naval battle. The room had a damp smell, as if not often used.

'Please sit down, Miss Lane.'

He ignored Tabby, but when I sat down, so did she. He remained standing, but ill at ease as if the surroundings were as strange to him as to us.

'Were they your assassins?' I said.

The twitch of his mouth might have been meant for a smile. 'You are determined to think badly of us, aren't you? We don't use assassins.'

'Don't use them or don't call them by that name?'

'Don't use them under any name. Those men were nothing to do with us.'

'But you knew about them?'

He sighed and sat down heavily. The outer corner of his left eyebrow was twitching. He pressed his fingers to the twitch to make it stop. His eyes, meeting mine, showed an instant of distress that anything should be out of his control.

'Yes, we knew about them.'

'They were foreign.'

The announcement came flatly from Tabby. If the table had spoken, Sir Francis couldn't have looked more surprised.

'How do you know that?' I said.

'I told you one of them shouted something before they shot the man. It was something foreign.'

'What did it sound like?' I said.

Tabby made a series of guttural barks like a terrier with laryngitis. I'd been relying too much on her powers of mimicry. It didn't resemble any language I knew. I could see from Sir

Francis's face that it didn't mean anything to him either. He looked relieved about that.

'Tom said the men that tried to burn us down were foreign too,' Tabby said, not at all put out by being centre stage. 'I suppose they were the same ones.'

'I see your . . . er . . . friend doesn't think quite so badly of us as you do,' Sir Francis said to me. 'I told you we had nothing to do with your fire. Do you believe me?'

'About the fire or the two men?'

'Both.'

'About the fire, I'll believe you. But if those two men weren't working for you, why did they shoot him?' I said.

'Because he'd failed.'

Sir Francis' words fell like drops of water in a cave. I waited.

'You will remember that we spoke in London on Friday, Miss Lane. You told me certain things of which we had not been aware.'

'About the deaths of Janet Priest and Peggy Brown.'

His nod acknowledged their names. We'd achieved that at least. 'Yes. That evening, back here at Windsor, Her Majesty entertained a large number of people to dinner, including several ambassadors. It was arranged that I should be sitting next to a certain gentleman from one of the embassies. Naturally we talked, as one does, about this gentleman's impressions of London.'

Tabby gave me a look from under lowered brows, asking what all this was about. I signed to her not to interrupt, now that Stone Man had decided to talk.

'My neighbour was properly impressed by our parks, Hyde Park, Regent's Park and so on. Naturally, I agreed with him that Regent's Park is a delightful place.'

I began to see. His fingers were clamped to his eyebrow again. I suspected that he'd had to struggle hard to stop it twitching during that civilized conversation with the gentleman from a foreign embassy.

'So many places near it of interest too,' he said. 'Could he believe, for instance, that just to the side of the park was a deep pit containing thousands of tons of ice, a regular little Arctic in the heart of London? So convenient to be able to bring ice so close to where it was needed.'

I was leaning forward in my chair now. I couldn't help it. 'And how did he react?'

'He entirely agreed with me. So very convenient. He must mention it to their own ministry of works when he next returned to his home country.'

'Was that all? Surely he must have understood,' I said.

He smiled. 'Of course he understood. For the rest of the dinner we talked about other things, but when we moved to the drawing room for coffee I noticed that my neighbour and several of his colleagues were absent. An almost unprecedented display of bad manners in diplomatic circles. They returned later, after what I'm sure was a council of war in somebody's bedroom. The ambassador did not look pleased. They knew they'd lost the game.'

'They'd lost their chariot too,' I said.

'Indeed. But that wasn't the decisive blow in itself. What mattered was that we had knowledge of their whole operation, and they knew it.'

'Knowledge we'd given you,' I said.

A slight shift in the angle of his head was the nearest he came to a nod of agreement.

'So what happens now?' I said.

'Nothing. The object is achieved. The attempt to destroy Prince Ernest's reputation is back where it belongs, in the fictions of hack journalists and various disreputables. You'll remember what Virgil says about rumour? *Adquirit eundo*: she gains strength by moving. Conversely, when rumour stops moving, she dies.'

He was flattering me with Latin, trying to draw me into his world. I didn't care for the reminder that, to the Romans, rumour was female.

'So all we have to do is stop talking about it?' I said.

A deeper inclination of the head.

'And what will happen to the people responsible?'

'One of them is dead, as you saw. Several of the fellows who operated the chariot are in custody.'

'Yes, and the men who planned it all are dining with the queen.'

The surge of anger I felt came from guilt. On Friday evening, Clyde's employers had discovered that the whole mechanism of their plot was known to the Foreign Office, because of what I'd told them. Thirty-six hours later, he'd paid the price of failure.

'I didn't make the world, you know,' Sir Francis said. 'Are we to break off diplomatic relations, risk war even?'

'The man who called himself Clyde knew what was going to happen,' I said. 'Those men were trailing him from Saturday onwards, waiting for their chance. I think he was watching that walk to church this morning, knowing that the person who'd planned the whole thing was there with the rest of the party. He was going to appeal to him directly for sanctuary, but the two men with the gun headed him off.'

Clyde been waiting for his chance, much as I'd been waiting. But the ambassadors had paced on with the rest of the important gentlemen, while Clyde died outside the walls. I was sure of that now.

Silence inside the room. The sound of an organ voluntary came faintly from the chapel.

'Making it public wouldn't bring those young women back to life,' Sir Francis said.

It was as near as he'd come so far to a direct appeal for continued silence.

'If you're hoping to get any kind of promise from me, you'll have to release Amos Legge first,' I said.

At least he didn't pretend not to know who Amos was. 'Your friend seems to have intervened in a somewhat impulsive fashion.'

'Amos Legge's anything but impulsive. He's the only one who's done anything useful and you've got him locked up in the barracks.'

'If he's innocent, I'm sure the processes of the law—'

'Why should he be subject to the processes of the law when nobody else is? He was nothing to do with the chariot, apart from carrying out a citizen's arrest single-handed. You should be thanking him. And incidentally, you owe him the price of a race horse.'

He looked surprised at my anger. 'Very well, I'll see it's attended to. But I'm sure an intelligent woman like you will take the point that—'

'I'm not discussing anything else until I see Amos a free man.'

Tabby clapped her hands. In the small room it sounded like a series of shots and Sir Francis flinched. He looked from me to her and back again.

'She means it,' Tabby said.

'Excuse me. If you'll be good enough to wait here.' He left the room abruptly.

'Well, are they going to cut off our heads or what?' Tabby said.

'Goodness knows.' I felt weary, past caring.

'Are they keeping us prisoner here?'

'We have to wait here in any case to make sure he brings Mr Legge.'

We waited. At some point the doors of the chapel must have opened because the organ music surged louder. Boots stamped on the cobbles as soldiers came to attention. The queen and her guests were going back to their routine Sunday, the afternoon walk on the terrace and the military band playing airs from Donizetti. Soon after the last strains of the chapel organ had died away, Sir Francis was back, looking harassed.

'Instructions are being given to free Mr Legge.'

'And bring him here?' I said.

'And bring him here.'

I expected him to leave us on our own again, but he sat down.

'Since we last met in London, I've been hearing more about you, Miss Lane.'

Impossible to tell from his expression whether those things had been bad or good. He was waiting for me to ask but I wasn't going to give him that satisfaction.

'I gather it's not the first time you've been able to do a service to Her Majesty.'

'I suppose you're thinking of what happened two years ago,' I said. 'I wasn't intending to do her a service that time, nor this time either.' It sounded ungracious, but I'd no intention of posing as a champion for Little Vicky.

'No. As you made very clear to me, you were working for a client. An unusual line of business, for a young woman.' He smiled. A more human smile this time, but tentative, as if not sure of his ground. I remembered he'd said he had a daughter about my age.

'I have a living to earn,' I said.

'You don't aspire to what most young ladies want?'

So I'd become a young lady now.

'What's that?'

'Marriage. A household of your own. A family.'

While Tabby and I had sat there waiting, my mind had gone to

Robert and how I could explain all this to him. I wondered what he was doing. Having lost track of anything that was happening outside immediate events, I couldn't even remember if the wedding in Ireland would have taken place yet. My face must have given something away, because Sir Francis was apologetic.

'I'm sorry. I'm trespassing.'

Trespassing on a sadness, his voice said. Well, he was right about that. All this had been such a blow to my confidence in my own judgement that I couldn't see a clear way ahead. Was it fair to inflict on Robert, with his own problems, a woman who could look down on Clyde's body, know what he'd done and still feel sad? Probably not.

'If you decide to persist in your . . . er, profession we may be able to offer you work from time to time,' Sir Francis said.

'For the Foreign Office?'

No answer. I guessed that the first rule was not naming names.

'So will you give me your word not to talk about what's happened?'

I'd thought about that too.

'There are people who will have to know something. Mr and Mrs Talbot for instance.'

A nod. They were approved, discreet. Also, there was the promise I'd made to Janet Priest's sister. I couldn't and needn't tell her everything, but at least she could know that the man who'd planned her sister's killing was dead. No need to say anything about that to Sir Francis.

'But you won't tell your journalist friends?'

How Tom would love it. And surely something was owed to Jimmy Cuffs.

'Wouldn't that serve your purpose?' I said. 'The best way of clearing Prince Ernest's name would be to expose the whole thing to everybody.'

He couldn't suppress a shudder. 'I think not.'

Because that would mean telling the world what another sovereign power had done to try to prevent a certain wedding. Bad diplomacy.

'I see. You'd rather keep it to use for a little quiet diplomatic blackmail next time you're negotiating a treaty.'

No response.

'So which was it?' I said. 'Austria or Russia?'

No response, but then I hadn't expected one.

Two or three sets of heavy steps sounded in the passage outside, then a familiar voice. 'If you're taking me to call on the queen, you might have given me time to change my boots and breeches.'

Amos, sounding as good humoured as on a summer morning in the stable yard. The door opened and he was in the room, towering over Sir Francis. When he saw Tabby and me he came to such a sudden halt that the officer behind cannoned into him.

'Don't tell me they've gone and arrested you two as well.'

Sir Francis made a sign to the escorting officer. He left, closing the door behind him.

'I don't think we're arrested,' I said. 'And you're not any more.' I glanced towards Sir Francis. He nodded.

'This is Sir Francis Downton,' I said. 'He wants to thank you for what you've done and apologize for locking you up.'

Sir Francis shot me a look that said that wasn't what he'd intended at all. But Amos was beaming at him, holding out his hand and his goodwill was too much for the forces of diplomacy. Sir Francis got to his feet, took Amos's hand and said he was sure they were all very much obliged to him. He didn't apologize, but that might have been too much to expect.

'So we can all go home?' Amos said.

Sir Francis looked at me, still angling for that promise of silence.

'Yes,' I said. 'We can all go home.'

Amos stood back to let Tabby and me through the door first. I turned at the door.

'So you'll be sending Mr Legge the money he had to pay for the race horse?' I said.

Amos started saying it didn't matter. I interrupted him. 'How much was he?'

Amos bent his head, shamefaced. 'Thirty guineas.' Then, apologetically to Sir Francis: 'That was a good five guineas too much, look, but you know what they say: "Needs must when the devil drives."'

'Needs must,' Sir Francis agreed.

Tabby, Amos and I walked out of the castle gate. There wasn't even a patch of blood where Clyde's body had been.

COURT CIRCULAR

WINDSOR, Tuesday. His Serene Highness Prince Ernest of Saxe Coburg is better.

The Bard of the Rifles attended at the Castle last evening and played the following pieces:–

March, "Kenilworth."

Overture, *Fiorella* (Auber), arranged by Weichsel.

Cavatina, *Ultimo Giorno de Pompeii* (Paccini).

Quartetto, *Puritani* (Bellini).

Galop, *Beniowsky*, arranged by Weichsel.

"Walza die Heimuth" (Strauss).

Prince Ernest is better.

The Times 6 November 1839

TWENTY-FIVE

Dublin. Friday 8 November.

My dear Liberty,

The thing is done: happy couple seen off on their honeymoon tour, leaving a castle full of bachelors with sore heads, brides-maids with worn-out dancing shoes and enough goodwill and gossip to last until the next gathering of the Fitzwilliam clan. As you see, we've reached Dublin and we face a final weekend of duty visits before the boat to Holyhead on Monday. All being well, London two days after that. I can't tell you how much I'm looking forward to seeing you and hearing all your news.

One thing I want to discuss with you. I've made friends with one of the regiment of cousins, a cheery fellow of about my own age who rides like a demon, drinks like a bosom friend of Bacchus and writes surprisingly good poetry. During his stay at the castle, he threw his heart at the feet of la belle Alice and was spurned. For some days he moped around threatening to drown himself in the lake but was happily persuaded against it by talk of the giant pike that inhabits it. A watery grave may sound fine and poetic, but not with saw-toothed fish in attendance. So he's adopted the next resource of a broken heart – travel. He plans to spend the winter in France and Germany then, in the spring, move on to Italy, Athens and perhaps even Constantinople. He's asked me to accompany him. At first I told him it was out of the question, though my heart leapt at the thought of Athens. Since then, I've been wondering if it may be just the thing I need. As you know, I'm nowhere near as well travelled as you are and I sometimes worry that I may appear dull in your eyes as a result. I've told him I will give him my answer in a couple of weeks. What do you think? I must hurry this to the post then change for dinner. Stephen sends his best respects to you. I'm so looking forward to seeing you, my dearest.

Another question there, beneath the one he'd asked me. He knew that and so did I. But I didn't know the answer.

Towards the end of November, *The Times* got round to announcing what everybody knew:

COURT CIRCULAR

The Queen held a Privy Council at half-past 1 o'clock on Saturday afternoon, for the reception of Her Majesty's declaration on the subject of her intended marriage with his Serene Highness Prince Albert of Saxe Coburg Gotha.

The Council was attended by 85 Privy Councillors, all of whom (with very few exceptions) appeared in naval, military, or official costumes, or in their robes of office, the members of orders of knighthood wearing their respective ensigns. Among the earlier arrivals were Lord Lyndhurst, the Earl of Durham, Viscount Beresford, Lord Wharneliffe, Lord Ellenborough, Earl of Ripon, and Lord Brougham. The last-named noble Lord came in forensic costume.

The Duke of Wellington appeared in his uniform as Governor of the Tower. His Grace, while entering the Council-room, took the arm of this brother, Lord Cowley. The noble Duke was warmly congratulated on his arrival by many noblemen and gentlemen present.

The Privy Councillors were ushered on their arrival across the grand hall and sculpture gallery into the library, where the Council was held.

The Queen's Guard was on duty on the Palace lawn, and received his Royal Highness the Duke of Cambridge on his arrival with the usual honeurs, the band playing "God Save the Queen."

When the Council had assembled, the Queen entered the chamber from an ante-room. Her Majesty retired after reading her declaration.

Formal announcement of the Royal Engagement
The Times, 25 November 1839

And Amos sold the bay race horse for one hundred guineas.